Heartbeat of the Moon

by

Jennifer Taylor

Rhythm of the Moon Series

This is a work of fiction. Names, characters, places, and incidents are either the product of the author's imagination or are used fictitiously, and any resemblance to actual persons living or dead, business establishments, events, or locales, is entirely coincidental.

Heartbeat of the Moon

Cover Art by *Angela Anderson*

The Wild Rose Press, Inc.
PO Box 708
Adams Basin, NY 14410-0708
Visit us at www.thewildrosepress.com

Publishing History
First Mainstream Historical Edition, 2016
Print ISBN 978-1-5092-0861-6
Digital ISBN 978-1-5092-0862-3

Rhythm of the Moon Series
Published in the United States of America

Ian glanced her way, finally.

"Do you think Josef has lost his wits?"

"I don't know," she said. "For we have seen stranger things than this, things I never thought were possible. And it's as if…"

"What?"

She shook her head. "It is fanciful and silly."

"Maggie, I have told you before." He came to her and took her hands. "Nothing you ever say to me will be taken lightly, for every word you utter is like holy writ to me."

She moved into his embrace, her hands on his bristled cheeks. He was very warm. "The spirit of the holy nun lives in me still."

He nodded.

"Something happened today."

Josef moaned in his sleep. "Let me in. The beast is out there, in the woods, and he comes for us. Where are your weapons? Where is Ana? Has she not arrived? The beast is coming; do you hear it? No, the floor is sticky with her blood, I slipped in it, I could not help it," Josef screamed.

"But I just saw her yesterday," he continued in a voice not his own. "She sold chestnuts in the market. How can this be her, neck laid open? She will not stop bleeding. Her eyes opened, she snarls."

And his own voice returned. "No, stop screaming, sister. We must bury her, bury her deep."

Fear rippled down Maggie's back.

Kudos for Jennifer Taylor's
MERCY OF THE MOON
Book One in the Rhythm of the Moon series

MERCY OF THE MOON won Second Place
in the Historical Category
of the 2013 Lone Star Writing Competition.

Dedications

To Wayne,
for thirty-seven years of kindness, love, and passion.
May there be many more.
~*~
To Emily, Leslie, and Geoffrey,
for your encouragement and humor.
~*~
To my beloved mother, Gloria,
for your boundless love and
living example of creative grace.
~*~
In loving memory of my father, Gene.
~*~
Many thanks to my childhood friend,
Anna Jean Bradley, registered midwife.
How cosmic that I would connect
with a childhood friend
who has over thirty years of experience
in bringing new life into the world!
Your knowledge and expertise is greatly appreciated.
I will strive to get it right.

Chapter One

King's Harbour, England 1735

Maggie Pierce awoke from a dreamless sleep and reached under the pillow for her husband Ian's letter. His scent rose from the foolscap, clove and bayberry, the sharp bright tang of the sea. She closed her eyes to let sleep pull her into its dark waters. Ian's words echoed in her heart:

My Dearest Maggie,

Every mile I travel across the Channel and through the mountains of Bohemia, takes me farther from you, and as I ride, I write your song. Distance has not dulled the memory of you: the grey of your eyes, dark as an undertow when you are vexed, your black hair spread like fine Chinese silk over my bare chest, your wide hips my comfort and compass. I yearn for you, but know the search for my affliction's remedy must continue. For us.

The urgency of singing you, possessing you with the words of my soul, grows with each step of the journey. Then, my heart plummets. I can never do you justice, for you are ever-changing like the moon. Oh, Maggie, look down upon me with your cool regard, rise above me with your passion, lie beside me so I might truly know you.

Until then, I remain your Most Loving and

Besotted Husband,
   Ian Pierce

Maggie tossed and turned. Ian had been gone for three months; why could she not get accustomed to sleeping alone? She slung her bare leg to the other side of the bed. The scent of clove and male musk rose from the warm sheet. Oh. The burn and glow of pleasure in her secret place were not the products of a dream. Ian had returned last night.

He stood by the window, utterly naked. "It is early still, my Maggie. You fell asleep like the dead as soon as we slaked our passion. Go back to sleep."

Not just yet. She must gaze upon him, all of him. Two hours ago, he had suddenly arrived, and the urgency to make love overpowered everything else. Now, in the dim light, the green glow of his eyes lit her body from the inside out. The lines of his broad shoulders, tapered waist, and long, muscled legs made her mouth water.

"You liked my letters?"

"Of course I did." She put the letter under her pillow again out of habit, and glanced at him, to see if he would make sport of it.

"Oh, Maggie, I hoped you would." The bed creaked under his weight, as he gathered her in his arms. He seemed impossibly big, the contained strength in his arms, the hard muscled planes of his chest warm against her bare skin. "Imagine my joy upon receiving the news of our child! Are you well, Maggie mine?" The tips of his fingers were rough as he caressed her back. "So soft, so smooth."

The rusty edges of his voice invoked twinges of pleasure in her limbs.

"Yes, I feel fine. My, your fingers are abraded."

He broke away from her and searched her face. "Am I hurting you?"

"No, of course not. I just wondered why."

He grinned, teeth white in his tanned face. "I worked on the boat. The hard labor is a good remedy for my restlessness."

"Ian, did you find what you were looking for, to ease your affliction?"

He took her face in his hands and kissed her. His sun-chapped lips made hers tingle. "Let us not speak of it now," he said. "It has been a long three months without you. Can we not celebrate our reunion? And then, my hard-working midwife, I insist you sleep some more."

He rose above her, clasping her hands and putting her arms above her head. He trailed his fingers down the underside of her arms, and to her breasts with the lightest of touches. Her body rose to meet him, and he smiled against her lips before he kissed her.

A pounding on the door doused their passion like a splash from the English Channel.

Ian bolted from the bed and bounded down the stairs stark naked. "Stay abed, my love. I'm sure I won't be long."

The door opened and Ian said, "Josef! You have arrived home! Why are you not in the arms of your Lena?"

"Ian, my friend. Give me all the millet seeds you have, and quickly! We must sprinkle them around the grave, for when the creature rises, he cannot resist counting them all."

Chapter Two

Maggie dressed and joined them downstairs. What brought Josef here at this hour?

Josef paced across the parlor, wringing his hands. His brown eyes were bloodshot, and a foul odor emanated from his weathered and filthy clothing. His black hair hung loose and greasy upon his shoulders.

"Josef, you are overwrought. Sit for a moment and have some of my wife's good soup."

Maggie first built up the fire, and before she could take the ladle from its hook, Josef said, "There is no time. We must bury Nikolaus before dawn. Help me, Ian."

Ian grabbed him by the shoulders. "Bury your nephew? Josef, what happened after we met at Boulogne?"

"I don't understand," Maggie said. "If the two of you met up in Boulogne, why did you not take the same boat for home?"

Josef trembled, wiry arms tense, hands hard fists.

Ian shoved a mug of ale into his hands. "Here, drink. Catch your breath." He took Maggie aside, keeping one eye on Josef. "Josef's nephew, Nikolaus, was coming back with him to learn the business of running an inn and making beer."

Josef had left the same time Ian had, for different purposes, Josef to fetch his nephew, and Ian to search for herbs for the apothecary shoppe, and a remedy.

"Nikolaus fell ill," Ian said. "He had a raging fever, and the captain feared smallpox. The ship's doctor would not allow him passage, but I left on it. Josef must have found another boat captain whose love of coin was stronger than the fear of disease."

Josef slammed his mug down on the table. "My Nikki is all alone in the ship's hold. We must bury him."

She had never seen the normally taciturn man so distraught. Surely he must be ill to be speaking so. And why the urgency for burial?

Lena's husband wrung his hands. "How will I tell my sister her only boy has died? I failed to get him away from the monsters in my homeland. If only I had left sooner. I have failed her, and my Nikki, my boy, is gone."

"The boy is dead?"

He nodded. Bits of dirt fell on the floor at his feet. "Yes, man. His condition worsened, and I had to take him down to the hold, for the sailors threatened to throw him overboard. I fought them off. And he died there, like an animal."

It must be a lethal disease indeed for him to have sickened and died so quickly.

Josef grasped Ian by the shoulders. "I went straight from the boat and dug the grave in the grove outside the Landgate. For the love of all we experienced as boys, please help me."

Maggie and Ian glanced at each other, mirroring their confusion. Surely grief altered his mind?

Josef ran into the apothecary shoppe, opening and closing drawers. "Your seeds, where are they? We must bury him now, millet seeds, poppy seeds, for if he rises, he is compelled to count them all, and he will never finish before the light of day. May the sun burn him and send him to his eternal rest before he can become a monster."

Ian lit a candle and handed Josef a basket for the seeds. "Let me grab my cloak, Josef. Maggie, I will return as soon as I am able."

"No." She grabbed her cloak as well. "I will not be parted with you so soon, and then have to wait here, wondering and worrying."

"I would rather you stay," he whispered. "I fear disease."

"No. If you are going, then so am I. You have only just returned."

Ian laid his palms on her cheeks. "I can tell you all about it later, when we have returned to our bed, and I have made you moan again."

"Do not try to charm me. I'm going."

"I can see there's no convincing you. Allow me to at least put on your gloves." He fit them on her hand, with a tug, reminding her of the fit of his member deep within her. His hand slid up her arm. She held her breath. Why did it seem he was broader, more powerful, despite the gentleness of his fingers?

"You must take care," he warned. "You are carrying our child."

"I do not require special treatment. It's not an illness."

"I would guard my treasures." He embraced her.

"Come on, man!"

"Josef, fear not. I'm coming."

As they followed their friend out the door, Ian

whispered, "I wish we were not venturing out on this grim endeavor tonight. It doesn't matter whether I understand what he is talking about. For I owe Josef my life, more than once." He kissed her thoroughly, his hands on her arms trembling.

"For God's sake, hurry!" Josef shouted.

King's Harbour rested upon a hill, with the church at the top above the market square. The decline to the docks was steep from Maggie and Ian's apothecary shoppe. The full moon guided their way, and the leafless trees cast their shadows on the cobblestones. The wind moaned its way from the sea.

Josef raced ahead. "Hurry."

Ian cradled Maggie's elbow as they approached the harbor. The fishing boat rocked back and forth, and the salt-tinged wind slapped her about the face, stinging her eyes. She closed them for a moment and, upon opening them again, discovered Ian's hair had whipped out of its tie. He looked as wild as the waves crashing against the pilings, reminding her of all the places he had been, and all he had experienced without her.

Then he smiled, the ends of his mouth curling, and as he helped her onto the deck of the boat, his whisper blended with the wind. "It's not how I imagined us spending our reunion."

She followed his gaze to Josef's bulk hurrying to the boat.

"I'll not let you stay up here alone. There's no telling who might be lurking around here," he said. "Follow closely."

Once in the boat, she trailed Ian through the torch-lit passageway, down to the ship's hold.

Josef stood waiting, wringing his hands. "God

forgive me. I could do nothing for him. I had to bring him down here, for he was delirious and raving, burning with fever. He was up on deck and would not cease yelling of how the light hurt his eyes. He was half blind with it, and I had to guide him down here, fighting him all the way."

As Ian stepped into the hold, he put his hand out to block her way. "Please. You do not need to see this, Maggie."

She shook her head. She had seen plenty in her midwifery work. Josef was Lena's husband, and a dear friend. She would try to be of use.

Ian gave a sharp nod toward the top of the stairs. "Maggie, I would not have you breathe this miasmic air. Go up the stairs a bit."

She acquiesced at the fierce glint in his eyes and was glad she did, for the stench hit her all at once. She reached in her apron pocket for the peppermint-scented handkerchief she always kept there. The sweet, sickly smell of death crawled toward her. She forced herself to breathe. How could she be of help holding onto a handkerchief like a delicate duchess?

In the dim light, Maggie eventually made out a figure lying in a corner, a rope wrapped around his middle, tying his arms to his side, a gag in his mouth. A blond fuzz covered his chin. She gasped. He'd died with a snarl on his young face, teeth bared wide, tongue hanging from his mouth, swollen and purple. His body was bloated. His skin swelled around the ropes on his wrists.

Josef knelt in front of his nephew. "I had to tie him, for he would have hurt me. He tried to escape up to the deck once, claiming he was thirsty, but he would not drink. He died growling, like an animal. He did not recognize me." He swiped his tears with the back of his hand. "I cannot cast him into the sea. I must bury him."

"I will help you do whatever needs to be done. Let's not delay." Ian handed Josef a kerchief to put around his mouth. He put on leather gloves, and he and Josef lifted the body and wrapped it in a canvas sail. Maggie led the way to the deck of the ship. With great haste they loaded the body into a wagon waiting by the docks. The horse's hooves echoed on the cobbles as they set out with the sea wind against their backs.

Maggie shivered as they made their way out of town through the ancient Landgate. The warmth of Ian's arm around her did much to chase the chills away, as Josef tried to dodge the ruts in the ancient road.

"This way," Josef called. "I remember this place from the smallpox, when those without coin could not afford to be buried in the churchyard."

They reached a grove of trees off the main path. Josef handed the reins to Maggie, and the two men jumped out of the wagon.

Ian took her hands. "I would ask you to stay in the wagon, but I know what your answer would be." He helped her down, and she walked over to the hole Josef had dug.

Ian held the boy in his arms, then without a word, Josef climbed into the grave and held his arms out for the shrouded body of his nephew. When Ian handed him the body, he gathered the boy in his arms and sobbed.

Ian joined Maggie. The wind had turned bitter as a spurned lover, and he tightened his hold on her as she shivered. There was nothing they could do but let Josef grieve. She remembered the flask she held in her apron pocket and handed it to Ian. He took a sip and gave it back. "Take care not to catch a chill, sweeting."

She swallowed a mouthful of brandy, and they waited for Josef's sobbing to subside.

Ian cleared his throat. "Josef. It is getting late."

Their friend embraced Nikolaus one last time. "Oh, my boy, I should have kept you safe." He adjusted the canvas sail as if he tucked him into bed. Ian reached a hand to Josef and pulled him out of the grave.

Maggie handed Josef the flask. He took a long draught with trembling hands. It seemed to brace him, for then he took the shovel and threw the first shovelful into the grave. Together Maggie and Ian watched as his nephew disappeared into the dark earth.

Ian began to sing in a foreign tongue, his voice carrying on the wind. The whistling of the bare trees provided harmony to his rusty tenor. It was a mournful song, in a most minor key, and Maggie could not stop the flow of tears.

Ian took the shovel from him and continued to sing.

"He was a good boy," Josef said between gulps of brandy. "Never hurt anyone. Strong and never complained, so kind. What must I tell his mother? And to die in such a way."

When the last bit of dirt was piled atop the grave, Ian put his arm around Josef, and Josef's bass joined him as together they raised their voices and sang to the trees, to the starry sky, to the heavens. Mayhap to God himself, for it seemed their voices carried on the wind, pure and plaintive. Every sorrow she'd experienced cut into her like a knife.

"Ah, my Nikolaus' favorite song," Josef said. "His mother taught it to him before he could walk." Without warning, he broke from Ian and ran to the wagon. "The seeds. We must scatter the millet seeds around the grave, for if we do not, he will rise undead."

And so the three of them, only one of them understanding why, walked around the grave, and scattered seeds.

Josef's voice carried across the wind. "It is said by the wise ones if the creature escapes from the grave he cannot help but count the seeds, no matter how many. And if it takes until dawn, the sun will rise and burn him and he can go to his maker. Or to hell. It is what they do in my nephew's village, to keep the evil at bay."

Chapter Three

Back at the cottage, Ian urged Josef to eat.

Josef shook his head. "No, I must go home to my Lena."

Maggie stirred the soup pot, in hopes the aroma of onions and potatoes would cover up the stench emanating from Josef, but to no avail. She cursed her delicate sense of smell. Had the man not bathed, or even changed clothing during his three-month journey? He stood by the fire and took off his topcoat. The odor of unwashed man, fish scales, and fear barreled into her senses like a runaway, dung-covered horse. Her stomach turned inside out upon spotting bits of unidentifiable grey matter swimming in his beard. She was well used to the reek of sailors and workmen getting off boats, but even she had her limit.

"Maggie, are you quite well?" Ian rushed to her side, taking her by the elbow.

"If he goes home to Lena reeking like a rotten haddock, she will greet him by casting up her accounts. Repeatedly. She has enough trouble keeping her gorge down. He will make her more ill than she already is."

Maggie had just been to see her good friend today, to experiment with another remedy for the morning sickness which had plagued her during her entire pregnancy. Perhaps the sight of Lena's increased girth would cheer Josef.

"He needs a bath," Maggie whispered.

Ian winked, eyes glinting with mischief. "A bit of Lena's ale will make him more pliable for a bath." Despite the ordeal of the evening, he fair glowed with vigor. "Sit down, man. You must have a bite to eat before you go home. It has been an arduous journey and a horrible night. Some of my wife's chowder will do you good."

Maggie ladled out the soup and handed it to the men.

Ian peered at her. "Maggie, you are favoring your shoulder, the one Edward Carter injured. I will take a look at it later. Sit down and eat." He waited, stern as a magistrate.

She settled onto the divan, and he handed her the bowl of soup, his long, tapered fingers lingering over hers. The fire reflected in his green eyes, making them glow like emeralds. He soon sat beside her with his own bowl, and she could not help watching as he brought the spoon to his mouth. Hours earlier, his mouth had covered her, and made her gasp, then he murmured against her tender skin, words from a distant land.

His sleeves were rolled up, and firelight danced on his tan, muscular arms. How could a man be gone three months and seem to have changed so much? It was not just the soup warming her center. How had his shoulders broadened so wide, his chest straining against the linen of his shirt, the bands of muscles in his neck shifting? She swallowed hard.

Josef had set his bowl on the fireplace and sat hunched over in the rocking chair, his hands between his knees, the bare pate of his head shining in the firelight. Ian rose and patted him on the shoulder. Fibers of his rough-hewn shirt fell to the floor.

"You will be delighted to see how much your unborn child has grown, Josef."

"Ah, my child!" For a moment, a light came into his bloodshot eyes.

"Yes, but before you go home to Lena, you need to bathe."

"Bathe?" He looked as if Ian had offered to chop his head off with a rusty scythe.

"Yes, man. Come on, you must bathe a bit." He guided Josef to the basin and bayberry soap, and set to work loading the pitcher with hot water.

Maggie, for the sake of Josef's modesty (which clearly he did not possess), and her sensitive nose, headed to the shoppe. "I will organize the…" She didn't bother finishing her sentence as the conversation between the two men became more heated.

"Take off your clothes."

"No need, no need!"

Maggie could not help but feel sympathy for the man, having suffered such a grievous loss. But his troubles would be doubled if he went home reeking.

Ian gave it another try. "Your clothes are falling off of you, man. Did you not change them the whole of your trip?"

"Why would I?"

"A wash will make you feel better."

"I want to go home to Lena."

"Yes, of course. But do you want her throwing up?"

"Why would she be throwing up still?"

"Just…never mind. Come on!"

Josef let out a yelp, and there were sounds of a struggle and ripping of cloth. "You bastard!"

"You'll feel better. Lean over the sink, and stop squealing like a lass. You'll wake the neighbors."

Maggie peeked through the door to find Ian washing Josef's hair.

"What in God's name is swimming in your beard? Here, wash it." He held the soap out to Josef.

Josef shook his head, flinging water droplets everywhere. He sputtered as Ian took him by the ears and lathered soap into the thick, black beard.

"Must I wash your ballocks for you as well? Have you no pride? Do I look like a bathhouse maiden? Precisely how many layers of dirt can you have on yourself?"

Maggie snickered and tucked her head back into the shoppe.

Ian nagged and persisted until at last he said, "Dry yourself with this. Ho, where did you get this nasty bruise? And some kind of bite or cut in the middle."

"What?"

"On your side here. It bears watching."

"Don't feel it."

'If you say so, brute. Well, it's a shame we didn't have time for a full bath. I have a set of clothes in my trunk I think will fit you."

He escaped into the shoppe and riffled through his trunk, muttering to himself like a harassed mother, and gave Josef the clothes. He faced Maggie for a moment and gazed toward the heavens. His linen shirt and breeches had soaked through, and she spied the nutmeg colored hair around his brown nipples and the muscled planes of his stomach. Josef entered, pulling at the new clothes, scowling.

Maggie nodded her approval. "Yes, Josef! There's the handsome man your wife knows and loves." She sniffed and smiled at Ian. He'd worked a miracle.

Ian held the door open for Josef. It was early yet, and the shopkeepers busied themselves setting up their wares and opening their shutters.

Ian glanced back, holding her gaze. "I will be home shortly, Maggie."

Did he always have those flecks of burnished copper amidst the leaf green of his eyes? She shivered. Contained within the hoarseness of his voice, a wild and restless animal waited, growling.

****

Across the street, Ed the butcher hung a ham outside his shop. He nodded at Ian and Josef, heavy brows knit in confusion. "Welcome back, gents! But why are you not in the warm beds of your women?" He shook his head and returned to his work.

They did not comment but made haste to the Siren Inn, where Josef had been proprietor for seven years. Josef's acquisition of the Siren Inn would live on forever in the history of King's Harbour. Old man Stowe had left the inn to his son, now nicknamed Full-Pocket Pete, and in a game of dice, Pete Stowe lost the inn to Josef, their indentured servant since his miserable childhood.

Another story for another time. Ian breathed deeply as Josef opened the heavy door of the inn. Ah! The smells and feel of one of his favorite places on earth made him catch his breath and sent the blood racing through his veins. The smell of pipe smoke, ale, and fish frying, and the musty overtones of an ancient inn.

Sabine, the young foreign girl from the Orient whom Lena and Josef had taken in, held a rag in her hand. Her eyes grew round upon seeing them. "Father Josef!"

Just then, a woman who looked somewhat like Lena, but so very thin, except for the considerable bulge of her pregnancy-surely this could not be hearty, robust Lena-came in from the kitchen, wiping her mouth with a handkerchief. She was pale as parchment. Bits of her white blonde hair peeked out of her cap.

She stopped, dropping the handkerchief. "Josef! Oh, my Josef." She ran over to him and into his arms, and they kissed.

Ian felt an intruder to their reunion and averted his eyes. He watched Sabine observing them, a light in her almond-shaped eyes.

He leaned against the bar and in Mandarin, Sabine's native tongue, asked her how she fared. She beamed, for Ian was the only one in town who spoke her language. He had spent some time in the Far East, her native land. She had been sold into prostitution by Edward Carter, and subsequently rescued. She lived with Josef and Lena now.

Edward Carter. Ian fought against the memory of the man who had endangered Maggie last year. Her shoulder pained her, he could tell. And no wonder, for she had done the work of two during his absence.

Then Josef's gravelly voice cut into the scene like a saw into teak. "Lena, are you ill?" He held her at arm's length. "You are wasting away." He rested his hand upon her stomach. "Except for the child, who has grown so much." He smiled and hugged her, keeping away from her middle as if the child would reach out and bite him.

He turned to Ian. "She could not keep the food down when I left. Mistress Maggie told me it would pass."

Lena blushed. "Most times it does, *Liebchen*. Some women do suffer from it until the babe is born."

He frowned. "But there is nothing to you."

"It is because every morning," she paused, swallowing hard. Her face had gone pasty again, as if the mere mention of her nausea would bring it on. "I am sick every morning, all day. I cannot keep food down, not even a biscuit."

His brown eyes clouded with worry. "My poor Lena."

Lena put her hands on Josef's cheek. "How fresh and clean you smell, my love. I have missed you so, dear Josef. And do not worry. I am strong, and now Ian is back, mayhap he will find a potion that will work for me." And as if the excitement was too much for her queasy stomach, she ran from him and vomited in a nearby bucket.

"Yes, I will indeed work on a remedy, dear Lena."

Josef ran to her, rubbed her back, and wiped her mouth with the clean handkerchief Ian had given him.

She recovered quickly enough. "Where's young Nikolaus?"

Josef backed away from Lena, as if the act of burying his nephew would contaminate her. "He is dead."

"Dead?"

Josef put his head in his hands. "I can still hear his moans, feel his skin burning with fever. Oh God, Lena. He died on the boat like an animal, and we buried him,

Ian and I, last night."

She held her stomach, and Ian rushed to bring a chair for her.

"Sabine," Ian said. "Pour him some ale. Josef, sit down. I will explain. We do not know why he died. He was ill with something."

"It is the evil in my town. I saw it with my own eyes."

"No, Josef, do not say such things." Lena held him in her arms as he sobbed like a child.

After a time, Josef quieted and fell asleep.

Ian exchanged glances with Lena and took Josef from Lena's arms. She stumbled as she rose.

Sabine rushed to her side. "Mother Lena, you are tired."

She shook her head. "I must tend to my husband."

Ian put an arm around Josef. "Come, man. I will help you to bed."

The man could barely walk, so pronounced was his fatigue, and the drink had finally taken effect as well. Ian stripped him of his clothes and tucked the covers under his chin.

Josef opened one eye. "Thank you, friend."

Ian patted his bearded cheek. "Would you like a bedtime story, Jo Jo?"

Josef scowled. "Go away."

Lena leaned against the doorway. "You are a good friend. My poor husband."

"Don't worry, Lena. I expect things will look a little brighter in the morning, when he's had some rest. And you must get some. I will return tomorrow with something for your vomiting."

Poor woman. She blanched at the mention of the

word.

"*Danke.*"

Ian nodded and left quietly. The weight of the day lowered over him like clouds, as did the burden of what he must tell Maggie. But could he not just serve her with his body and forget all else? Mist fell upon his face, reminding him of the droplets of Maggie's sweat last night, as he rolled her on top so she could have dominion over him. He quickened his pace, the exertion helping to quiet the urgency humming through his veins.

Chapter Four

Maggie was dressing her hair upstairs when Ian arrived home.

He stood in front of her, head cocked. "What are you doing?"

"It's time to start the day. I have mothers to visit, and you must open the shoppe."

He bent and kissed her forehead. "The people of King's Harbour can do without us for a spell. I have kept the 'closed' sign on the door." He grabbed her hands from the top of her hair and put them in her lap, undid her hair, then led her to the bed. "Your mothers are not the only thing you need to see to today." He held her hand against the bulge of his desire.

"I want to touch you Maggie, as I dreamt of doing those long three months. Like this." He tangled his hands in her hair and kissed her, lips firm and tasting of cloves. He cupped his hands under her breasts. "Ah, see how your breasts have grown so ripe, so full."

"My body has changed much since you left."

"You are even more beautiful than I imagined, with our child growing inside you." He skimmed his fingers from the top of her breasts to the nipple, and circled it, slowly. She gasped at the hard feel of his muscled body, soon naked, warm and hard. His tongue mimicked the light thrusts of his hardened member against her soft center. He slid his hands up her ribcage with

21

painstaking slowness, fingers trailing along the sides of her breast. With one deft movement, an arm around her waist and the other under her bottom, he lifted her onto the bed as effortlessly as a cup of tea.

She ran her hands in his hair and drew his face closer to hers, kissed him harder, for she longed to inhale him, bring him into her to keep him there.

Damn him. She had lived her whole life without his touch, without his bright essence pumping into her, and how she yearned for him, even as her center tightened and pulsed around his hard strength, sending waves of pleasure washing in warm rivulets from her limbs to her fingertips. And one last thrust cast her weightless and rising in the morning light.

Later, they lay facing each other, his hand resting on her stomach. She tucked her nose into his neck, so she could inhale him, the scent of oranges, cloves, a hint of bayberry. They had not had a chance to speak alone about Josef.

"Surely it is just ignorance and suspicion," Maggie said. "A creature rising from the dead, kept from malicious mischief by counting millet seeds?"

He turned to her, gathered her hair, and spread it over her breasts. "The two of us have seen things no one else would believe. A supernatural being assisted me when I suffered the throes of my affliction and gave me clarity when I needed it most. A holy nun ministered to you in your darkest hour. Is she still with you?"

Maggie nodded. "Even more so, since my pregnancy. It is a feeling often without words. A presence."

He sat up. "Sweeting, I need to look at your

shoulder. I can tell it is bothering you. Why have you not said anything?" He sounded inordinately fierce to her ears.

She sat up and shrugged, wincing despite herself. "We have had other things to worry about. I am fine."

"Could your sister not have manipulated it like I showed her?"

"If you recall, we ran the shoppe in your absence and took care of our mothers and mothers-to-be. And Sarah's babe is extraordinarily mischievous, requiring more care than the average child. We did all we could to keep things afloat in your absence." She heard the shrill tone in her voice.

He grew still. "I know. I am sorry. I don't want to leave you, Maggie, and never meant to burden you. Had I known you were with child, I never would have left."

When would she learn to still her tongue? "I'm sorry. I know you must go, to find this *litio*, the remedy for your condition. Did you?"

"No. I don't think so. I don't know what I'm looking for, which makes it difficult. I must only go by instinct, by smell and taste and hope I will recognize it, feel a change within me, when I try it. I sampled many things, but the remedies were not what I needed." He wrapped her in his arms and buried his face in the space between her breasts. His lips as he spoke tickled her tender skin.

"I'm sorry."

She kissed him. "I have seen you in the throes of your affliction and would not have you suffer so."

"Here." He lifted her, and seated her between his spread legs, laid her thick hair to one side. "Black silk."

She sighed at his compliment. How she had missed

23

hearing his flights of fancy. His thighs were so hard, his muscles bigger from what she remembered. How much he'd changed, but he was the same—tender, passionate. Soon, thoughts left her head as his strong fingers kneaded her shoulder. The vibration from his humming resonated on her back.

He paused. "Am I hurting you?"

"It feels wonderful."

Vigor radiated from his body. "To continue our discussion, I did find all manner of interesting herbs and medicines, spices too. And several ancient tomes I cannot wait to delve into, but…"

So much he had experienced, so many places he had gone, and she, serviceable Maggie, stayed the same. Would he not tire of her? And soon his child would tie him down.

He kissed her, his eyes glowing into hers. "But there are other things I would like to delve into, just now. Do you want me, Maggie?"

He waited, clenching his jaw. She did. But was it not indecent to admit it?

"A part of me says it is shameful to be with child and still yearn for you so." She averted her eyes.

"Does it feel shameful?"

"No."

He laughed. "We bring each other joy, Maggie, and there is no shame in it."

She could not argue with him, not when he touched her there, just so.

Later, as she dressed, she said, "It is frightfully late."

He stood in front of the window in broad daylight, not a bit of clothing on, his hands loosely propped upon his narrow hips, as powerful as a knight of old. Foolish! She'd become such a fanciful midwife. But she could not resist a feeling of pride and fierce joy.

"Ian, what are you doing? Someone might see you standing there naked."

"What? I was just thinking how much I missed not having you by my side. Mayhap a combination of things will make this *litio*. I was thinking next time you could come with me on my trip."

His eyes were iridescent green, like the wings of a dragonfly.

"We could be like gypsies, sleeping upon the ground at night in summer, wandering the countryside, dining on wine, cheese, bread and berries, making love in the mountain meadows in the soft grass, wildflowers in your hair." He tied her shift, fingers trembling with his excitement. "We could camp by the sea, mist cooling our skin."

Was he raving mad? "I have never been truly idle, except for our wedding night."

"And what a night," he sang, and she laughed despite herself at the enthusiasm of his delivery.

"Might I remind you, we were quite busy." His eyes burned up and down her body, making her breasts tingle.

Something about him seemed almost feral, and she found herself drawn into it. She smirked at him to hide her confusion. "I really don't know if it would suit me."

"You should find out. I will ply you with enough wine it shouldn't be a struggle at all." He tucked a stray piece of hair into her cap, standing very close. "Unless you'd like to struggle—a bit."

She broke away. "We have *work* to do, wicked

man. Besides, I cannot leave the town. I am way too busy birthing its babies to wander about like a wanton."

"Someday, Maggie. You will see."

****

After a hasty breakfast, Maggie sipped a cup of tea in the apothecary shoppe and watched Ian open his steamer trunk. He had shaved, his high cheekbones glistening with the bayberry shaving lotion he used. Ah, she had missed the smell of him, the sound of him.

Ian knelt and flung open the trunk. A most unusual scent wafted to her: spices, incense, bitter and unpleasant musty smells as well, the odor of dead plants.

"Oh, I have something for you," he said. "But it's for later." He waggled his sandy eyebrows. In usual breakneck speed, he rummaged around and pulled something out of the bottom of the trunk. "Ah! Here it is."

It was square and wrapped in crimson silk, tied with a ribbon. He shot over to the wooden counter and before he set the package down, wiped the counter with a rag. And then slowly—oh it must be special indeed for him to unwrap it so slowly. "I still cannot believe I have this. Surely the old man selling it did not know its worth."

As she suspected, it was a book, ancient and discolored.

She looked over his shoulder. "What is it?"

"It is Galen's book. The great Greek doctor and philosopher. Not the original of course, but a fair copy."

She blinked.

"He is indeed one of the fathers of modern science."

She could not help but be wrapped up in his enthusiasm. "How interesting. I will look forward to reading it, when I am not so busy."

He cocked his head. "I will read it to you later."

She scowled. "Read it to me? Am I a child of five? You know I can read, well or better than you." The old woman who had schooled her in midwifery had also taught her to read. "Do you think I am not intelligent enough to understand it?"

He grinned, tapping his fingers on the counter.

Aggravation prickled her skin like stinging nettles.

His eyes followed the blush burning from her cheeks to her bosom. He stepped back in mock alarm, and she gave in to her rage. Insufferable man!

"Do you think you are far smarter than I? Do you think because you have travelled to the ends of the earth, seeing more in one trip than I have seen in my life, you can lord it over me?"

His lips quivered. God help him if he smiled. He reached out his hand, and she backed away.

"I will not be patronized like a child. Read it to me?"

He grasped her hands and brought them to his lips, despite her struggle. "Maggie."

Did he think her nothing but a lowly midwife from London's slums? What kind of rare women did he meet, travelling so far away from her, for him to think of her in such a way?

"Maggie."

His voice caressed her inside with long, slow strokes. His lips lingered enticingly near, firm, long, and tilting at the corners. He had a small nick on his chin from shaving.

"What?" God curse her, she squeaked.

"It is written in Greek."

"Oh." She had to admire his composure. She could not blame him if he laughed. She was such a fool. What had gotten into her, yelling at him like a shrew? "You speak Greek?"

"Yes, of course."

She laughed. "Of course." How was it he could speak so many languages? Mandarin, German, Greek. Unnatural man. She pulled away from him and went behind the counter to cover her embarrassment. He joined her, yet suddenly she felt so far away from him. Due to their sudden marriage last year and his frequent trips abroad, at times he still seemed like a stranger. She had no more control over him than she did the cycles of the moon, the timing of her women's trials. Or how she wanted him.

But dear God. He stood in front of her with not a trace of anger at her outburst. He held her hands at her sides and kissed her very softly, as if in question. "Have I offended you somehow? What can I do to make you feel better?"

She put her arms around his neck and kissed him, because she could not ask for forgiveness. Why did he move her so, make the warmth flow through her, squeeze her heart with pain and joy combined, and the only way to soothe her was his lips, his body upon hers? She felt his smile under her lips.

In the silence of the room, their ragged breaths mingled, became one and his tongue found hers until she broke away.

"I'm sorry if I seemed boastful," he said.

"No, it is just that you were gone for so long. I

thought I knew you, but there is so much about you I do not know."

"It doesn't matter," he murmured. "I love you, and we have time to learn the rest."

She kissed him, and he put his arms around her, long fingers splayed over her bottom.

They didn't hear the door open and close, but remained in their embrace until Ian said, "Why do we not go upstairs, sweeting? Let me quench the fire I started."

A hawking and resultant splat on the floor cooled Maggie's ardor.

She started and pulled away. "Captain Jacobs." Maggie faced away from the door and retied her bodice, smoothed down her overskirt. How did she manage to let Ian get her in this condition?

Another hawk and splat upon the floor.

She turned. "Captain Jacobs, with respect, sir, how many times have I told you not to spit on our floor?"

The captain was stooped at the shoulders and wiry thin, with bushy white eyebrows perched over bloodshot blue eyes. A brown bit of snuff hung from his bushy white beard. "My apologies, mistress," he graveled. "But to tell the truth, I walk in here and think I'm in a bordello, the way you two are carrying on." He blinked, a wide grin creasing his weathered face.

Ian came out from behind the counter and bowed to the old man. "Good to see you, Captain. And my apologies, for I did just return last eve after such a long absence, and she is so beautiful I cannot..."

"Never mind," Maggie interrupted. "Look at what the man has done to our floor."

"I will take care of it, love."

"I tell you I didn't come here to watch the two of you cavorting like two pigs in heat," he rasped. "Just got in yestermorning myself."

Maggie opened her mouth but only air came out.

"What can I do for you?" Ian motioned for the fisherman, as Maggie gathered the necessary supplies for her rounds. "Come to the counter, man, and I'll take care of you."

"Me bones ache something fierce since I woke this morn."

"Let me see if I can find you something to ease your pain a bit." Ian wrapped his hand around his chin and tapped his cheek. "I'll wager you've a headache as well."

Captain Jacobs nodded.

"Show me a sailor whose head's not pounding after the long journey, and I'll show you…oh!" He opened a drawer and pulled out a vial. "Wood betony for your head." He reached under the counter and brought out a mortar and pestle, well worn, with a chip out of the side at the top. "I use this one," he stage whispered to Maggie, "because it looks more impressive."

He ground the wood betony. "Put a teaspoonful into a glass of water."

The captain harrumphed. "Why drink water when there's wine or ale, young fool?"

"Well then." Ian grinned and handed the packet to the old man. "It might help your rheumatism as well. But in addition, I will give you horsetail and wintergreen."

He set the two items in the mortar and pestle and began to scrape a rhythm with the pestle inside the mortar.

"I came upon a mermaid,
Her hair as white as pearl.
It swirled around the water,
She was a buxom girl.
Her eyes they looked upon me
And softened up my soul,
But hardened up my nether parts,
And therein was the goal.

Captain Jacobs nodded his head to the rhythm, then guffawed. "So you heard it on your trip, did ye?"

"No, but it came to me on the boat from Boulogne."

He set to humming again to the rhythm of the pestle against the stone, as if everyone composed a shanty while concocting herbal remedies. She could not seem to tear her eyes away from him, or leave the shoppe. She sighed. She had duties she must attend.

"Ay, it's a good'un." The old man chortled. "My crew will thank me when I sing it to 'em."

"You must use the horsetail and wintergreen in a tea," Ian said. "I will mix it up for you. Why do you not sit down and rest yourself, my good man? I'll fetch you a cup of ale. Your remedy will take a bit of time."

He guided Captain Jacobs to one of the chairs lining the wall, gave him his ale, and met Maggie in the doorway to their private living area. He slipped one arm around her back and cradled her neck in his other hand, while the old man leaned his head against the wall and sipped the ale, a beatific look upon his face.

Ian bent to kiss her, running two fingers in a circular pattern on the base of her skull, sending a rush of heat to her center, like a waterfall to a deep pool of desire. He released her to fetch her cloak and wrapped it around her. "Where are you going today, Maggie mine?"

"I'm going out to the McCall's."

The McCall family lived a mile outside the Landgate, and the roads were some of the worst in the county.

He knit his brows. "You're going all the way out there?"

"Yes, believe it or not, I have continued to make my rounds, in town and out of town, while you were away. The world did not stop because you left."

"I did not think it did. I would accompany you, but I fear I must make my presence known. I have some new remedies I learned from the gypsies and must unpack my trunk. I have a combination of herbs I'll bring to Lena for her morning sickness. Poor thing. I am glad you do not suffer from it." His eyes darkened. "I do not like the idea of you walking alone."

"May I remind you, I travel most places day or night without harassment? There is nothing to fear, for even the smugglers have women who give birth. As long as I keep my mouth shut, I'm fine. And I have my knife, which has come in handy before."

He nodded. "I don't like it."

"I've been fine without you," she said.

He winced, then sprang over to his steamer trunk. She had forgotten how active he was.

"I have a gift for you, unique as you are."

He bowed and presented the wrapped object to her, as if she, plain, serviceable Maggie, was a queen.

Her unwrapping revealed a cloth ball of sorts, with a slit-like opening. She spread the slit open. Inside of the opening lay a panel of cloth, and above it, another opening, where a baby's head waited. As gently as if she attended a real birth, she guided the head out of the cloth womb, and then the babe emerged, legs drawn up and arms folded across its knees. There was even an umbilical cord! She pulled on the cord, and the afterbirth emerged, attached of course to the babe's belly. It had thick threads throughout, resembling the veins and arteries.

Maggie gasped, realizing she had been holding her breath. "Ian, a model of a babe inside its mother's womb. It's amazing. To be able to show my birthing mothers what is going on inside their bodies."

He grinned. "So I have pleased you?"

"Oh yes! How many of my mothers are afraid, because they don't know what is happening?" She carefully placed the baby back in the womb and pulled it out again. "I can explain to them the pains have a purpose, to help bring the baby out."

He handed her another object, a cloth ball, resembling a large nut, but with the privy passage at one end. Inside the womb, twins lay curled together, a thin partition separating them, the cords draped around their bodies. One had its feet at the mouth of the womb, and the other its head facing down, so they fit perfectly together.

"Twins, often fraught with difficulty," she murmured. "See how the babe by the privy passage is going to be delivered feet first, unless they change position? And look at the cords, which could so easily be around their necks. But see how God has made them fit together just so, making room for each other to grow."

"As do we." He kissed her forehead.

"My husband, thank you!" She blushed. "No one has ever given me gifts before."

"More's the pity. It is my mission to make you happy, and I would do anything to bring the glow of joy to your face. Of course, upstairs lies my favorite way." He trailed his fingers down her neck and along the line of her bodice. Maggie's breathing quickened.

Just then, Full-Pocket Pete Stowe's mother walked in. According to rumors, Margaret Stowe had once been a great beauty. Even now, her face was smooth and pale, but for two deep groves around her mouth. She held her tall frame straight as a boat paddle.

She must spend hours upon her hair in the morning, Maggie mused. Her faded blonde hair was streaked with grey and powdered. It lay in neatly curled rolls around her face, her cap pinned just so behind the curls. She glanced at Maggie, blue eyes glinting like a crow's.

Maggie nodded. "Good morning, Mistress Stowe."

"I require some pennyroyal and be quick about it, Mr. Pierce."

She cast a withered look in the direction of Captain Jacobs, who had fallen asleep with his chin on his chest, clutching his empty mug of ale like a long lost dolly. Ian tried to wrest it out of his hand, and the old man started, jumped to his feet with surprising agility, looking around frantically. "Man the masts," he yelled. "Step lively, lads!"

Ian laughed and guided him back to the chair. Has the medicine done you any good, sir?"

He nodded. "Yes, I will fetch myself summat to eat now. Thank ye, young Ian." He nodded to the two women and exited the shoppe, whistling Ian's mermaid tune as he went.

Maggie shook her head. The medicine had done the old man wonders. Or was it Ian's solicitude? It certainly worked for her.

Mrs. Stowe huffed and marched to the counter. Ian leaned forward over the counter and smiled at the older woman, the same smile he used on market day to sell his wares. No one seemed able to resist it, except Mrs. Stowe, apparently.

"Now then," he said. "What can I do for you?"

"It's not for me. It's for my poor boy."

Maggie inwardly scoffed. Poor boy? Full-Pocket Pete was five and thirty years old.

"Pete?" Ian winked at Maggie. Poor man. He was still trying to charm the sour woman.

"Well, who else?" Mrs. Stowe's voice was sharp enough to cut a mutton chop.

"The lad has been in pain, ever since his unfortunate beating last year, and the loss of his thumb." Mrs. Stowe pointed her sharp nose at Maggie, as if she were responsible.

Maggie's fists tightened at her sides. She must calm herself. It would serve no one to engage the woman in an altercation, and getting angry could endanger the baby's health… Ian didn't seem the slightest bit perturbed. The woman defended the man who'd been so busy taking bribes last year, hence the name "Full-Pocket Pete," he couldn't be bothered with bringing to justice the blackguard who'd nearly buried her sister alive.

Mrs. Stowe's next statement snapped Maggie out of her reverie.

"My poor boy has the most terrible pains in his

hand, since his unfortunate victimization."

She should just leave so she didn't have to hear this rubbish.

Mrs. Stowe continued. "And the spot where his thumb was, it aches, as if it is still there. He cries and moans so."

"Hmm," Ian said. "Let me think."

"He has not even been able to work, so fearful have the pains been."

Maggie knew why Ian turned his head to look at the drawers behind him. She could not hide her smile either. Pete Stowe spent his days at one of the ale houses, or the Siren Inn. His ability to provoke fisticuffs was not inhibited by his missing thumb and was equaled only by his ability to drink himself under the table.

To be fair, no one deserved the torture Pete Stowe endured from Edward Carter. She had heard his screams when she and Sarah languished in the underground tunnel. And at times they still echoed in her dreams. Mrs. Stowe, Maggie surmised, blamed Maggie and Ian because of their connection with Edward Carter. But her son's greed had been his undoing.

Ian ground wood betony and wrapped it. "Seems to be a popular remedy today. It might give him some ease. One teaspoon in a cup of ale or wine."

"Oh, he does not partake, as a rule."

To give him credit, Ian's expression did not alter in the least as they exchanged coins. Surely she was just trying to fool herself. "If you bring him in, I'll look at his hand. Perhaps I can be of help."

"Oh, it's not necessary. I am skilled at nursing my

boy."

Maggie stifled her laugh with a cough. No truer words were spoken, for though he was a full grown man, his mother still held him as close as an infant on her teat.

"Thank you, my lady." Ian bowed.

She ignored them both and stalked out the door.

Maggie blew out a breath. "Why does she continue to blame us for her son's dishonesty and shiftlessness?"

"A mother's affection?" Ian shrugged.

"Misplaced motherly love can be as crippling as a missing finger," Maggie said.

"How did you get so wise, my heart?"

"Mayhap it comes from having no mother to be wise for me."

He nodded, laying his hand upon her head in sympathy. "The Stowe family always did like to hold a grudge."

"Yes, old Mr. Stowe never did forgive Pete for his lack of work ethic, and you can't blame him for growing fond of Josef. I hear he was like a son to Mr. Stowe."

"Josef worked for Mr. Stowe way past the terms of his indenture and was a hard worker." Ian's eyes grew dark as a storm-churned sea. "I remember how Josef used to come here with bruises from Mrs. Stowe. He suffered so, and my mother's tender ministrations softened the way for him on a regular basis." He brightened. "She always tried to get him to wash behind his ears."

"She tried but did not succeed." Maggie smiled and kissed Ian behind the ear. "I'm glad she succeeded with you." She breathed in the bayberry scent and forced herself to break away from him. "I must go."

He held the door open for her. "Take care, my beauty. And heed what I said about the road to McCall's."

She nodded and set off, both amused and peeved at his concern. Had she not taken care of herself while he was gone? Was she now helpless just because he'd returned?

Chapter Five

If she had a farthing for every time she had to search for her worthless son...and of all places for him to be lurking. Margaret Stowe avoided the eyes of a group of merchants sitting at a table by the door of the Siren Inn. How could Pete shame the family by abiding here? Look at them laughing. See how they made sport of her, entering her former home, and what manner of son she must have who would lose the family inn, and then return there for a glass of ale. Her face burned with embarrassment. She had not set foot in the place since they'd had to vacate. She blinked her eyes to rid herself of the flush of shame and took comfort in her smoldering rage. The humiliation!

There he was, in the corner, leaning against the wall like a ne'er-do-well. She motioned for him to rise, but he buried his face in his ale. He either pretended not to see her, or blatantly ignored her, she couldn't tell which. Just a year ago, he was a proud man, the constable, not exactly the proprietor of the most popular inn in town, but at least she could hold her head up high. At least he had some influence then.

The insolence of the lad, ignoring her. She grasped his arm. "Did I not tell you to purchase a cut of meat for dinner while I went to the apothecary shoppe?"

"My thumb was paining me, and I thought some ale would help." He pulled his arm out of her grasp.

"Must you scold me like a child, Mother?"

"Do not act like one." She sniffed. "It's little I ask of you."

"I am not a housemaid to be sent on errands."

"No, you're more useless. And you will do as I ask. Your actions have reduced our means drastically," she hissed.

"You never cease to remind me of it."

"I'll not spend another minute in this place." She shuddered. "How can you come here, knowing it was once yours, and you gave it away?"

He stared at her, eyes wide and unblinking. "The alewife makes the best beer in town." He tipped his mug to her.

"You know I never drink."

"Mayhap it might sweeten your disposition, Mother."

He made a big show of drinking the rest of his ale and put his payment on the table. He paid coin to a place rightfully theirs. Did it not bother him?

"Mother, do you know you have a twitch? Below your right eye. Even in this dim light I can see it."

It was getting harder and harder to control him. "You impertinent sluggard. We are leaving now."

He stood, swaying.

She put her arm in his and felt him stiffen. "I cannot fathom how you would make me come in here. Thank Providence the alewife and her husband are not around."

Once outside, she blinked against the light. He looked for all the world like a dutiful son, holding onto her arm, assisting her like any fine gentleman would. Little did these ignorant bumpkins know she held the drunken sot up. She would not have him shame her in the street. How many mugs of ale had he managed to drink?

"You should have seen the apothecary and his wife today. No shame. All over each other like rutting beasts. And treating me like any other customer, not the least bit apologetic for ruining your life. Had it not been for them meddling in Edward Carter's affairs, you would not have landed in the dungeon and suffered so, my poor boy."

"Mother. I'm a man, not a boy. Can we not move toward the future and put the past to rest?"

She must tamp down her rage. It did not help to lose control. "A man does not give away his birthright in a card game."

"When will you forgive me for a mistake I made when not in my right mind?"

"Because you were drunk? I'll forgive you when you redeem yourself." She drew away from him to make her point.

"Did you hear about the alewife's husband? He claims his nephew will rise from the grave as a monster."

"Really? How ridiculous." She stopped. Was the *esteemed* owner of the Siren Inn, the boot-licking indentured servant, losing his mind? Intriguing, and full of possibilities. "What else did you hear?"

He cocked his head. "Something about spreading seeds about. I don't know, Mother. I wasn't listening." He grasped his hand. "The pain."

"Be a man. It's a thumb, not a leg." He looked every bit like a little boy who'd gotten his ears boxed. God knew it happened often enough.

They had reached the kirkyard at St. Agnes' church.

Old Widow Jenkins appeared, making her way between the gravestones.

Margaret put her arm through her son's again, leaning toward him solicitously and suddenly raised her voice. "I will treat your thumb with the herbs the apothecary gave you. Do not despair."

He'd better get the insolent grin off his face, or she'd slap it off.

"Good morrow, Mrs. Jenkins," she called.

The old woman glanced up. "Good morrow, Mrs. Stowe. I was just paying me respects to Mr. Jenkins, God rest his soul." She eyed the two of them up and down, eyes rheumy but alert. "What brings you out this morning?"

"My son's wound is troubling him. We visited the apothecary to find a remedy." She glanced at Pete. "Then I thought we'd pay a visit to the vicar to discuss the troubling, and quite frightening rumors about Mr. Josef's nephew dying."

"Oh, aye, I've heard my share of tongue-wagging already this morn."

Mrs. Stowe stepped forward, so close she could see the rotten black pillars of Mrs. Jenkin's bottom teeth.

"You wouldn't be paying those tongue waggers any mind, would you? Seems not long ago the gossip was about your son."

The backs of her eyelids burned as the visage of the old woman faded and turned to red, the black-red of her gnarled hands pressed on the hot coals, the screams, hoarse with fear and pain. She smiled. *Better.*

Would the crone never cease her yapping?

"Lena is a good woman, kind to me she is. Her man as well, though he doesn't say much. Mayhap the shock of his nephew dying has addled him."

"This morning I heard tell he saw Satan, in his homeland of Bohemia." Nice touch.

"Oh?" Mrs. Jenkin's eyes lit up. Her wrinkled lips moved, mouthing the words so she could repeat them, no doubt. "Ooh, how frightening."

At least the old woman would set more tongues wagging over her last tidbit. What else could she, a mere woman, do to get their rightful property back?

"Where are we going, Mother? I thought we were headed to see the vicar. He's always kind to me, though he's a bit daft."

"No, it's not important."

Pete moaned and listed sideways. Why had God forsaken her by giving her such a weak son? Must it be up to her to regain the family pride?

"Look," she said. "There's the midwife, grinning like a fool. What do you suppose she's so happy about, the little doxy?"

Pete righted himself. "Well, I wouldn't say she's a doxy."

"Oh shut up."

Chapter Six

Maggie stopped for a moment, holding her face up to the sun tucked amidst the grey clouds. Ian was home, and she could not stop the joy from singing within her and putting a smile on her face. She straightened her features. It would not do for people to see her look too happy. They would know exactly what she had been doing with him.

The town of King's Harbour sat upon a hill overlooking the sea with the church of St. Agnes the Virgin at the top. She and Ian lived on Market Street, a short walk to the docks.

The muscles in her calves pulled as she climbed the steep hill and stood near the church to catch her breath. She then hastened her speed downhill, to the ancient Landgate out of town. It towered over her, formidable in what it had witnessed in over five hundred years, holding within its stone the scent of fire and strife from the French, darkness and fear, lives loved and lost.

She hurried out the other side and shrugged off her fanciful self like an itchy cloak; mayhap her uneasiness was due to the burial and Josef's grief. She picked her way down the heavily rutted road, travelled for hundreds of years by merchants and even the occasional monarch. She kept a wary eye out for ne'er-do-wells, those who would rob her of coin and take pleasure from her fear. It was easy enough for them to slip into a boat and escape into the blue.

And what a rare blue sky today! She let the breeze cool her cheeks. Her heart lightened despite the strange and sobering burial. Ian had returned. Not accustomed to feeling joy, other than the simple pleasure of a good meal, or the exultation of a child safely brought into the world, she had gone her whole life without feeling the heartbeat in her throat that came with merely meeting his eye, the joy of joining flesh with him, rising in passion. She had gone her life without feeling such pleasure. And once experienced, she could not do without it.

Still deep in thought, she crossed the bridge. Her foot sank into a soft spot in the wood, and she extricated it carefully from the hole. She should take more care. It was a wonder she hadn't sprained her ankle, or hurt the babe. Why the bridge was still there, she did not know, as it served no purpose, merely arched over a long dried-up river leading to the sea.

It felt good to stretch her legs; she was sore in spots she had not been for a while. She forced herself to slow her pace, for after this much walking, her limp became more pronounced. It was a daily reminder of a midwife's incompetence during her own birth, and a constant reminder to take care with her patients. Maggie had emerged feet first, and the impatient midwife had pulled her out by one foot, giving her a permanent injury.

She took a small rutted side road into a wooded area, following the sound of bleating sheep. She walked along a row of cottages with parcels of land behind them. The McCall family had an ideal situation, with their house at the end of the road, giving them more land to farm their sheep.

The sounds of children at play greeted her as she reached the McCall's cottage. They played in the field behind the small dwelling. She stopped for a moment to view the scene. A burly sheepdog, white spotted with black, romped in the field with four children. The youngest, Thomas, barely one-year-old, tried to follow his older brothers and sisters, who were calling the dog in turn, so he would chase them. The poor little lad, curls bouncing, tumbled down, and upon hearing his cry, the sheepdog returned and prodded him up with his nose, cropped tail wagging. The baby grabbed him by his ears and rubbed his face upon the dog's muzzle. The dog in turn licked Thomas, causing him to sputter and giggle.

The dog stayed with the tot until he was running again, leading strings flapping behind him, and herded him toward his siblings. Tall Katherine no doubt suddenly remembered her duties as the eldest, stopped short, resulting in knocking down her brother behind her. Before she could reach down and help him, the dog came along and nudged him up.

Maggie smiled. The sheepdog was a competent nursemaid indeed.

Mr. McCall leaned against the fence, his eyes alight on the children, ruddy face beaming. "Mistress Maggie! Have you come to see my wife, then?" With obvious effort, he rose and caught his breath as he put weight on one slightly bowed leg.

"Are you injured?"

He grinned beneath his red beard. "Oh no, I'm right enough. Bit of a tussle with my old tup. Nasty disposition, but the ewes cater to him, they do. It's the only thing keeping him from being mutton this winter. Ach, I'm sorry. I have you standing out here, and ye've got yer basket and all." He was a stocky man, well-built and vigorous.

"I would swear young Katherine is growing taller on a daily basis," Maggie said. "I saw her a fortnight ago, and she seems to have grown two inches."

"Aye, she eats like a draft horse, my lass does." He beamed with pride, ruddy cheeks glowing. He shifted his weight on his leg.

"You will let my husband know if your leg doesn't improve, won't you?"

"Ah, he's back, then? Jolly good!" Adam and Ian had been friends since childhood.

He bowed slightly, wincing as he did so. "I thank you, Mistress Maggie, but I'm sure I'll be fine in no time. It's my wife I'm worried about." He rested his hand on the door knob, and lowered his voice. "She's big as a barn door. I've never seen the likes of it, even in my biggest ewes."

She snorted. "I can see why you whisper."

"Yes, she wouldn't be fond of hearing the comparison."

"Don't worry, Mr. McCall, a woman in travail can do astonishing things, and your wife has delivered of four robust children."

Adam smiled. How very satisfying when a few words of encouragement could lift an expectant father's spirit so.

Just then, the door opened and Bethan, Polly's sister appeared. "Mistress Maggie, how good it is to see you!"

Bethan embraced her, squeezing her so hard she

47

squeaked.

"Oh, I'm sorry. I don't know my own strength sometimes."

Maggie had to crick her head to meet the young woman's flashing blue eyes. Bethan was certainly tall for a woman, as was her identical twin, Elunid. Her glossy brown hair pulled up in a simple chignon accentuated her widow's peak and arched brows.

"Oh! Congratulations on your pregnancy."

"Thank you, Bethan. How fares your sister?"

Bethan bent slightly to whisper in Maggie's ear. "She frightens me. She's so immense."

Maggie laughed. "Bethan!" Honestly, the girl became more impertinent with every visit, but she could not help but be drawn to her like a flower leans toward the sun. How could she be so joyful, with the burden of her sister always upon her shoulders? One twin was perfectly sound in mind, and the other without an anchor to sanity.

"Is your twin inside?"

"No, Elunid left shortly after dawn this morning, in search of inspiration for her new needlework. She said she must finish it soon, for *they* were demanding it."

"They? Who?"

Bethan grimaced. "She is convinced she pays penance, for what sin I do not know. But it does no good to convince her otherwise. She'll return when she finds what she's looking for." She straightened her shoulders. "That's Elunid. There is no changing her."

Maggie nodded.

"But I apologize." Bethan put her hand on the door knob. "I am keeping you from tending to my sister." She smacked her hand on her forehead. "Oh! Elunid is almost out of thread. I must get some for her today."

Maggie was about to inquire further into the matter when the sound of chanting made them look down the lane.

"Hark, a walking tree!" Bethan joked. "And singing."

Indeed, it seemed as if a tree had uprooted itself and marched down the lane. The scent of pine sap from a massive pine tree wafted their way. Maggie would know Henry's rumbling bass anywhere, though she could not see his face, or his son, George's.

"Heft it up, lad. Heft it up. Use your legs, lad. Use your legs. Right. All your life you must work, you must tend to your body, young George. Sing with me."

Bethan murmured beside them. "Who is that?"

"Have you not met Henry?"

"No. What a deep voice he has. And well-muscled calves," Bethan added, so softly Maggie was not sure she heard her correctly.

They carried the tree between them, and Maggie could not help but admire the well-formed, deeply muscled calves of the night soil man.

Adam headed toward them, clapping his hands. "Ah, there you are."

"Here we are, neighbor. Two able-bodied men ready to work."

"Ah, the tree speaks," Bethan quipped.

"Adam, where do you want this?" Henry said. "Or should we be dancing around with it all day?"

Adam took hold of the tree's midsection, and they carried it to the small lean-to barn lying next to the cottage.

"Easy now, George. On the count of three, we will

lower it. Watch you don't bang your hands. One, two, three." A thump reverberated on the ground as they laid the tree down.

Suddenly the men materialized. Henry arched his back, groaning, then straightened and glanced their way. He grinned, teeth white in a neat black beard. He had a broad chest and powerful arms, the sleeves of his homespun shirt rolled to the elbows. "Good morrow, Mistress Maggie."

Bethan's hand dropped from the doorknob, and a hiss of breath escaped her.

"Good morrow, gentlemen."

Henry reached Maggie and bowed.

George stood behind his father, dark hair tousled and dirt besmeared on his face.

Henry turned toward George. "Say hello, son."

When he turned around again, and saw Bethan at first glance, he took a step backward and trod on George's feet.

"Yow, Da!" George knit his brows in reproach.

"I'm sorry, lad."

Maggie watched in amusement as Henry regained his balance. His ears had turned bright red, and color crept along his neck. But Maggie had to admire his gallant recovery, as he bowed toward Bethan, then raised his head, eyes the color of treacle pudding.

"I'm sorry. I don't believe we've met, mistress."

Oh, most interesting. Maggie glanced between Bethan and Henry, who met each other's shocked gaze. They seemed oblivious to George's restless shuffling, the yipping of the sheepdog.

Bethan nodded. "Pleased to meet you."

"Henry, Bethan is from Llandudno, northern

Wales," Maggie said.

His dark eyebrows rose. "Ay? I've never travelled so far north."

"It is quite beautiful," Bethan said. "And wild."

"Much like yourself?" Henry searched her face, eyebrows arched.

A deep pink stained Bethan's cheeks. She gave her head an odd little shake.

"I would like to venture there," he said.

"The lighthouse is quite majestic," Bethan murmured, eyes the color of ripe blueberries.

"Yes." Henry nodded.

An awkward silence hung in the air.

Maggie said, "Henry is the night soil man."

Bethan stepped back, put her hand over her mouth, and bumped into the door. "You are...the night soil man?" She looked as if she'd been pelted with a shovelful of shite. Then, as if realizing her rudeness, she slowly lowered her hand.

Henry lifted his chin. "It's our bread and butter, my lady."

Maggie snorted. Not what she would call it.

It was Bethan's turn to blush. "I'm sorry to offend." She paused, a corner of her mouth quirking. "But it seems you do not..."

"Reek?"

She reddened. "Yes."

Truth be told, Maggie had often asked herself the same question about Henry and George. Currently, the pleasant smell of pine sap wafted from father and son.

Henry straightened, seemed to grow taller and broader. He put an arm around George's shoulders. "Indeed, milady, it's an honest profession, and we would all spend the day holding our noses without it." His full lips twitched, and Bethan leaned against the door.

Maggie's glance ricocheted between the two. She repressed the urge to laugh. She'd not expected to be entertained, and as much as she enjoyed this little distraction, she had work to do. "What are you doing with the tree?" As long as they'd been lingering, poor Polly could have delivered the child by now.

"I've come to help Adam build a new pen for his ram."

Just then, Adam joined Henry. "Are we going to get on with it, man? Or will you stand here talking the day long?" He turned to Maggie. "The ram and the last lady he tupped broke it, they did. It keeps them confined, like. So I don't have to chase them." He grinned.

Speaking of mating, the air between Henry and Bethan held the sweetness and promise of a ripe peach. Maggie recognized it, for she'd just experienced it herself.

Henry nodded at Maggie. "I have my orders." And with one last penetrating glance toward Bethan, he tipped his cap.

George bowed. "Good morrow." He looked to his father for approval.

Henry clapped him on the shoulders. "Nicely done," he whispered.

The door opened and young Katherine stood at the threshold. "W-welcome, Mistress Maggie."

"Katherine, so lovely to see you."

Katherine curtsied prettily. Her face, upon rising, had flushed to apricot, and her eyes were a piercing dark blue, like her aunt's. She was slim as a reed with her father's red hair and her mother's pale coloring.

On their way in, Bethan muttered, "Night soil man? He looks nothing like our man back home. And he would never dare to be so impertinent."

Maggie did not know much about the northern Welsh town in which Bethan had grown up, but remembered Polly talking about how angry her mother had been when she'd run away with Adam. Adam had asked for her hand, but her parents felt she'd be marrying beneath her, for while they were not aristocrats, they were monied. But a happier couple Maggie had never met, and beautiful children they'd produced.

"Mother said it's almost time for tea."

Maggie followed her into the cottage. A welcoming fire roared in the hearth, and stalks of lavender strewn about the neatly swept floor sweetened the air like spring. Polly's splendid embroidery hung on the whitewashed walls, giving the impression one stood in a meadow, with bright birds and flowers, knights and ladies of old. A new piece hung on the wall, medieval and threatening, with skeletal figures scaling their way up castle ramparts. There was an air of desperation to it, and it did not resemble Polly's usual work.

"My, how you have grown, Katherine." Maggie smiled at her, hoping to coax her out of her shyness.

Polly stood by the fire. "Mistress Maggie, how lovely to see you. You are just in time for tea. It is miraculous how fast Katherine is growing. We had to let the hem out of her skirts last week. And she has a lovely straight even stitch."

"She is taking after her mother," Maggie said. She

tried very hard not to let alarm show upon her face. Polly *was* immense, but beautiful with the lush intensity of a woman close to her term. She had blonde hair, whereas Bethan and Elunid were dark.

"Polly, how are you feeling?"

Polly smiled wanly. "Well enough. I feel like I'm walking in a vat of molasses, though."

Maggie nodded, though apprehension skittled in her belly like a crab. How could this petite woman carry such an immense burden?

Polly smiled at her daughter and put a hand upon her shoulder in approval. "Go now, child, and set the table for tea."

"I'll pour," Maggie said. "Sit down, Polly."

Polly obediently perched at the trestle bench. "Ah, wonderful," she groaned.

Bethan clapped her hands. "Tea time."

As soon as Polly sat, the one-year-old toddled over to his mother and peered over her belly. "Ma."

The dog galumphed over to Polly and put his head on her thighs.

"Ung!" The baby indignantly shoved the dog's head away. "Ma."

Unfazed by this treatment, the dog shuffled over to the fire and plopped down. Baby Thomas raised his arms to be picked up.

Maggie bent to lift him, one hand under his bottom, and the other wrapped around his chubby body. "Ho! He's a hefty little lad!"

He laid his hot little palms upon her face and grinned, cheeks plump as fresh rolls. She ruffled his blond curls and allowed herself the luxury of sinking her nose into the creases of his neck, breathing in the scent of milk, baby, and innocence. A most curious warmth enveloped her. Perhaps the two babes, hers unborn, spoke to each other in a language known only to them. Or perhaps he'd just wet his clouts, who knew? She set the babe on the trestle bench beside his mother. Polly put an arm around the little lad, and he leaned his head against her side, thumb in mouth.

Maggie used every bit of her professionalism not to stare at Polly's immense belly. What manner of child resided within? Would it pose a problem at her time of trial? She needed to examine her.

Polly set her chin on top of the little lad's head. "I know what you're thinking, Maggie. I'm huge."

Polly had a fortnight before her time, but every instinct Maggie possessed said she would deliver before then.

"All shall be well, Polly."

"I made scones with some raisins left over from last summer's grapes," Katherine said.

At the mention of raisins, the other two boys looked up from the dog.

"Peter, Adam, come greet Mistress Maggie." Polly's soft voice demanded instant obedience.

The two boys, almost the same size, had their sister's coloring, and their father's sturdy build. They approached Maggie and said in unison, "How do, Mistress Maggie?"

"Very well, thank you. And you?"

Fidgeting, they eyed each other. "We are well, thank you."

"My." She turned to Polly. "What well-mannered children you have." This engendered a huge grin from both boys and they filed to the table, beaming.

"Mother," Katherine said. "Should I not call Father and the night soil man in to tea?"

"Very thoughtful of you, Katherine, but you know how men are. Until they have finished the job, they will not stop to feed themselves, even if we wave it in front of their faces."

The door flung open and a girl, looking eerily like Bethan, swept into the room. But of course it was her twin Elunid, dark hair snarled around her face, eyes blue as troubled seas. She stood on the threshold.

Bethan had just buttered and smeared a generous amount of blackberry jam on her scone. She took a deep breath and rose. "There you are. Look at you. There are bits of straw in your hair, and you have torn your skirt." Bethan adjusted her sister's clothing, took the pins out of her hair, and set it to rights again, while her twin gazed at the wall hangings.

Maggie was amazed anew at the mirror image of Bethan. But not quite identical. They were exactly the same height, but Elunid seemed shorter, for she stood with her shoulders hunched and her head down. She was paler and had not the light in her eyes her sister possessed.

"Where have you been, my girl?"

She did not respond but continued to stare at the wall hangings. Bethan grasped her hands. "My poor dear. What have you done to yourself? Your hands are all scratched up, and your nails are torn and filthy! Here, we must go outside and brush the dirt and straw from you."

Again, no response from Elunid.

Bethan put a quilt over her shoulders. "You are so cold. Have you lost your cloak again?"

Polly whispered to Maggie. "Bethan takes it as a personal affront if the poor girl is less than immaculate. I think she feels it's one of the few things she can control. She has been taking care of her since they were fourteen."

Bethan led her sister outside. Polly and Maggie exchanged glances.

"She has good and bad days, and days like this, where she is not aware of the outside world," Polly murmured. "And we can do nothing for her but try to keep her safe. Mother has not the patience for it."

The two girls soon returned, and Bethan led Elunid to the table and sat her down. "You must eat." She sat and smiled, patted her hair in place. "You needn't have waited for us."

The simple meal consisted of cheese, scones, jam, and good black tea. Once the initial hunger had been satisfied, they began to chatter, interspersed with Katherine's admonitions for them to mind their manners.

"Katherine," Maggie said. "These scones are delicious."

"Thank you." She blushed.

"Now tell me true, Polly. Have there been any changes with you?" Maggie asked.

"I told you, I've been fine enough."

"Have your ankles been swollen?"

Polly paused mid-sip. "Just a bit, in the evening. But they're fine by morning."

A quiet, self-assured woman, Polly thought before she spoke, but always had a kind word for someone. She had been an invaluable helping hand when smallpox ravaged the town a few years back. With each of her children, the second child born when Maggie first came to town, she never complained, and was one of the calmest delivering mothers Maggie had ever seen.

There was the sound of scraping boots at the front door, and Adam filed in. Henry and George stood behind him, mouths open, both of them rubbing their chins with their thumb and forefinger.

Maggie stifled her amusement. Like father, like son.

"Come join us," Adam said. "What ails you, boys?"

"I think they did not know Bethan had a twin." Maggie laughed.

"Ah," Henry started. "Please pardon my rudeness."

George tapped his father on the shoulder. "Da, there are two of them."

Bethan burst out laughing. "Yes, George. We are twins, a strange and sometimes wonderful phenomenon."

"As if one of you wasn't enough," Polly said.

Bethan placed her hand on Elunid's shoulder. "This is Elunid. Is it not a beautiful name?" She smiled kindly at George, who had forgotten his manners and was chewing with his mouth open.

"George," Henry whispered. "Close your mouth."

Maggie eyed Elunid and shivered, for it seemed Elunid's body was present but her soul had disappeared.

Just as suddenly, the sensation left Maggie when Elunid cocked her head and gazed at George without blinking.

"Elunid is the quiet one," George said.

"You are a smart boy," Bethan said.

He took a large bite of a jam-topped scone and made a big show of swallowing first before he said, "No one's ever called me smart before, except for Da."

"Your father is right," Bethan declared.

Henry beamed at her and met her gaze. She blushed and averted her eyes.

Polly shifted in her seat. It must be uncomfortable to carry such weight. Maggie hoped she would not be as huge.

Katherine brought another pan of scones to the table, and Henry smiled as George shyly thanked her. Eating resumed and pleasant chatter filled the table.

Adam held his cup out to Katherine for more tea. "Mistress Maggie, tell us about your husband's travel adventures."

Word certainly got around fast, even out here.

"I have not heard them yet, but I'm sure he had many. He usually does."

"Well, I look forward to hearing them when I go into town. Henry, what's this about Josef returning and bringing the devil with him? I heard it from the miller."

Henry shook his head.

"And sometimes lurk I in a gossip's bowl
In very likeness of a roasted crab."

Bethan's head shot up from her plate. "It's Puck." She looked round the table for affirmation.

Maggie's confused expression mirrored her fellow tablemates.

"Yes!" Henry laughed. Admiration gleamed in his eyes like a sea-kissed agate. "Shakespeare's *Midsummer Night's Dream.*"

"Indeed, it's one of my favorites."

Maggie hadn't the slightest idea what they were talking about, but she could not mistake attraction's glow, as if the sun shone only on them.

"How come you to know the quotation, Mistress Bethan?"

"Stormy winters at the lighthouse are a perfect time to read the old bard." She ran her index finger round the rim of her teacup and peered up at him. "A better question is how a night soil man comes to know Shakespeare."

"Oh, I know all manner of things, Lady MacBethan."

Bethan giggled.

Adam cleared his throat. "Henry, why are you not eating, friend? Do you dislike my daughter's cooking?"

"For pity's sake, husband," Polly said.

"Father!" Katherine cried.

Henry nodded at Polly and Katherine in turn. "Oh no, ladies. Everything is delicious." Upon saying the word delicious, he peered at Bethan, whose cheeks turned pink as a peony. Polly rose from the table gingerly and bid the children clear the table. Katherine carried the babe to the rug by the hearth and called the boys over.

Just then, Elunid stood, eyes wide and staring at the needlework on the wall. "I have no more thread. They did not like my work and said I must try again." The voice lay dull and flat in the air, and the scone she held crumbled as she brought her fist to her mouth. "If I have no thread I must unravel some," she murmured and walked woodenly over to where the odd needlework hung. It must be Elunid's.

"No, Elunid. You will not *unravel* now." Bethan

grinned at her play on words and shrugged her slender shoulders, suddenly looking years older. "If I did not jest about my sister's condition, I would cry." She lifted her dimpled chin. "I hate to cry."

Then Bethan rose and joined her hand with Elunid's limp one. "I will fetch you some thread. I have some squirreled away for just such an emergency." She shot a look over her shoulder at Polly, who nodded her head and lumbered over to her sewing basket. Elunid laid her hands on the wall hanging of a knight on his charger on a background of blossoming fruit trees.

"I think I have some as well." Maggie rummaged in her basket.

"They will not like it," Elunid repeated, hoarse with desperation. "I have seen them, crawling up the gaping hole of hell. They cannot scale it, and their nails fill with hell's ashes." She beetled her brows at Bethan. "The perfect shade of Satan's punishment is hard to find."

"Stop, sister, you will frighten the children. You must work on something else."

Bethan turned to Maggie. "I can distract her for a while, but there are certain givens in this situation, and one of them is she must have thread. I will go to town this afternoon."

She put her hands on Elunid's shoulders. "Where is your needlework cloth?"

Elunid pressed her lips together. "I mustn't tell, sister. They said I must bury it and be ashamed, for it did not honor them."

"You buried it?" Bethan grabbed her cloak and put it on her twin. "We must find it, for you have spent many hours toiling." She exchanged glances with

Maggie. "Our absence will allow you some privacy to tend to Polly."

"Wait," Henry called. "I will accompany you."

"No, we can manage alone."

"I'd be happy to help."

"It's best if we go alone," Bethan said. "She behaves better."

"She's probably right," Adam said.

Henry grabbed his cloak and draped it over Bethan's shoulders. She glanced over her shoulder, and his hand stilled. Elunid began to hum in a hoarse monotone, words indistinguishable.

The children lifted their heads as one. The youngest put his head in Katherine's lap. "Never mind, boys," Katherine soothed.

"Come, my dear. Lead me to where you buried it."

Adam rose and kissed his wife upon the cheek. "We must get back to work." He motioned to young Adam. "Come, lad. You can help us today."

"Can I, Da?" He rose, remembered his manners, and turned to Maggie. "Good day, Mistress Maggie."

Henry rose. "Thank you for the delicious tea, mistress." He tapped George on the shoulder.

"Thank you, Mistress McCall."

Polly smiled, nodding her head graciously.

Maggie stood for a moment, breathing in the harmony. Despite the sheer number of children in the small space, there existed a sense of everything in its place and everyone knowing their worth. It spoke to the child within her who still yearned for unconditional love. Indeed, it was a feeling akin to the peace and comfort the holy nun had given her when she'd needed it most.

But she had not come to see to her own wellbeing. Polly needed looking after. "Katherine, would you mind keeping your brothers occupied while I examine your mother? We must see how the baby is doing."

Katherine nodded, eyebrows creased in concentration and back straight. "Yes, Mistress Maggie. Boys, I will fetch the cup and ball Aunt Bethan brought us." She reached up onto a shelf and retrieved the toy, then took the children to the far corner of the room. The dog curled up by the fire and watched them.

Maggie smiled at Katherine's imperious tone and motioned Polly over to the corner where a pallet lay, covered with an embroidered spread. "Lie down, and we will see how your baby is doing."

Polly chuckled. "Lie down in the middle of the day? I feel like royalty."

"And indeed you are for the moment."

She soon had the young mother lying in comfort with a pillow under her hips.

"Ah, it feels heavenly." Polly sighed.

"You should do this often. It is good for you and the babe."

"With four children and an ungainly sheepdog?"

"I see your point." Maggie laughed.

She knelt and pulled Polly's skirts up, while at the same time draping a blanket over her legs to preserve her modesty. Then with both hands, she felt her stomach, searching for the babe's body parts. She pushed her fingers lightly at the top and received a responding kick from the babe. "Good morning, little one," she exclaimed.

"He is active, isn't he?" Polly grunted as her massive belly undulated.

Maggie palpated the mound again, feeling a bump here, a bump there. *Oh.* It might be a knee, or perhaps an elbow. A rump, and another kick under Polly's ribs, and a kick low, right above her privities. A kick up above and a kick down below? No babe could manage those contortions, unless it was a monster.

Anxiety sat like a clump of ice in Maggie's stomach; what if the babe were monstrously malformed? It happened, and with the constant worry of Elunid's activities, distress could play a part in harming the child. She'd never seen it, but had heard of it from the old midwife, and countless others.

No, how foolish of her. There were just too many body parts for one child, so it must be—she lifted her hands off Polly's belly.

Polly lifted her head. "Is something amiss?"

"No, not at all." The wonder of it! And how extraordinary Ian had given her the model of the twins this very day. A warm breeze entered her, melting the ice in her stomach as the spirit of the holy nun visited her, and the words, "All is well," echoed within her.

She placed her hands upon Polly again, closed her eyes, and saw two babes within their mother's womb. One lay with its head at the top, the other's head lay at the bottom. They were curled together, legs crossed at the ankles, thumbs in their mouths. The two umbilical cords pulsed between them.

As quickly as it came on, the vision cleared when the back door opened, and little Thomas wailed.

"Shame on you, Peter," Katherine scolded. "Give Thomas back the toy." She stood over the boy, with crying Thomas perched on her narrow hips. "Now."

The three-year-old handed the toy over to Thomas

and eyed his sister, who held a rag doll in her hand. "Here," she said, sounding beleaguered.

Maggie usually brought a treat for the children, and today was no exception. She reached into her bag and gave each of them an orange. Peace reigned again as they sat at the table, and the smell of oranges wafted over to the two women.

Maggie put Polly's clothing to rights. "Why do you not close your eyes for a moment and enjoy the respite?"

"It will last only as long as the oranges do," Polly said. "I have the most fearful dyspepsia when I lie down. Have you anything for it?"

"Yes, I will give you some meadowsweet to steep as a tea. And it's no surprise you do. I have made a discovery, Polly."

Polly's eyes popped open.

"You are carrying twins."

Her face blanched. "Two babes?"

Katherine appeared with a piece of orange in her hand. She forgot her dignity for a moment, and hugged Polly. "Two? Oh, Mother!"

"Twins." The color began to bloom in Polly's face like a newly opened rose. "Oh my."

"They seem healthy," Maggie said. "And I see no reason for concern, other than you must rest more." In truth, delivering twins was always fraught with difficulties, and these babies seemed huge in comparison to the other set of twins she'd delivered this year.

"I will help you, Mother! I pray they are girls. I need sisters."

Maggie reached into her basket again and handed

Katherine two more oranges. "Would you peel these for your mother? One for each baby."

Katherine giggled and handed her mother the orange piece. "I forgot. This is for you, Mama."

"Thank you. You're a good lass." A look of affection passed between mother and daughter, and a longing rose within Maggie for her mother who had died in childbirth so long ago. She held her hand upon her stomach. She would be a mother like Polly.

Katherine skipped over to the table.

"Poor girl," Polly said. "She is already doing the work of a full grown woman."

"I think she enjoys helping you. She seems a happy girl."

"And old beyond her years."

Maggie helped Polly sit up. "I will have my husband make you a tonic to strengthen you and the babes."

Polly said, "I don't know why I am so shocked, when twins run in the family."

"Speaking of twins, it must be a bit wearing to have them here."

"It is both helpful and wearing. Bethan deals with Elunid; she always has. The burden falls on Bethan. I must admit it is a bit worrisome, because we never know when Elunid will become…unhinged. And I must say she does frighten the children at times."

Just then, Adam and the boy came in, letting in a gust of cold air.

Katherine ran to her father. "Father, Mother has two babies. I do hope they are girls."

He stood stock still. "Pardon?" Henry and George stood behind him, wearing identical looks of shock.

Polly came up to him, placing his hands upon her stomach. "It is crowded in there. With two."

He took a ragged breath and then rallied round, embracing his wife. "Wondrous! How clever of you, dear Polly!"

Thomas, the soon-to-be dethroned king of the family, pawed at his mother's skirt.

Adam lifted him into the air and swung him around, much to the boy's uninhibited delight. "You will not be the baby of the family for long. Best prepare yourself, lad."

Soon the other boys gathered round for their share of roughhousing, giving Maggie a chance to speak with Polly. "Now, remember to rest when you can, and send your husband for my sister or me if anything changes."

"I will be visiting you in the next day or so, and my most hearty congratulations."

"Thank you, Mistress Maggie."

As Maggie stood on the threshold, Bethan and Elunid walked up. Bethan whispered in Elunid's ear, an arm around her thin shoulder. Elunid clutched a piece of cloth in her hands and nodded as Bethan spoke.

Bethan seated her in the chair by the fire. "Are you feeling better now, dear?"

Elunid nodded.

'Good then. Here is the thread, and I will go into town this afternoon to get more." She turned to Maggie. "Do you mind if I walk with you?"

Henry, who'd been rubbing his chin as he watched the scene, cleared his throat. "Miss Owens?'

Bethan glanced up, cheeks coloring. Maggie had never seen the girl color before. "Yes?"

"I would be happy to give you both a ride in my

wagon."

She gulped. "Your night soil wagon? I do not think…"

Henry cocked his head, a glint in his eyes. "Clearly this lady looks down upon me for doing an honest day's work," he stage whispered to Adam.

Bethan held her hands in fists against her dress. "Well, I only meant you do gather shite…'

Polly gasped. "Bethan. Your language."

Bethan tossed her head. "What else can one call it?"

"Da and I clean it every morning, Miss. It hardly stinks at all."

A smile tugged at the corner of Bethan's mouth. "Well, the sooner I buy thread, the better."

"Don't worry, Bethan. I've ridden in it many times, and it was not unpleasant," Maggie said. "And I would appreciate a ride to the Siren Inn. I need to see how Lena fairs."

Before long, the four of them set off toward town, George perched in the back of the wagon on a piece of burlap.

Maggie sat next to Henry on the narrow bench, with Bethan hunched up on the end, braced for disaster, it seemed. She held a handkerchief over her mouth.

Maggie tilted her face to the sun. "Mild day, is it not?"

"Yes, even as we worked last night, we were quite comfortable."

"It is all the more pleasant for being fleeting. Do you not think so, Bethan?"

Bethan's eyebrows knit above panic-filled eyes. She nodded.

"Never known you to be speechless before." Maggie nudged her playfully.

The horse stopped short before the bridge.

"Easy, Clyde." Henry turned toward the two women, brushing a black curl out of his eyes. "He's a bit bridge shy. Mayhap he sees how silly it is to be there, as there's no water under it anymore."

He leaned over and caressed the bay's neck, rumbled endearments in a deep bass. Bethan gulped and slowly lowered the handkerchief.

It was plain to see. Bethan would very much like to be the horse right now.

"Ready then?" Henry gave the horse's neck a gentle pat and the wagon moved forward. "Easy now. Easy."

He tended to the road then, veering around a pothole. "So, Miss Owens, your sister is a talented seamstress. What is your talent?"

She scowled at him. "Must one have a talent? Is it not enough for one to be a good person, to be kind?"

The reins went slack in Henry's hands. "I did not mean to offend, mistress. I was just curious." He peered sideways at her. "Despite my lowly occupation, I do like to make conversation."

"He talks all the time," George yelled above the rumble of the wagon.

"Bethan has many talents," Maggie said. "She plays the pianoforte quite beautifully. A pity Polly doesn't have one."

"Indeed, I would like to hear it," Henry rumbled.

"I must confess I will miss it while I'm here," Bethan said. "But Elunid has been keeping me quite busy of late, so I wouldn't have time to play it in any case."

"Miss, I consider the caring of a family member with such tenderness to be a rare talent indeed."

A blush rose from Bethan's neck to her forehead. "She is my twin," she whispered. "I could do nothing less."

"She is dark and you are light, like a full moon," George said. "E'en though you look the same."

"What a clever boy you are, George."

"Oh no. I am stupid."

At this, Bethan turned full around in her seat. "Who says so?"

"Some of the children."

"Well, you mustn't listen to them, for it is they who are lacking," Bethan said forcefully.

"Thank you, mistress."

The rest of the way into town, Maggie made a mental list of what she and her sister Sarah would need to do to deliver Polly safely. Certainly they would have to visit her more often, every few days at the very least. She did not carry the babes low yet, but things could happen quickly when twins were involved. How in the world could she and Adam house so many people?

She wondered what Ian would say when she told him about the vision. How miraculous to have seen the babes within the womb. She lifted her face to the sky. *Thank you, Holy Mother.*

They soon arrived at the Siren Inn.

"Thanks very much for the ride." She meant it, for in truth, her foot pained her, as it tended to do after a long morning.

Henry headed for the other side of the wagon. Before he could assist Bethan, she scrambled out of the wagon, murmured a thank you and farewell to Maggie, and headed up the street toward the notions store.

Maggie shook her head in amusement. Bethan behaved very oddly indeed. Perhaps the strain of caring for her sister affected her? No, this was something else entirely. She eyed Henry, who stood with his hands on his hips, watching Bethan stride down the street until she disappeared out of sight.

As Henry helped Maggie out of the wagon, a group of customers scurried out of the old inn.

"What's come over the man? He's gone balmy."

"How can I enjoy a tankard if he's spouting such nonsense?"

"Let's go to the Shipwreck Hotel."

What had transpired? She had seldom seen a customer leave the inn unhappy. Her stomach growled. The babe within demanded food, and soon. As she entered the ancient inn, the scent of roasting meat and the comforting aroma of ale and pipe smoke enveloped her.

Josef leaned toward a customer, wiry arms folded on the counter. "I tell you man, you must beware. The horror I've seen in my native land would bring a man to his knees. I have brought this evil to our village. We sprinkled the seeds, but I fear it may not work, and he will rise. I must go watch the grave tonight."

Chapter Seven

Clearly Josef had taken no heed of Ian's warning to keep still about the circumstances of his nephew's death. He topped off a sailor's ale and slammed it on the scarred but polished counter. The amber liquid splashed in the sailor's sunburned face. He gave Josef the gimlet eye. "I paid to drink this, not wear it," he yelled.

"Shut your gob, man."

What possessed Josef? This was worrisome indeed. Of all the inns in King's Harbour, the townspeople flocked here, in big part because of the food and Lena's excellent ale, but also due to the even-tempered, albeit taciturn Josef. He had a way of tamping down the embers of conflict before they flamed, making the Siren Inn a convivial place to be.

"Josef, I see you are back at work in earnest. You must be tired after such a long journey."

He shook his head. "What does it matter, when I must write my sister and tell her Nikolaus is dead?"

The seaman nodded to Maggie in a pronounced manner indicative of the very drunk. He eyed her with great appreciation. "Lass, care to bide a spell with me? I'll tell ye a story. Ye can even sit on me lap." He leaned toward her, foul breath blowing like an ill wind.

She was used to this type of behavior; her look of contempt usually dampened a man's ardor faster than a fishwife could gut a haddock.

Suddenly, Josef lunged over the counter and grabbed the man's shirtfront, knocking over his ale. The room grew silent.

"Does she look like a doxy to you?" He growled. "This is a respectable lady, and I'll thank you to stay clear of her, you poxy scab of a bastard."

The sailor stood, swaying, and looked about for his comrades, she guessed. Finding himself alone with no reinforcements, he sat back down.

Was Josef so altered by grief and fatigue, he had forgotten his responsibilities as proprietor? She would have to intervene.

"Now, I am sure no harm has been done, eh?" She smiled at the sailor. "Sit and I'll pour you another drink." He'd had enough to be easily manipulated, especially by a woman. He'd drunk the fight out of himself, and what he wanted right now was a warm bed, and an even warmer woman. She put the ale in front of him and took Josef aside.

"Is all well with Lena, Maggie? She is never sick. She started the morning retching and hasn't stopped. She's thin and sickly, except for her belly."

"Don't worry, Josef. She'll be fine. Many mothers suffer from this for their entire term, and the remedy I have with me today may help."

His face brightened again, making him look years younger. "It is a son, no doubt, to have such a strong effect on his mother."

She chuckled. "Could be. There is much mystery in the begetting of a child."

He nodded. "I cannot believe it. It is a miracle! After so long."

Perhaps now she could talk some sense into him. "Josef, you have suffered a great shock. But there is nothing you can do for your nephew now. You must concentrate on Lena and the baby. It is all the more reason you should not speak of what happened last night."

A group of merchants called out for their dinner.

"Please," she warned Josef. "Heed our advice. You need only remember what happened last year, when superstition overpowered the common sense of these good people."

He nodded, but did he really understand?

"Is Ian coming tonight?"

"We spoke of meeting up here," Maggie said.

"I have something for him," he said. "He can use it in his travels." He wore a sly, furtive look, the one that made Lena bristle like a hedgehog. He glanced back at the main room, where a crowd of dock workers had just come in, and the song they sang would grow hair on a woman's chest.

"I must get back to work," Josef said. "I know this crew."

"I will go see if I can help your wife with her morning sickness," she said. "Josef, you must get some rest. Your wife and unborn child need you."

He nodded and made his way back to the counter. She followed him behind the bar and walked into the kitchen. Sabine stood at a table, measuring grain with one hand and holding her baby on a hip with the other arm.

She smiled. "Good after—noon," she said haltingly.

"How are you, Sabine? You look well."

74

"I am well, Mistress Maggie."

Ian was teaching Sabine English; little Ruthie, Maggie's sister Sarah's daughter, helped as well. The baby was a year old and gazed at her mother with a beatific smile. Her eyes, like her mother's, were almond-shaped and the color of toffee.

Lena stood over a large pot, stirring a mixture of grains with a giant wooden spoon. The smell was most agreeable. The room was steamy and fragrant. Lena's face glistened with sweat.

"Maggie!" She smiled. "Sabine's *kinder* has grown, no?"

"Lena, you are working hard as usual. Did you not make ale last week?"

"*Ja*, and it's gone. The damn sailors drank their weight in ale and small beer Saturday."

"You must take a care for yourself, Lena."

"I'm healthy as a horse but for the vomiting all day. Once it's over, I feel myself again." She grinned.

"You have the biscuits by the bed like I suggested?" Maggie reached into her basket. "Cinnamon in warmed wine. Keep it by the bedside. Mayhap it will help."

"*Ach*, wine. For aristocrats and Frenchmen." She made a face. "But this wort. Ugh. It does not smell right."

"It smells like it always does, Lena. Wonderful."

She wrinkled her nose. "No, it makes me…" She gulped, put her hand over her mouth, handed the spoon to Maggie, and ran over to the basin to vomit.

Maggie's gorge rose in sympathy. Oh no. It is a bad thing when a German ale wife cannot stand the smell of her own ale. Maggie stirred, shook her head, and stared into the boiling pot of wort, the brown bits of grain that eventually transformed itself into beer.

It would be easy to tell Lena she had nothing to worry about. Sometimes her responsibility to her mothers to see them safely through their travails weighed heavily upon her, and she had only so much knowledge at her disposal. With Lena, it was especially worrisome, for a few years ago, she had delivered Lena of a stillborn. She straightened her shoulders. She would do everything in her power to see nothing would happen to this child. Or Lena.

"I'm sorry, friend. Perhaps the wine will agree with you."

Lena nodded, beads of sweat pooling on her pale forehead.

"You must rest when you are tired. Drink, to replace what you have purged, or your humors will suffer for it."

Sabine stood quietly at Lena's side. "Mistress," Sabine said, "I will finish." Her normally soft voice adopted a tone brooking no argument. She handed the babe to Maggie, eyeing Lena sternly. "You rest."

"She's right, Lena. Come put your feet up. You are getting too big to be working so hard."

Lena nodded. "*Ach*, you are right." She took a plate off the stove. "I made strudel today from the apples we gathered last summer. I know how much you like it."

"You are such a good and kind friend, Lena. Making things for me when you feel so poorly."

Lena laughed, holding her middle. "And here you are caring for me, when you should be home tasting your strudel of a man. Eat, they're still warm."

They left the kitchen and went through the public

area to Lena's private sitting room.

Maggie placed a stool in front of Lena. "Put up your feet when you can."

They sat in companionable silence. Maggie took a bite of the strudel. The day of apple picking had been one of the most pleasant times she could ever remember. They had taken the ferryboat to Winchelsea and spent the afternoon in the apple orchard. They had picked a bushel and taken a nap underneath the apple trees. As it turned out, the owner of the apple orchard had bartered with his apples for Maggie and Sarah to deliver his child in a few months. A fair trade, apples for babies. She smiled.

"How are you feeling, Lena?"

Her friend leaned her head back and closed her eyes. "Like I wobble on a spoon in a vat of wort. Seasick. Wort-sick."

"Try to keep something in your stomach all the time," Maggie advised.

Lena gave Maggie the gimlet eye. "Every time my stomach convulses, it is so strong, like I am in labor, and I think, the child, like the one before, will be expelled."

"No, Lena, one has not to do with the other." Maggie grasped her thin arm. "It is a good sign. The child makes its presence known. Your body is just growing accustomed to having it there. And indeed it is growing! I swear I will do everything in my power to keep you and the babe safe."

"You cannot perform miracles, Maggie."

She couldn't; it was true. "I will do what I can, Lena. And what your body says to me is despite the power of your nausea, the child grows. Now, let me examine you."

If she could only look inside and see how the child fared, like she'd seen the twins. She shut the door to the parlor and washed her hands at the pitcher and basin in the corner. With the utmost care, she laid her hands upon her good friend. "I feel the movement of a healthy babe. He seems not troubled by all the upheaval."

"I promise you this will not last. And I have something I hope will help."

Lena sighed. "I have had it almost eight months now. Does it mean the child is ill?"

"Some women cast up their accounts their whole term."

Lena flinched. "*Meine Gott*." She smiled. "I thought Josef would swoon this morning. He has never seen me sick."

"As I said, it means the child has taken root in you and makes his presence known."

The wrinkles upon Lena's pale forehead had lessened, and Maggie was glad she could reassure her friend.

'It is easy for you to say." Lena smirked. "You do not suffer from this, and I am glad of it."

Maggie laughed. "Yes, I'm sure I'd be whistling another tune. But do you not admit it is good you followed my advice months ago? Ten juniper berries in the morning may have led to your fertile belly."

"*Ach*, enough of your talk."

"I am sure you are glad to have Josef back."

"*Ja*." Lena sat back up again and leaned toward Maggie. "I cannot believe what my poor Josef has gone through. Such a horrible thing. I never met his nephew, but he was like a son to him. It is my husband's health we should be worried about. Did you notice how thin he is? But I cannot get him to sit and eat, so distraught he is."

"It takes time to heal from grief."

"And he can do nothing but talk about it. To have his nephew die so horribly. Such strange, frightening things he says." She shivered.

"We have told him to keep quiet about what—or what he thinks—transpired."

Lena nodded. "It cannot be true, what he is saying."

"Lena, you mustn't worry. I'm sure he is just overwrought. Now, close your eyes and rest. I will go see if I can help Sabine."

She went behind the bar and silently took Sabine's tray. "Where to?"

Sabine smiled her thanks, showing a fetching set of dimples, and pointed to the table.

Later, Maggie sat at the bar to rest for a moment, and spotted Vicar Andrews in the corner, gawping at Sabine. He had the dazed look of someone who'd been hit with a mallet. His wig was askew, white powder falling on the table in front of him, his hazel eyes not blinking. His head rested on his hands, his pasty forgotten in front of him.

When had this begun? Vicar had a perfectly good cook, and no real need of coming to the inn for supper, except obviously, for companionship. He looked barely old enough to be a vicar, with those smooth cheeks, and a wide smooth forehead like a child's, unwrinkled by cares or worries.

Then he squinted, and she followed the path of his eyes as they tracked Sabine around the room while she served food and refilled drinks. She had a quiet dignity about her, stately posture, and had put on weight in all the right places since Lena and Josef had taken her in.

"My Maggie is woolgathering?"

She jumped. How had she not seen him come in? Ian's warm breath caressed her neck. Lands, she had forgotten how he could sneak up on a person. She glanced toward the vicar and Sabine.

"Oh ho!" He smiled. "I wondered."

"How could you possibly? You've not been here for months."

He sat beside her, bringing the cool air from outside, a hint of salt and sea. "It didn't take long for me to see he is besotted, and she is completely unaware."

"Are you sure? She is a woman. Women know." She shook her head. "Poor boy. A vicar and a former prostitute."

"He's a man of marriageable age. You ought to know he's looking to settle down, for he had his eye on you, did he not?"

"It's a match destined for disaster."

"Maggie, you are such a pessimist. Nothing is impossible. Who would have thought a flighty musician like me could have landed a woman like you? But wait!" He grasped her hands. "Come outside. I have something I must show you before it gets dark."

He pulled her off the stool, his hands so warm they made her skin tingle. His high cheekbones were red, and the wind had blown his nutmeg colored hair around his face. He tried to lead her toward the door. She resisted. She was quite comfortable; her shoulder had started to hurt during her stint as barmaid, and it had finally stopped throbbing. She was ravenous.

He gathered her hands to his lips and kissed them. "You must come outside." His sea eyes pulled her forward like the tide coming in. She had not the power to resist his enthusiasm. Neither did anyone else, for upon hearing the excited sound of his voice, people began to gather around them.

Josef stood by the door, arms folded.

"My love," Ian said. "Josef has been too kind to us and has sold it to me for a song. It is ours now, our ticket to freedom, to…"

"What is it?"

Chapter Eight

Josef opened the door. A gypsy wagon lit up the dusk.

"Come, my queen. You must see it from all sides."

The entire wagon was painted a bright yellow, bordered all round with red and blue flowers. In the center posed a shepherdess with a lamb in her arms, her bosom pouring out of her bodice like clotted cream.

"How do you like it? Come closer."

Come closer? Every instinct said to run away. She opened her mouth, shut it, opened it again. "No words."

"Yes, quite right!" He grinned. "I had your same reaction—utter awe—upon seeing it the first time." He hugged her. "Come look on the other side."

"But we don't need a wagon," she said, drowned out by the babbling crowd of onlookers. A wagon? Not just a wagon, but a…a monstrosity!

They walked through the crowd to the other side, and her jaw dropped open. In the center stood a ram with fierce eyes and horns, and gigantic stones hanging below his belly. His face seemed almost human, a lecherous grin upon his face.

The men oohed and awed. The women gasped.

"It is ours," Ian sang. "Josef sold it to us for a song." He took her hand, and she felt the energy coursing through him.

"But we don't need a wagon. Or the horse," she

sputtered.

Widow Jenkins cackled, a spectator to Maggie's humiliations, as always. "What have you got there, apothecary? A travelling medicine show?" She pointed her gnarled finger at the ram. "You should be home servicing your wife."

The crowd roared.

"You see?" Maggie said under her breath. "We are already the laughingstock."

But there was a beatific look upon Ian's features, and he hummed under his breath.

He eyed the ram with pride. "Well, I am glad we can be a source of entertainment. People need to laugh. I do not mind being the source of it, if it entertains them."

No, he did not mind being the entertainment. In fact, the man had travelled all over the world, performing for royalty, selling his herbs, and gathering new ones in search of cures, and one special cure, for his affliction. He certainly didn't look afflicted at the moment. Perhaps he'd just got tired of being here in this town, being with steady Maggie, always the same.

"Well, *I* do not like being a laughingstock," she hissed. "The difference between you and me, for I need to be taken seriously in my work. I need to be someone the women can respect." Her throat had grown dry from the hissing, and she clamped her mouth closed.

She watched the movement of his Adam's apple as he hummed and ran his hand along to the other side of the wagon, dangerously close to the woman's bosom bursting enticingly over her peasant blouse.

She tried one more time. "Ian, how do you expect them to take your doctoring seriously when you go about in this garish embarrassment?"

Utter surprise widened his eyes. "And why would they not take me seriously? Don't worry so much, my love." He wrapped an arm around her shoulder, pulling her close. "Zounds, you're warm as a cinder. You shouldn't overheat yourself so, Maggie. Do not worry. They will get used to it."

"Well, I will not," she muttered. "Where did it come from?"

"Josef had been working on it for some time."

"He painted it?"

"Yes, is he not talented?"

"Erm." She had to admit it was skillfully painted.

"Who knew he had such talent? To think he has been keeping it a secret all these years. I made an offer, and well…"

Her husband had paid for this miscreation? The heat rose in her chest and boiled over her face like an unwatched pot. Yet she bit the inside of her lip to keep from talking. A wife cannot tell her husband how to spend his money, could she?

His hair flew about his face in nutmeg-colored wisps. His eyes fair glowed green like new grass. As his arm encircled her back, she felt the quiver of excitement coursing through him.

For the life of her, she did not understand. The man returns from a three-month absence, and the very next day he buys a frivolous wagon they have no need for.

"Maggie, I can take you to birthings. You can take the birthing chair. This can be a birthing wagon!"

"What birthing chair?" She had wanted Samuel to make one per her instructions, but there had been no time.

"The one I'm having shipped here."

She dug her feet in. "We don't need a wagon."

The crowd listened to their argument with gusto. She clamped her mouth shut. She would not argue with him in everyone's presence. And there were too many other things to worry about.

A group of sailors stood around Henry's son, George. The boy gaped open-mouthed at the shepherdess, his hands tracing the swell of her bosom. "Oh, she's beautiful."

"Cop a feel, simpleton." One of the seamen cuffed him on the head. "For it's as close as you'll ever get to a real woman."

Bethan shoved her way through the crowd. "Leave the boy alone, or you'll find my fist down your throat." She towered over the sailors, eyes blazing fire.

The women gasped.

"Ooh, look what we have here. An Amazon!" One bushy-bearded gent approached her, close enough to put a finger on her bodice. Ian stepped forward.

Faster than the blink of an eye, Bethan slammed the heel of her boot into his instep. She laughed, fierce and humorless, and circled the group wielding a knife in her hand. "Tell me, is your manhood so…questionable you must harass this good boy? Shall I test my theory?"

They dispersed, stumbling like the drunken sots they were. "No harm meant, mistress. She's crazy, ain't she?"

Bethan laughed. "If you think I'm crazy, you should meet my sister."

She put her arm around George and led him from the public eye. The crowd parted for her, fear and fascination on their faces, and Henry burst out of the door.

He grabbed Bethan's hand and kissed it. "Thank you. I was in the kitchen frying fish and someone came in and told me what happened." He dropped her hand like a hot coal and stepped back. "I apologize for taking liberties. I am just…grateful. How brave you are."

"Da, she was fierce, like those warrior queens you read to me about. Like Minerva, or Queen Isabella of Spain."

"Yes, indeed. I'm impressed you remembered those names."

Widow Jenkins clutched Maggie's sleeve. "Yon girl is unladylike, but she gets the job done."

Bethan, for all her beauty and grace, had likely learned how to fight to defend her sister from ridicule.

Maggie joined Bethan. "Are you all right?"

Bethan nodded. Henry bowed, met Bethan's eyes. "Thank you again for your defense of my son."

Bethan inclined her head. "It was only right." She smiled." I must take a look at this wagon." She smirked at Maggie.

They followed as Henry led George to the ram side of the wagon. George's eyes grew round, and he backed away a bit. "Da." He turned to Henry. "How does he hold them up?"

A voice in the crowd said, "Ian, my man. Did you model your monstrous cods for this work of art?"

The corners of Ian's mouth twitched up. "A gentleman never brags about his prowess."

"Well, you're no gentlemen."

"True enough." Ian grinned, pretending to undo his breeches. "I'll show you, then."

Maggie fumed. Whoops and hollers, and everyone laughing at her expense!

Ed the butcher quipped, "It's a wonder you can even walk, or your wife."

Men and women alike roared with laughter.

A few minutes later, Adam arrived for Bethan.

"Can you stay for a pint?" Henry asked. "You must have run the whole way here."

The beleaguered father nodded, gasping for breath. "No, I'm sorry. I would like to, but Elunid is distraught. She has run out of thread."

Bethan smiled. "I now have plenty of thread. Thank you for fetching me, Adam."

He laughed. "Truth be told, the walk did me good. Too many hens in the hen house."

They said their goodbyes, and Henry said, "Again, I thank you for your kindness, Mistress Owens."

Adam glanced from one to the other. "You must explain your behavior on the walk home." He pushed past the crowd, Bethan in tow.

The humiliation of the wagon and Bethan's defense of George had turned into the biggest event in King's Harbour since the county fair. Lena slid next to her, wrapping a shawl around the both of them. "Getting chilly, is it not, my friend?"

"I doubt any of these fools would notice."

The nearly blind Widow Jenkins stood nose-to-bosom with the shepherdess. "Where did you get this grand wagon?"

"Josef has been hiding it outside of town for some time, amusing himself bit by bit with adorning it."

Vicar Andrews stood a good distance from the wagon, as befit a holy man, but stared fixedly, two spots of color on his cheeks. He straightened his wig as if he expected to see the lass come to life and kiss him on the cheek. Maggie had to admit, the woman looked realistic.

"I didn't know Josef could paint such a thing," Lena said. "Do you see she has my hair?" She exchanged a glance with her husband, and his eyes softened in response.

Maggie grimaced. There Ian was, holding court with the other fools. "He is so impulsive, this man. Just arrived home last night and buys a wagon. No offense to you or Josef, Lena, but we had not even discussed a wagon, or even a need for one."

"Would you not have some use for it, Maggie?" Lena murmured.

"I do not need it. I do not like it."

"But look at the pleasure it gives him. He's bursting with it. Sometimes we do not understand what our men do, but we must allow them their pleasures. And it is not another woman, *ja*?"

She nodded. "I suppose."

"Maggie, you will find in a marriage there are things to be angry about and things you must let go. He is the master of the house. You have the wagon, so enjoy it."

Maggie stalked over to the horse. "So I am victim to every whim he has? And what of this horse? More expense."

"Well, he did not pay much for her, I bet," Lena said.

Maggie eyed the grey nag. Although old, she seemed sturdy enough. She ran a hand along her neck and received a nudge in response.

Ian appeared beside her and rested his hand on the small of her back. "You will find this wagon will come in handy for your work, Maggie."

"I am not a travelling salesman, selling…what?"

"Fecundity, of course! You are selling fertility!"

The horse suddenly jerked its head and flared its nostrils. They turned around to see what caused it.

Pete Stowe strode up, a whip held in his good hand. His mother stood behind him, contempt upon her face. He lunged forward. The horse shied, eyes rolling, and backed the wagon up amidst yelling and cursing.

"You almost ran me over," someone yelled.

Maggie held the horse's bridle. "There now. Settle." The horse quivered.

Pete Stowe laughed. "What have you got here, Pierce? Just what I'd expect from the likes of you."

"Yes." Ian stood in front of him, dwarfing him with his stature. "Isn't it grand?"

"Grand for a lunatic, to be sure."

Maggie held her breath. Everyone in town knew Ian was afflicted, but no one ever mentioned it, for it was as much a part of the town's landscape as the English Channel.

"Yes, it's a fine wagon for transport to Bedlam."

The crowd grew still.

Ian merely stood, head cocked. "Your wound, Stowe. It is putrefying. If you come to the shoppe I will treat it for you."

Full Pocket had sandy hair, a sharp nose, and brown eyes swimming in red, no doubt due to the drinking and his dissolute ways. His entire hand was swollen to twice its size, and pustules of green drained from the angry red. The stump where his thumb had been was a hard dry crust of dead tissue. *Escar, an eating sore.* He held his dead tissue gingerly against his stomach. Even with the odor of the crowd, a sickeningly sweet smell seeped from his pores.

"I don't need your help." He shot Ian a look of contempt.

"You will lose your hand if it isn't tended to."

"Yon wagon looks like a travelling whorehouse. Or transport to gaol again. 'Twill ease the way for your jailers, to be sure."

Henry stood beside Ian. "Where were you last year, when innocent people were being terrorized? Got yourself in a bit of trouble then, chumming around with the likes of Edward Carter. Didn't you, Stowe?"

Stowe blanched, no doubt remembering his ordeal in the hands of Carter. Some nights Maggie still heard his screams echoing in her dreams.

Henry turned to Ian. "Why do you not just pop him one? He's nothing but a coward."

Ian raised an eyebrow.

The crowd yelled, "Aye, pop him one!"

Ian held his hands aloft and examined them. "I'd rather save my vigor for tonight, my friend. For I plan on making love to my wife in such a manner she'll never forget."

Laughter all round.

"And why give him what he wants? He hopes I will lose control. But you see, it will not happen, for I'd much rather enjoy my wife's charms, just now. But first I must feed her, for she bites if I don't."

He turned and held his arm out to Maggie. She glared at him, but truth be told, she was quite proud at his restraint regarding Full-Pocket Pete.

Pete Stowe hawked and spat at Maggie's feet, then skulked off with his mother beside him. "Come, Mother. Let's go to the Shipwreck Inn. The company is more congenial."

"Not when you're around," Henry said.

She grabbed his arm and hissed, "You let him get the best of you again, dolt."

The crowd parted respectfully as Maggie, Ian, and Henry walked into the Siren.

"My hand was itching to whack him a good one," Henry said.

Ian slapped him on the back. "I know, good friend. I know."

They were nearly knocked over as Josef emerged out of the inn, his head down.

Lena followed him. "Josef, stay here."

"No, I must go be with the boy." He tried to push past them, but Ian and Henry blocked his exit.

"What are you doing, man?" Henry clapped an arm around Josef, but he shook him off.

"I go to my nephew, for darkness is nigh."

"No, Josef!" Lena took his arm. "Stay here."

Josef grasped Lena's shoulders. "You don't understand. I must wait to see if he emerges from the grave. I must protect the town from him."

Chapter Nine

"Please, do not speak of it, Josef." Ian pleaded. "Stay home with your wife and unborn child. You can do nothing else for Nikolaus."

"No! I must guard the grave. What if he rises tonight and the evil destroying my village threatens us here?"

He tried to shoulder past them. Ian and Henry each took an arm and hauled him inside. He fought them, swinging, and hit Henry in the gut. Lena backed away, her hand over her mouth.

"We need to get him away from the customers. He is frightening them," Maggie urged.

"Let me go. I must guard him. He must not rise."

Ian nodded. "I know, man. But it's late, and you are very tired."

Josef shook his head, showing the whites of his eyes.

They strong-armed him into the private living quarters. Suddenly, the fight went out of him.

"My friend." Ian sat Josef in the rocking chair and covered him with a blanket. "I will visit the grave with you tomorrow."

Lena put her arm around him and whispered, "Come, *Liebchen*. You must rest. You are still tired from the ordeal. Take me to bed, for I have missed you."

He met her gaze, bushy brows raised.

"Let me comfort you," Lena whispered.

"But the babe…"

"The babe will not be harmed by our affection." Lena kissed him upon the cheek.

Maggie mixed a sleeping draught in a cup of ale and handed it to him.

He gulped it and shuddered. "You do not understand," he cried, throwing off the blanket and rising again. "In my country, when the sun sets, the demons rise from the earth."

Ian pressed him down into the chair again. "You are causing alarm among your customers. They will go elsewhere to take their refreshment, and everything you've worked for will be for naught."

Josef did not heed him but stared fixedly at the door, quivering. They could only wait for the sleeping draught to work.

Lena stood over Josef, wringing her hands in her apron.

"Lena," Ian said gently. "You must rest."

She sighed and took her seat beside the fire.

"Maggie," Ian said. "I see the way you're holding your shoulder. Is it bothering you?"

She shrugged, then winced at the movement. "I am fine."

He led her to the divan and sat her down, then paced so rapidly it made her head spin. One arm crossed his chest to brace his other arm, fingers tapping. Slumped in the armchair, Josef drained his ale and held the mug out for another one. Ian poured the women some as well.

Maggie nodded her thanks. "Why do you not sit

down, husband?"

He paused in front of her. "Indeed, I cannot." His eyes burned into hers. "I am thinking."

"Can you not think sitting down? You make me tired just watching you."

He stopped. "I'm sorry. You know I cannot help it."

She nodded.

They waited in the quiet of their parlor, the sounds of revelry drifting under the door.

Ian stood behind Maggie, massaging her shoulders. When she winced, he asked, "Why did you not tell me your shoulder was hurting?"

"I had other more important things to worry about."

"When you suffer pain, I do as well." His eyes reflected the blazing fire.

He was angry with her? She was only going about her business in his absence.

Josef slumped in his chair and stared sightlessly at the fire.

Ian ceased his ministrations and laid his hands upon her head. His fingers nearly burned her with his restrained power. "I put more sleeping draught in his ale."

Lena leaned her head back and closed her eyes, while Ian resumed his manipulation of Maggie's shoulders. "You would not hesitate to tell your friend to rest. Why can you not take a care for yourself?"

The words fought their way up her throat. "I did what I had to do, since you were gone so long. Indeed, I did the work of two people. I am not complaining. I just feel it necessary to remind you, for you seem to have forgotten."

She had not meant to say it aloud, but she would not stomach his anger, for she had only done what was necessary.

His hands grew still, and he moved to stand in front of the fire, long back stiff, hair undone about his shoulders. "You know I had to go," he said, voice low. "I wish I could be the perfect man, without affliction. But I am not, so I will find the remedy for what ails me." He turned, and her heart clenched as anguish assaulted his features.

"I am sorry, Maggie. I warned you what you were in store for when you married me. Even though you had no choice in the matter."

A flush of shame washed over her. Damn! Could she not keep quiet? He could not help it, could not control it. "Ian. I'm…"

Josef rustled in his chair. "He was such a good lad, my Nikolaus."

"I am sorry, old friend," Ian said.

Indeed, they had known each other since childhood, when Josef had come from Serbia as an indentured servant.

"You people do not understand." Josef's voice echoed in the quiet room. "In my village by the Moldova River, evil is afoot at night. Monsters prowl with teeth bared, attacking the innocent. One such animal must have attacked my Nikolaus, I am sure of it. I fought for his life upon the ship, as he moaned and burned with fever."

"The sedative has calmed him," Ian murmured. "But nothing will take the pain of loss away."

The firelight fell upon Ian's throat, highlighting the

powerful muscles and the bulge of his shoulders, as he stared at Josef with deep concentration. "Fever? It sounds like disease, but I know not of any disease with such strange manifestations. I will study on it."

"They wanted to throw him overboard. Even as he lay there, dying."

Perhaps it would help Josef if he could continue to talk about his experience. But soon his head began nodding in the ale, and Ian gently removed the mug from his hand and laid him on the divan. Maggie covered him with a blanket.

"I cannot predict his behavior," Ian said. "But he cannot continue repeating his tirade tonight. I think we should stay for a while, to make sure he will sleep."

His eyes avoided her. If she could only touch him, soothe the stiffness away, tell him how sorry she was. She should not punish him for something he had no control over. And he hadn't left on a lark to enjoy the pleasures of travel.

"He must be exhausted from his ordeal," Maggie said. "To have seen the things he thinks he's seen."

Ian glanced her way, finally. "Do you think Josef has lost his wits?"

"I don't know," she said. "For we have seen stranger things than this, things I never thought were possible. And it's as if…"

"What?"

She shook her head. "It is fanciful and silly."

"Maggie, I have told you before." He came to her and took her hands. "Nothing you ever say to me will be taken lightly, for every word you utter is like holy writ to me."

She moved into his embrace, her hands on his

bristled cheeks. He was very warm. "The spirit of the holy nun lives in me still."

He nodded.

"Something happened today."

Josef moaned in his sleep. "Let me in. The beast is out there, in the woods, and he comes for us. Where are your weapons? Where is Ana? Has she not arrived? The beast is coming; do you hear it? No, the floor is sticky with her blood, I slipped in it, I could not help it," Josef screamed.

"But I just saw her yesterday," he continued in a voice not his own. "She sold chestnuts in the market. How can this be her, neck laid open? She will not stop bleeding. Her eyes opened, she snarls."

And his own voice returned. "No, stop screaming, sister. We must bury her, bury her deep."

Fear rippled down Maggie's back.

Josef's face contorted in pain, and he tossed about, crying.

"Josef, wake up." Ian clutched him. "You are dreaming."

"Josef." Lena kneeled beside him. "Josef, wake up."

Then, as quickly as it had begun, the nightmare stopped. He rolled over and began to snore.

"Lena, get up." Maggie lifted her from her kneeling position. "It was just a dream."

Maggie tamped down her fear and looked to Ian for reassurance. She did not receive it, for he wore the same stunned expression she knew she must have.

"I had best go out and help Sabine," Ian said.

"We will take good care of Josef," Maggie said.

Lena nodded, her face pinched with concern. "He

is so changed. When he saw how much the babe had grown, he was happy, I could tell. He has long wanted to be a father, but he could not stop talking about these horrors. What if they are true, Maggie? What am I to do?"

"He just needs time to recover, Lena. He will come to his senses."

Lena nodded, concern casting shadows on her hollow cheeks.

"Try not to worry. It is bad for the child."

Sabine arrived carrying a tray with sandwiches and tea. Good. Lena needed to eat. Maggie reached into her basket and pulled out a flask.

"Here, Lena. Drink this first before you eat. It is a remedy for morning sickness we haven't tried yet. Ian brought it back. Sip it."

She took a timid swallow and made a face. "Blech! What is in this?"

"Do you really want to know?"

Lena shook her head. "I am not hungry. How can I think of eating when my Josef is in such a state?"

"You do it for the child."

She sipped a goodly amount of the mixture and took tiny bites of the sandwich. Indeed, Lena would not approve of the contents: powdered steel mixed with cinnamon and white wine, stoppered and left in the sun for eight days. She had exhausted all other remedies, and if this did not work, poor Lena would likely suffer her entire pregnancy.

Later in the evening, Maggie was heartened at the absence of retching. Perhaps this remedy would work. Ian arrived shortly and carried Josef to his bed, as if he were a small child.

"Lena," he said upon his return. "Send for me immediately if I can be of service to you."

She nodded. "Thank you, good friend. He will not need anything tonight. Mayhap he will be a new man tomorrow, once he gets some sleep."

****

The wind had picked up as they made their way down Siren Street. It was quite late, and her shoulder throbbed with fatigue. Indeed, her legs ached with all she had done today, coupled with the late night and lack of sleep. Ian held her arm and hummed under his breath, an energetic little tune. He seemed not the least bit tired. Josef's story echoed in her mind. Surely it must be a figment of his imagination. But it seemed so real.

The cold air from the English Channel slapped her face, chastising her fanciful thoughts.

When they arrived at the cottage, Ian built up the fire. "I will heat some water for your bath. You need compresses on your shoulder."

"You need not fuss over me."

She watched him as he leaned over the fire, at the muscles in his powerful thighs and buttocks. She would swear he was more muscular than before. How was it possible?

Despite her fatigue, she could not draw her eyes away from him, as he brought the tub in front of the fire, the muscles of his upper arms straining against his linen shirt. He made a pallet of blankets upon the floor.

"The hot water will help your shoulder." He set the soap out for her.

"Thank you. And Ian?"

He met her gaze. "Yes, my love?"

"I am sorry I was harsh with you."

He shook his head, hair falling into his eyes. "I deserve it."

"It is not your fault."

He nodded, came to her, and undid her bodice, untied her shift, and faced her to hold each of her breasts in his hands. "They have grown so ripe with the coming of the child." He cocked his head. "I know in time, these beauties will not be for me. But for now, will you allow me to worship them?"

Her nipples hardened in response.

"Sit down, Maggie." He led her to the divan and knelt in front of her. He held one of her breasts in his hand, circling her nipple with the lightest of touches, then wrapped his lips around it, drawing on it lightly. He ran his tongue around it, then began to suckle again, increasing the pressure. Her womb tightened.

He met her gaze and kissed her. "Does this please you?"

She moaned. "You know it does."

He held her other breast. It waited, heavy and wanting, jealous of the attention its partner had gotten. Maggie sighed as he suckled, and warm honey flowed through her limbs as her womanhood grew soft.

He caressed the swell of her stomach in long circles, around the outside, meeting in the center, and slowly up again. "I have never seen anything so magnificent, Maggie, your skin so white and lustrous, an offering."

He kneeled to remove her stockings, fingers lingering, and helped her into the tub.

"Now then." He shrugged off his shirt. The muscles in his chest rippled in the fire's glow, the nutmeg colored hairs adorning him were tipped with gold. Something seemed different about him; she could not put her finger on it. But, oh God, she wanted to put her finger on every part of his body.

His eyes glowed like a nocturnal predator and demanded she feel his heat. She followed the path of his long fingers down his legs as he slid his breeches down, his hot gaze upon her.

He climbed into the tub behind her. "Get thee between my legs," he rasped. "Lean against me. Soap, please."

She moaned with pleasure as he kneaded and massaged her neck and shoulders. She leaned back against his hard chest, the coarse hairs rubbing against her tender skin. He reached his arms around to her breasts, covering them with his hands, slippery with soap, the rose scent reminding her of summer. He caressed them with his palms, in a circular pattern, tortuously slow, taking her nipple between his fingers and tugging it to the edge of pain.

One hand on her breast lightly teased her nipple, and the other lay upon her rounded belly. "You carry our child," he whispered. He spread out his fingers and made slow circles around the swell of her belly. The water lapped against her womanhood.

She ground her bottom against his engorged member, and he held onto her hips as she struggled to turn so she might join with him.

He kissed her neck, nipping it gently. "We must adjust our lovemaking to accommodate your swell, my beloved. Perhaps the tub is not the place for our coupling." He reached between her legs and found her pleasure bud, and she leaned against his hand. The warm water surrounded her, and as she found her joy, his member throbbed against her bottom.

He helped her out of the tub and dried her with utmost care. She took the towel from him and slowly dried him off, taking pleasure at the feel of his wet body under her fingers. His member stood stiff against its nest of curly hair. He threw back his head and moaned, and joy filled her at his response. She took him by the hand and led him to the pallet he had made on the floor.

Now it was her turn to command. "Lie down."

He obeyed immediately, and she straddled him, her belly resting gently against his chest. She kissed him, her tongue melding with his. She bent to hold his cock, gasped at the hard silk feel of it, weighed the heaviness of his stones with her other hand. She rubbed his tip against her wetness and in one fluid movement, filled herself with him. He grasped her bottom and held her still, thrust into her once, and then she was lost in him, as waves of pleasure crashed over her.

Later, as the fire crackled before them, she lay against his shoulder, her body humming with warmth.

"Maggie, I am concerned about your shoulder. It should not be paining you after a year's time."

"It is a trifling matter."

He scowled. "No doubt you have been overusing it."

She opened her mouth to reply and vowed she would not repeat herself. It would serve nothing to remind him of what she'd done in his absence.

"Ian, did you find anything beneficial for your condition on your journey?"

She did not understand this manico-melancolicus, the bouts of frenzied activity plaguing him, sometimes followed by deep despair.

"I did not find anything abroad. I am sorry."

"Perhaps you do not need a remedy anymore, for you seem at peace to me."

He gathered her against the hard contours of his body, his arms wrapped around her and resting lightly on her breasts. Their knees nestled as one, her bottom rested against his engorged manhood.

A puff of breath tickled the fine hairs on her neck when he laughed without humor. "Oh, I assure you I am not at peace. I have periods, Maggie, where I'm not afflicted, but it never lasts long. In the past when I have travelled, it calmed my spirit for a time. The excitement of new experiences and new people inspired me and my music. On this journey, all I could think of was you and how to find this *litio* so I don't have to leave you again. Perhaps the remedy is closer to home, and we can take the wagon, explore the countryside together."

She drew away from him. "I do not want to talk about the wagon just now. And you know I cannot leave. I have responsibilities here and always will. And what of your duties as the town apothecary?"

"I know," he said. "Abide with me now, Maggie. Let us enjoy each other without being burdened by what has taken place since I returned. Let it be only us, your body against mine, like so."

He kissed her lips, neck, the hollow of her throat, and as he did so he sang her name, a hoarse baritone making her skin tingle with chills. She pushed against him, needing his hard strength inside of her again.

He sank himself into her with agonizingly slow thrusts, sliding the long length of him to her center, then withdrawing, only to plunge into her again.

When they had reached their pleasure, he said, "I want to stay like this forever, Maggie, feel your warm passage clasp me, soft and welcoming. It is the only passage I want to travel, for you comfort me so."

Later, as they lay entwined, she discovered he had fallen asleep. She rarely got to see him at rest. A small smile played upon his lips, wind burnt cheeks and the scar running from his chin to curl around his ear. He lay with one arm above his head, the upper arm heavily muscled, the dark blond hair under his arm strangely erotic.

She could not put her finger on it but knew he had changed, become more powerful. How could this be? His chest rose and fell with his breathing, and the smattering of hair on his chest led in a line to his manhood resting on the side of his thigh. She smiled, for he was not entirely still: his toes beat a rhythm under the sheet. Did he always hear a tune in his head, even in slumber?

As she lay propped up by one elbow, perusing him at her leisure, his lips moved, and she leaned closer.

"So sweet, so warm, woman wise." He sang in sleep.

His cock stirred and sprung to life. The singing stopped and he awoke. His eyes, green and bright, like kelp drying in the sun, brought tears to her eyes.

"What is it?" He stroked her cheek.

"You are beautiful and you are mine," she said. "And I am bearing your child."

If only she could possess the parts of him she didn't understand.

Chapter Ten

The next morning, Maggie rolled over to find the bed empty and the sun peeping through the drawn curtains. It was market day, and she had planned on starting her rounds early. But now nothing appealed to her more than returning to bed and staying there all day, sampling tidbits, loving Ian, drinking wine, as they did on their wedding night.

She turned on her other side, irritated at her wayward thoughts.

Just then, Ian bounded up the steps, carrying a tea tray, with bread and cheese.

"Good morn, my love." His hair hung loose and flowing over his shoulders, making him look primal and powerful. His chest was bare. She held her hand out for the teacup but stared at his neck, the ripple of muscles on his chest, the dark nipples, with swirls of hair around them, the powerful column of his throat.

She sat up and cleared her throat. "You need not serve me, Ian. I was going to rise."

He handed her the cup and poured the tea. "I prefer to wait upon you. You have a full day of work ahead, with mothers needing your attention." He put the tray down on the bedside table and handed her a plate with buttered bread and fresh farmer's cheese.

"It will be a fine market day if the weather holds." He sat at the edge of the bed and watched her mouth with great concentration as she sipped her tea.

"Will you be selling your wares today?"

"No, I need to catalogue what I brought back with me, if there's time between customers." He grasped her knees and gave them a squeeze. "'Tis a shame I can't attend, for I could use the wagon to display my wares. You could ride along." A corner of his mouth twitched.

He would try to tease her, but she would not take his bait. The man had the very devil in him! She would not discuss the wagon, or ride in it, ever. Foolish purchase.

He eyed her, smiling and humming to himself.

"What are you humming?" she asked between bites.

"The song I'm writing for you, always in my head. Just when I think it is perfect, I find it does not yet do you justice." He shrugged. "No matter. The joy is in the doing."

His eyes journeyed from her eyes, to her lips, lingering on her bosom. Her nipples hardened against her night rail. She became aware of a silence in the room, and the only thing she saw was his face, his lips, and the things he'd done with those lips, not so long ago.

He smiled and removed the teacup from her hands. She felt soft, moist and wanting.

"Oh, Maggie, I yearn for you." He growled, nipping her ear lightly. He lowered his head to her breasts, running his tongue around her nipple through the linen. She reached back and untied her shift, let it pool at her middle. With green eyes glowing, he watched her reaction as he took her nipple in his mouth. She felt the pull from deep within her womb.

The door downstairs opened. Josef bellowed, "Ian!"

"Zounds," Ian muttered against her breast. "From now on the accursed man shall be called "Sir Interruptis.""

She chortled.

"Ian! Are you ready to go to the grave as you promised, man?"

He kissed her with great care and concentration. "I will see if I can get him to eat and settle a bit."

She came downstairs in a few minutes to find the two men sitting at the trestle table.

Ian stood, offered up his seat with a courtly bow. "My lady, sit ye down. I will pour you some more tea and slice some ham. I have also saved you an egg, which I put by the hearth to keep warm. Also, there is some pottage for you with fresh cream and honey."

Josef seemed improved in health from last night, but at the moment, he gawked open-mouthed at Ian.

"I must make a preparation for Captain Jacobs," Ian said. "He will be in soon to pick it up, and I said I'd have it ready."

Josef followed Ian into the apothecary shoppe. "Are you a woman now, who must prepare meals for his wife? Never heard of such a thing."

Ian chuckled. "Josef, she works quite hard. In truth, she does the work of two men. How is she to have the vigor left over for my quite considerable prowess? I take care of her, and she will take care of me, if you catch my meaning."

Josef laughed. "Ah, I see. You have always known your way around women, my friend. But I would not lower myself to serving a woman."

Ian waggled his eyebrows at Maggie. "Ladies first."

She blushed. To be certain, it had always been Ian's practice, but really! Her hand fair itched to slap her husband. It was one thing to enjoy the pleasures of his flesh in private, but for him to speak of it to others? There would be no charming of her tonight. Ian winked at her. Ah. He had succeeded in distracting Josef from his mission to visit the graveyard, and angered her in the process. She smiled in spite of herself. Her smile faded. What did Josef mean by Ian knowing his 'way around women?'

"Have you eaten this morning, Josef?" Ian said in accompaniment to his pounding pestle.

"No, I must hurry to the grave. I do not deserve to be lingering at table while my nephew is in the ground."

"You must eat, friend. Remember, there's a son inside your Lena who needs his father strong and hardy." Ian glanced at the door, and upon seeing they were still alone, said, "Josef, we must urge you again, for the sake of your unborn child and beloved wife, to keep still regarding the circumstances of your nephew's death. If you must speak of it, speak only to us and to Lena. For God's sake, you can't come in here bellowing about graves and the like."

Josef nodded.

"How is Lena feeling?" Maggie sat back down at the table.

Josef smiled. "The medicine you gave her seems to be helping. She only threw up twice this morning, and none so bad."

"Ian, we must go. Make sure you bring the seeds,"

Josef said.

Ian cast Maggie a bemused glance. A cool wind swept in as they opened the door. The lovely weather from yesterday had changed to a more typical March bluster.

A while later, Maggie navigated the narrow closes on her way back from young Hester Anders' cottage, which lay behind the church and down toward the Landgate. Satisfaction warmed her against the cool air. Young Hester had just delivered her second child a mere ten months after the first one. Like anyone in her shoes, she felt a bit overwhelmed, despite help from her competent mother.

The oldest child had still been on the teat, and indeed Hester was so distraught and nervous, the new babe wasn't nursing well. She spent a goodly amount of time reassuring her, propped her up with pillows, the babe at her breast, and placed a mug of Lena's ale in her hand. She would be fine, given time.

As Maggie exited one of the dank alleys, she stopped short. Pete Stowe and his mother hurried down Landgate Street, as if someone chased them.

Mrs. Stowe leaned on her son. "I have hurt my back, thanks to your weakness, dolt. Just as I predicted, I had to do the bulk of the work. I may not be able to move tomorrow."

"I'm sorry, Mother. It's my hand."

"Nothing a strong will won't overcome, which you've never possessed. And apologies will not fix my crippled back, you sorry excuse for a helpmate."

Maggie sighed and shrugged. Interesting how a mother can brag a son up in public and berate him in private.

She headed toward Market Square. It was early yet, but crowds had already gathered, and merchants were putting up their stands. Martha, the baker's wife, ruddy-faced with exertion, straightened from her work and waved at Maggie.

"Your man is home, I hear?" She smiled, showing a gap in her teeth. "You need a bit of my gingerbread to keep your strength up." She handed her a chunk of the fragrant treat.

"Thank you, Martha." Maggie bit into it. "Ah! It is still warm. Everything on your table looks and smells wonderful. You have been hard at work."

Martha nodded. "I hear some entertainers are coming to land soon. A trio, two men, and a woman with the voice of a nightingale. It is said they have performed for royalty here and abroad. Called the 'Wandering Wastrels,' or something."

Maggie wondered if Ian knew them, for he had once been a travelling performer.

Martha lowered her voice. "I was abed during the hubbub last night, but I hear Josef is back and brought evil with him."

"He's had a shock, Martha. When someone we love dies, it is not unusual to feel altered for a while."

"Yes, but they say his nephew was a beast, a monster."

Maggie sighed, endeavoring to hide her impatience. Why did people jump so quickly to conclusions? Could they not see more than one possibility?

"Oh, Martha, I am sure he is just overwrought. We must do all we can to help Lena." There was not a person in town who did not like Lena. And her beer.

Martha beamed. "Ah, she is a love, isn't she? Is she feeling better?"

They passed a few minutes in friendly discussion about their mutual friend.

Martha handed her another slice of gingerbread.

"You are too good to me, Martha."

"I can tell by the glow on your face your husband has been good to you." The older woman waggled her brows. "Never have I seen a man with such vigor…"

Maggie had an idea. "Martha, I know you hold Lena in high regard. For her sake, would you consider helping to dispel the rumors circulating about Josef?"

Martha wrinkled her brow. "I don't know. What if it's true?"

"Have you ever known Lena to be anything but kind? And Josef, although quiet, has always treated his customers and friends fairly."

"Yes, 'tis true." Martha nodded.

"You are well respected by everyone. Your good opinion of Lena and Josef would go far."

Ian suddenly appeared at Maggie's side. Would the fool man never cease sneaking up on her?

He bowed, eyes alight with mischief. "Now, dear lady. Would you do a good deed for good people? For you have such a saintly nature and a charming way about you. 'Twould warm the coldest heart."

Martha grinned, eyes alight. "Oh now. You do know how to flatter a woman, don't you, Mr. Pierce? Since ye ask so nicely, I suppose."

Honestly, her husband could charm the skin off a kipper.

"Thank you, Martha." Maggie turned to Ian. "I'm off to do my rounds now."

He kissed her upon the forehead, lingering indecently close to her.

She said her goodbyes and set off on her morning rounds.

Chapter Eleven

The rest of the morning flew by as Maggie checked on several women in various stages of motherhood, like young Becky Myers, whose baby was but a month old. He had a problem with suckling, despite the girl's plentiful supply of milk. There was no explanation for it, but the child required extra care and attention if he were to survive. For truly nothing frustrated her more than a babe who wouldn't eat. She would consult Ian about a tonic for him.

By the time she walked into the midst of the market, the sun had been swallowed up by heavy clouds, but its absence in no way dampened the enthusiasm of buyers and sellers. Folks from surrounding counties gathered at their stalls, and the noise could deafen the ear. A crowd of people sampled Ed the butcher's sausages, and the soap maker's daughter had attracted a group of young boys, eager to compete for her attention. Voices mingled over the mooing of cows and clucking of chickens.

Over by the chandler's stall, a flock of people suddenly scattered. A little body barreled through the crowd, a babe of one with a mop of curly black hair and blue eyes blazing with mischief. It was her niece, Grace, with older sister Ruthie following, holding onto the child's leading strings. The ties were sewn on the back of babies' dresses, so their caregivers could keep them from falling as they learned to walk. In this case, poor Ruthie could barely keep up. The child seemed quite precocious for having just turned one year of age.

"Stop, Grace. You must stop." Ruthie's face was red, not only from exertion but from embarrassment, Maggie guessed. People pointed and laughed as they dodged out of her way.

Maggie was as fascinated as the rest of the crowd to see how Ruthie would handle her charge. She headed right in her direction, and Maggie scooped up the little girl.

"Me down, me down!" Indeed, the child was young to speak so clearly, punctuating her speech by kicking her legs and screeching.

Maggie held her tighter. The child would learn who was in charge. She took the leading strings and wound them around one hand, then turned the child to face her. "How now, my Grace? Where is it you are headed?"

Maggie then kissed Ruthie's flushed cheek. "Good afternoon, Ruthie dear."

"Hello there, Aunt Maggie!" Ruthie tried to catch her breath. "She is an imp. I do not know what to do with her." She eyed the babe with a combination of love and distrust. "She has been so naughty this morn. Mummy asked me to go ahead to market and give Gracie some air. She never stops." Ruthie shook her head.

Maggie stifled a grin at Ruthie's beleaguered look.

"Ruthie. I think you have earned a treat, don't you?" She reached into her apron and handed her a coin.

Ruthie's eyes lit up.

"Go and enjoy yourself. I will tend to the little

beast."

Ruthie embraced her. Goodness, she was growing so tall. "Thank you, Aunt Maggie." She curtsied, eyes on Maggie's face for her approval.

"Very lovely, Ruthie! You could be presented to the queen with such a gracious curtsey."

"Truly?"

"Yes, truly."

"Oh, I should like to meet them." She grinned and set off with her coin.

Meanwhile, the child had occupied herself by untying Maggie's cap and throwing it on the ground, chortling at her success.

Ian appeared out of nowhere. "Here, let me assist you." He ran his fingers through her hair. "I'll put it right." His fingers lingered on the back of her neck. She slapped his hand away, and just as quickly, he disappeared again.

Maggie spent an agreeable time talking to her neighbors, admiring the growth of Joannie's children, particularly the twins she had delivered last year. She enjoyed the feel of the child in her arms, warm and still slightly squirming, but content now with watching the crowd.

A large crowd assembled for this market day. It did indeed brighten up the winter days, when people could gather to talk, gossip, spread the news to folks who lived farther out in the country. The biggest topic of gossip was Josef's strange tales of evil. He must keep still, or he and Lena would lose their customers and perforce go to the poorhouse.

She kept her eyes open for the McCalls. She didn't expect to see Polly but hoped Adam would come to sell fleece or the odd garment or blanket from the sheepdog's abundant fur.

She strolled over to see the candles at the chandler's stall. Mary, the chandler's wife greeted her with her mouth almost closed, eyes downcast. It was well known she suffered from rotten teeth and terrible toothaches but refused to see Ian, even though currently, her jaw was swollen black and blue.

"Greetings, Mistress Smith."

She looked up and nodded, wincing at the movement.

"You have some lovely candles. How much for this one?"

She hissed the price through her slightly open mouth.

Poor woman. Other than her injured mouth, she was quite lovely, with a trim figure and clear, green eyes.

Maggie peered around to see if anyone lingered near. She would not hurt the woman's pride. She leaned toward her. "I see you are in considerable pain, mistress. Why do you not come to see my husband? He will give you something for the pain and perhaps pull what needs pulled."

At the last bit, the woman's eyes grew huge with horror. She backed away.

"He is quite gentle."

She felt a tap on her shoulder and jumped.

"Indeed I am."

"Why must you sneak up on me, you fool?" She smacked him on the shoulder. "You're leaving the shoppe untended?"

Mistress Smith smiled slightly, wincing again.

"As vexing as the man is…" Maggie waited for her heart to stop pounding, as it did after one of his sneak attacks. "He is a fine doctor."

"Here." Ian reached into his pocket and took out a packet of medicine. "Something for the pain at least. We can barter for a candle. Mix this with a bit of wine or ale. Swish it around in your mouth, just so." He demonstrated, puffing up his cheeks and mimicking a spit. The babe laughed uproariously, and he handed the medicine to the chandler's wife, who surreptitiously snatched it with a gleam in her eyes.

"Why have you left the shoppe untended?" Maggie shifted Grace in her arms.

"Everyone is here." He shrugged.

He prized the babe from Maggie's arms. "See my beautiful niece? Is she not glorious?" The babe put her hands on both his cheeks and kissed him smack upon the mouth. Ian laughed with utter abandon, eyes closed, head thrown back, powerful throat exposed. The babe began to wail.

"Oh, I am sorry, my little dove. Did I startle you?" he crooned.

Was there anyone he couldn't charm? Of course, children adored him, for they recognized one of their own. Just then, as if he could feel her thoughts upon him, he set his chin upon the baby's curly head and speared her with his gaze. The warmth of spring in them, green shoots of "yes" with a hint of speculation, travelled down her bosom and rose again, as if asking a question, and the chaos of the marketplace disappeared. She sucked in her breath as she felt the deep draw of desire, as if she'd plunged off a cliff to land softly in a bed of feathers.

A particularly loud squawk from a wayward chicken broke the spell. Maggie turned to Mistress Smith. "Come see us if you need more relief."

The good woman shoved a candle in Maggie's hand and lowered her eyes again, glancing under her eyelashes at Ian.

Maggie sniffed.

"Are you cold, love? The wind has picked up." Great bunches of clouds scudded across the sky from the direction of the Channel.

"No, I'm fine. Thank you, husband. Did you and Josef, er, finish your task this morning?"

"Yes," his voice lowered. "I persuaded him to go home to Lena and return to his duties as innkeeper."

He was very persuasive, she knew. "Well done."

Perhaps returning to his occupation would give Josef the comfort and distraction he needed.

Suddenly there was a shout and the slap of something wet on the table, and everybody headed for the fish sellers, the rippiers, who had arrived late and just started up in earnest now.

People moved as one body to their stall.

"Oh, I do love to watch them!" Maggie took his arm, and they followed the crowd.

The Booth brothers were a longtime fixture at market day. Ben was barrel-chested and sported a long black beard, and the other, Timothy, was wiry and short, with nary a hair upon his head.

"We're late, too true, because we're just off the boat. Such a harvest, a catch the sea stirred up just for you." Ben, the burly one called out, his voice gravelly and loud enough to carry over the crowd. "Look at this plump haddock." He held it up above his head as if it was the crown jewels. "Lively, 'init? Lots of meat on it, good for smoking, or roasting or frying, even. Since the sea has been so kind to us, we'll be kind to you. Going for a song—what say ye?"

A woman raised her hand. "Aye, I'll take it!" Ben threw the fish to his brother. The crowd grew quiet in anticipation. Brother Tim was known far and wide for his skill with the cleaver.

"'Twill even gut it. Do ye want the eyes, mistress?"

She shook her head, jowls shaking with mirth.

The little man cut off the tail, the head, scraped the innards out with his thumb in the time it would have taken Maggie to blink. He tossed it again to his brother, just for show, and he wrapped it in cloth and threw it to the lady, who caught it with a squeal. She beamed, handed him the coin, and stood aside, prize in hand.

"How does he do it without cutting off a finger?" Ian wondered aloud.

They watched the spectacle until Maggie's sister, Sarah arrived. While Maggie possessed a robust body and dark hair, Sarah was slight, with pale skin and blonde hair.

"My brother-in-law, so glad to see you home."

Ian bowed and kissed her on both cheeks, continental style.

Sarah spoke, and they cocked their ears in order to hear her soft-spoken voice.

"Sister," Maggie said. "You must speak up. I can't hear you over the din."

"I said where is Josef? Samuel wanted me to fetch some of Lena's ale. He is usually sold out at this hour."

Maggie filled Sarah in on Josef's bizarre behavior. She eyed her sister. "Are you feeling well, Sarah?"

Ever since the events of last year, when Sarah languished halfway between death and a dream, Maggie had watched her carefully for signs of ill health.

"Nothing a good night's sleep wouldn't heal."

Grace held her arms out to her mother.

"My best mama." She patted Sarah's pale cheeks.

"I am your only mother, wicked child, and the only one who would put up with you."

"My best mama," the babe repeated.

"Is she not young to be talking?" Maggie asked.

"Most assuredly." Sarah kissed the baby's cheek.

"Given the unusual circumstances of the child's birth, it makes sense she would be unusual." Ian said.

"She only sleeps two hours a night." Sarah yawned.

"Must be why you look unwell."

Sarah shot her a pained look. "How kind of you to notice."

"I didn't mean to offend." Maggie grinned.

"Thank you for tending to her. I had a bit of a lie down. Where is Ruthie, the poor girl? The babe is letting no one sleep. And you know how surly Samuel gets without his rest." She laughed. "Ah, there she is, over by the chickens, of course. And look!" Sarah pointed toward the docks.

In the hubbub, no one had noticed the boat docking. But soon, no one could ignore the brightly clothed group of three emerging off the boat and singing their way up the hill. The leader was a tall, dark-haired man dressed in green satin, his tenor voice booming with jovial greetings to the town. He had a lute strapped against his torso. A petite woman dressed in the most brilliant purple sashayed behind him, and bringing up the rear, a drummer beat a complicated rhythm on an old snare drum, held onto his shoulders by worn leather straps. He had on a most unbecoming bright yellow suit.

Ian groaned.

"What is it?"

His face burned with a combination of bemusement and embarrassment. He fidgeted from one foot to the other.

"Whatever is the matter with you?"

"I know this bunch. Quite well. A lifetime ago." The trio made their way into the center market like exotic, colorful birds amidst a flock of sparrows.

"Ladies and gentlemen," the tall, black haired man began. "We, the Wayfaring Wastrels, are delighted to be off the boat, and in your lovely town. I am Reginald, the leader of the Wayfaring Wastrels, and we are at your service."

He motioned expansively to the thin drummer. "Mortimer, the finest drummer this side of the continent."

To prove him right, the sour-faced man beat on his drum, a foot-tapping, magical rhythm with many layers.

"Well done, Morty," Ian murmured.

Then, without warning, the drummer threw his sticks in the air and juggled them. A snaggle-toothed smile lit his face as the crowd cried out in amazement. But where was the woman? Ah, she hid behind the tall man.

"I have saved the very best for last, my friends. Please meet and greet this lovely creature behind me, the nightingale of the north, south, east *and* west, Miss Charlotte Appleton."

He glanced at the drummer, who began a sinuous cadence, and the woman slowly danced to the front and center, a siren's dance, her hips moving in rhythm to the music, wrists bending and fingers curling in an invitation of delights.

She was exquisite, with honey blonde hair elaborately done on top of her head, and she gazed upon the crowd with an air of command. She wore a purple cloak lined with the palest blue to match her eyes. She inclined her head, and Reginald removed her cloak to reveal a purple satin gown. Although she was tiny, no taller than Ruthie, her full breasts presented themselves to the crowd like two sugar plums. Her complexion glowed like an apricot ripening in the summer sun.

"She's quite beautiful," Maggie said.

"Not the words I'd use to describe her," Ian said under his breath.

Then this Charlotte began to sing. Her soprano voice rippled as clear as a mountain spring and seemed to carry through the whole town. She sang a merry song of two lovers courting, a roll in a haystack, and a hasty marriage. People clapped, and it didn't take long for the crowd to sing along, at her queenly invitation.

Peculiar! Ian did not sing. "Ian, why are you not joining in the festivities? Surely you know this song."

"The song was a lifetime ago."

Maggie shook her head. She could not begin to understand the man.

Next, Reginald joined Charlotte in a love song. Tears glistened in the eyes of bystanders as they forgot their troubles for a time.

After a few more songs, Reginald bowed. "Good

ladies and gentlemen, we are happy to announce we will be staying in town for a few days to rest from our journey. We look forward to entertaining you more. Now, our throats are quite dry, and we ask for your indulgence as we slake our thirst."

The crowd cheered, and Charlotte curtsied, offering her bounty for all to see.

"She may be a strumpet, but she has the voice of an angel," Maggie said under her breath.

The trio wound their way through the crowd, and Reginald approached Maggie and Ian first. "Oh ho! Ian Pierce, my old friend! I did not know if I would find you here, but I was hoping very much I would."

"Reginald." Ian grinned. "You look the same."

"Oh no. I'm older, and wiser, I assure you." He smiled at Maggie, a playful glint in his dark eyes. "Introduce me to this beautiful woman. She is entirely too lovely for the likes of you."

Ian put his arm around Maggie protectively. "You might be older, but wiser? Clearly not. Don't even think about it, Reggie. This is my…"

Just then, the strumpet appeared at Reginald's side. She was even more delicate and perfect up close.

"Ian, is it truly you?" She fluttered her lashes, eyes brimming with tears. Even her tears were perfectly shaped. But why would she shed them for Ian?

"Yes, it's been a very long time," Ian said, flatly.

Reginald eyed the marketplace and grimaced. "I've often wondered where you were, lad. But never could I have imagined you in this provincial little town."

"A lot can happen in five years." Ian kissed Maggie upon the cheek. "Reginald and Charlotte, I am proud to present to you my wife, Maggie."

Reginald took her hand, raised it to his lips, and kissed it, while gazing into her eyes. Ian stiffened.

"Congratulations, man. You are most fortunate."

Maggie removed her hand.

"You are married, Ian?" The strumpet touched his sleeve, and he jerked it away.

"Yes, we've been blissfully married for a year now."

"Oh." For a brief moment, Charlotte's eyes went dull. While her singing voice was rich and full, she had the speaking voice of a little girl, and a pout to match.

Maggie felt like a giant beside her.

Charlotte inclined her head toward Maggie. "How do you do?"

"So very nice to meet you," Maggie said.

Reginald laughed as if all of life were a lark. "You, Pierce? Married to this delectable creature." He turned to Maggie. "No doubt Ian has told you all about us."

"No, not a word," Maggie said. And why not?

"Allow me to educate you then. For nigh onto three years, Ian sang and played with our quartet. We've been a sad trio since he left, I assure you."

"Oh come now, Reggie."

"You're right." He laughed. "We're magnificent. But people still talk about your exploits and fine music. Do you not miss the life of a Wayfaring Wastrel?"

"Not in the least," Ian said. "I am the most fortunate of men."

"Congratulations, Mistress Pierce. Your gain is my—our loss," Charlotte said.

Maggie's skin prickled with unease.

"I look forward to seeing you again." Reginald bowed. "But now I must slake my thirst."

"Yes, remember what an *appetite* performing gives you?" Charlotte widened her eyes at Ian.

"No, I don't." Two spots of color flamed on Ian's high cheekbones.

Did the two of them have a history together?

Reginald took Charlotte's arm. "Come along, dear."

"I see Reggie hasn't changed a bit, the asinine rake."

"Charlotte seems to know you well."

"Maggie." He turned to face her. "I will not lie to you but can only assure you it was all a lifetime ago."

Of course he had a past, she chastised herself. Did she think he came to her a virgin?

A commotion suddenly ensued at the edge of the square. Josef appeared, pushing through the crowd. "He is gone," he screamed. "My Nikolaus is gone!"

Chapter Twelve

Josef veered through the crowd, knocking over the potter's booth. Dishes crashed to the ground.

"Damn you, man! You will have to pay for this," the potter yelled.

"Help me," Josef screamed, his face a mask of fear.

"What is he talking about?"

"The man is mad."

"No, possessed."

The whites of their eyes shone in the gloaming of dusk.

"Sarah, take the children home." Ian took off after him.

Maggie followed. Some of the men tried to catch Josef, but he evaded everyone, dodging between stalls, knocking people down.

Ian grabbed him by the arm.

He struggled to free himself. "Let me go, man!"

"Josef, you must calm yourself. What ails you, my friend?"

Josef fought him off. "His body! It is gone!"

"Come, let's go home, Josef."

Josef gripped Ian's wrist and shook it. "No! We must find him, for he is undead." He searched the crowd, black hair wild around his head, pupils black as the coming night. "You will see when you come with me, and we must hurry."

No doubt anticipating more entertainment, the crowd followed Josef as he headed toward the Landgate.

"We must hurry," Josef yelled.

The crowd grew as they left the town. Some people had even fetched their lanterns. "Where is the madman going?"

Once out of the Landgate, Josef turned toward the graveyard.

Ian waited for Maggie and took her arm. "It is impossible to talk sense into him. I recognize the nature of the beast."

Cries of alarm burst from the townspeople as they realized where they were going. "Sweet Jesus, what is he about?"

"You must believe me, he is gone." Josef ran ahead into the graveyard. Maggie gasped as lanterns cast shadows upon the grave, and the piles of dirt and an empty hole where the body had been.

"You see?" Josef screamed. "He has risen. We must find him, or he will take the blood of the innocent, like the monsters in my village."

"Where is the body? He rose from the dead? What is this evil he's talking about? Is he insane?"

A pulse of fear beat through the townspeople and into Maggie's heart.

"Josef." Ian took him by the shoulders. "There must be another explanation. Please. Do not incite the fear of these good people anymore."

Ian raised his voice. "Please, my friends. Do not panic. Have sympathy for our friend Josef, who has ever been a good friend to you."

Maggie didn't know whether the chill was from the

biting wind or the fear and panic in the crowd.

Captain Jacobs yelled, "I've heard many a tale about the creatures, while I was abroad. Yon Josef has brought this to our town."

Shouts of alarm rang through the woods.

"Please forgive me," Josef screamed. "But it is not too late. We can find him and lay him to rest."

"He is crazy," someone yelled. "Out of his mind."

"Yes." Captain Jacobs made the sign against evil. "Or he will roam the town, massacring and go back to his grave, full of the blood of the innocent."

As one, the crowd surged toward Josef.

Someone prayed.

"Here now." Ian spoke above the rising panic. "Let us not turn against our friend, who has been kind to you all. He is distraught with grief, and confused. Do not read anything else into it."

Ah. She saw Ian's intent. If they could steer the crowd one way or the other, they could merely discredit Josef and let people think he was crazy with grief. He put his arm around Josef. His arm shook with the force of Josef's quivering.

"I'm sorry, Josef," Ian whispered. "I know you are not crazy, but you must be silent, man. You have started something here, and we must put it to rest."

The constable stepped up. "Now see here, what is the meaning of this?"

"Fear not." Ian assured him. "Josef is merely overwrought with grief."

"You must stop your caterwauling. You are frightening the townspeople."

Pete Stowe stood at the edge of the crowd, hunched over. "Why is it when there's trouble in the town, Ian

Pierce is involved?"

"Shut your face," the constable yelled.

"I'll take Josef home," Ian said. "He is ill with grief."

"See you do, and waste no time about it. Go home, people." The constable stood, hands on hips.

At this show of authority, the crowd began dispersing.

"I've heard the tales about the monsters coming out of the grave when the sun sets," a sailor said. "They are called vampires."

"I'm barring the door tonight."

Josef began to cry in great gasps.

"Get your friend under control," the constable said. "I can't be responsible for mass panic as these stories come off the boat and into our town. I heard a sailor talking the same kind of nonsense today. We do not want a repeat of last year's hysteria."

"No. We will take him to our cottage until he calms down. I don't want to alarm his wife. Come on now, Josef."

They made haste to the cottage. Ian administered a strong calming draught, and their friend, though still agitated, had calmed down a bit.

Ian paced across the floor, running his hands through his undone hair. "Maggie, we helped Josef bury his nephew. Josef was not mistaken, for we visited it just this morning. Where is the body?"

Chapter Thirteen

"We cannot continue dosing him with strong sedatives."

"They don't seem to have the desired effect, quite." Ian glanced at him. "The only thing stronger I can give him is opium. And I will not do it."

Josef was still wide awake, eyes glazed, limbs twitching. "I need to find the body. We both know it was buried there. We need to find it, find my nephew, for the sake of the townspeople who took me in and made me welcome." For the first time since he'd arrived, he looked at Ian with recognition. "Had it not been for your mother and father, I would have starved."

"Mistress Stowe is a cruel woman," Ian said.

Maggie gawped at him, for she'd never heard him say an unkind word about anyone.

"Josef and I grew up together," Ian explained. "Despite his being an indentured servant, he was like a brother to me. As I became older, and the affliction rose within me, no matter how erratic or shattered I became, he remained my friend. He will be run out of town if I can't help him soon."

"Help me," Josef implored Maggie and Ian, eyes bloodshot and rimmed with tears. "He is out there alone in the dark, my boy, wandering somewhere."

"Josef." Ian handed him another cup of the ale mixed with sedative. "Nikolaus is dead."

Josef shook his head, rising, and Ian pushed him back into the chair.

"You must rest, Josef. There is an explanation for this beyond what you are saying. No one rises from the dead."

"If they are really dead," Maggie murmured, remembering last year's events. "But there has to be a logical, plausible explanation for what happened."

"Perhaps there was malice involved. Who would want to discredit you, Josef?"

It was hard to imagine Josef making enemies, for he treated everyone with even-handed fairness, despite his quiet demeanor.

Before long, the medicine began to take effect. The best thing to do was to secret him back to the inn, before Lena became alarmed at his absence. He would surely sleep now, considering the amount of ale he'd consumed.

Ian bundled Josef up. "He is just awake enough for me to guide him home." Ian glanced at her. "I can carry him if need be."

Yes, of course he could.

"Will you not take your cloak?"

"No, I am overheated. The fresh air will do me good."

Indeed, she could feel the heat radiating from him.

"Will you be up when I get back?" He grinned wolfishly.

She nodded.

"Come on, my friend. Let's get you home. If we meet anyone on the way, they will merely think we have been drinking."

After they'd left, Maggie picked up a pair of his

breeches to mend and just as quickly threw them down. It was selfish of her to think so, but could life not be tranquil for just one day? She hoped he would not take long, for she could no more control the urgings of her body than she could control Ian's changing moods. It was like trying to harness the moon.

She should be ashamed for thinking of herself when Josef suffered so, and Lena as well. What were they to do with Josef? How much of his story was real, and how much merely a product of his grief?

In truth, she was tired, and as more time passed, she prepared for bed. A few hours later, she awoke to find him still gone.

Later, before dawn lit the sky, the bed gave way as Ian lay down, bringing with him the scent of oranges, ale, and sandalwood. She smelled something else she could not identify, carried on the winds of his travels. He wrapped his arms around her and nestled his lips against the crook of her neck.

"Did you sleep well, my love? I thought to stay with Josef until he fell asleep. It took longer than I anticipated."

She turned to him, luxuriating in his warmth, brought the blanket up around them, and molded her body to his in the early morning light.

****

Several hours later, Maggie walked up the lane to McCall's cottage. The sheepdog ran to her, barking and shaking his hind end in glee.

Adam McCall mended a fence, casting an eye toward the cottage every few minutes.

"How are you, Mr. McCall?"

He smiled. "Truth be told, I'm hiding from the

hens." He cocked his head toward the door. There was an uncommon din seeping from the cracks of the cottage.

"No mistake, it's glad I am to have them here." He lowered his voice conspiratorially. "But Bethan never stops talking and Elunid stares and fidgets in her odd way. When she has her fits it gives me the chills, it does."

He grinned and rose from his task. "No more delay. Onward and upward. Polly and the twins will be glad to see you."

She opened the door to find Bethan sitting on the floor with the children. The youngest one tugged on her skirts.

"Hallo there, little gent." She picked him up.

He tucked his curly head into her neck, and she inhaled the scent of milk, outdoors, and baby.

As a result of a pointed stare from their aunt, the children greeted her one by one.

Polly lay on her pallet with her feet upon a pillow. "Good morrow, Mistress Maggie."

"I am so glad you're resting. No, don't get up."

Maggie couldn't help but stare at Polly's immense belly. Could it have grown overnight? Her attention was diverted by Elunid, who stood against the wall and fingered one of Polly's wall hangings.

"The king and his nephew," she murmured.

Maggie marveled anew at the wonder of twins. Bethan and Elunid were eerily identical, except in behavior. She knew Elunid by the slope of her shoulders and the smudge of shadows below her eyes.

"Hello, Elunid."

Maggie doubted the strange girl would respond,

but she turned her head toward her, nodded, then resumed her perusal of Polly's handiwork.

"She's been reading legends again, and once engaged in something, she cannot let go of it," Polly said matter-of-factly.

"What smells so delicious?" Maggie sniffed.

Katherine stood. "It's *bara brith*. I made it."

"Did you now?"

She nodded, face flushed with pride. "Will you join us for tea, Mistress Maggie?"

She glanced at Bethan for approval. Bethan nodded.

"I would be delighted, Katherine."

The little girl took the pan out of the hearth, set the table, and made tea with an efficiency much like her mother's. "Tea is served," she announced regally.

The women gathered at the table, and the boys, still involved in their game, did not heed her.

Katherine raised her voice. "Pardon me, brothers, but did I not call you to *tea*?"

She raised her voice on the last bit, and the boys lifted their heads as one, as if familiar with the tone and not wanting what might be forthcoming.

Maggie helped Polly out of bed, and they had a most delightful repast with the delicious Welsh fruit bread.

Out of her trance for now, Elunid said in a monotone, "You have mastered the art of *bara brith*." She fixed her gaze upon Katherine, spoon held in midair. "It bodes well for you."

Katherine wriggled her slender shoulders, as if shaking off a chill. "Thank you, Aunt Elunid."

When a few minutes had passed and Elunid

continued to stare, Katherine began to squirm in her seat.

Adam broke in. "Delicious, Katherine. I'd say this earns you some time at play, before the weather turns. When we finish, you may take your brothers outside."

The sheepdog had been lying by the table under the baby waiting for fallen tidbits. Upon hearing the word "outside," he promptly rose, whacking the baby with his massive bobbed tale.

Bethan poured Polly another cup of tea. "I will be out soon to help you with your brothers, Katherine."

The children and dog headed outside.

Due to the size of her stomach, Polly had to sit with her body far removed from the table. With as much dignity as possible, she reached forward, and Adam handed her the tea, first stirring in a generous amount of sugar.

"Thank you," she said. "Maggie, it was very kind of you to come out again, but not necessary. I do not feel anything forthcoming."

"I would rather err on the side of caution, Polly. And I'm glad your sisters are here to assist you."

A fair amount of time passed in congenial conversation, then Maggie rose to attend to her duties with Polly. "Come. Let's see how the babes are coming along."

Just then, they heard the dog barking and growling in turn.

"Something's wrong," Adam said. "He never growls."

With the exception of Polly, who had already gone to lie down, they rushed to the door.

In the far side of the field, a large brown dog stood,

teeth bared. No more than two feet away, the sheepdog stood, hackles raised. The children hid behind him, Katherine carrying the baby, and when the other dog tried to advance, the sheepdog snarled and snapped at him.

"The sheepdog is protecting the children," Maggie said.

"Yes. Good dog." Adam grabbed a pitchfork and thrust it toward the strange dog. Bethan gathered the children and took them inside.

Their dog stayed with Adam, trying to get between him and the strange brown cur.

"Get away, you!" Adam yelled, until finally the dog ran toward the forest.

Bethan comforted each of the children in turn.

"Were you frightened, Katherine?" Elunid asked.

"Yes, but I knew Laddy would protect us."

Adam and the dog returned to the house. "He's gone."

The children all embraced the dog. He licked them in turn, tail wagging.

"Good lad. You've earned your keep today." Adam gave him a chunk of cheese, and he hunkered down to make quick work of it.

"I've not seen the dog before," Adam said.

'I hope he's gone for good," Maggie said.

"Was he mad?" Eluned asked without turning from her perusal of the needlework.

"I doubt it," Adam said. "There's not been a mad dog around the county for many years."

Maggie had just finished her visit with Polly when a clatter of wheels and hoof beats brought everyone to the door again.

"Ian, my man! And Henry. What brings you here?"

"Good to see you, Adam." Ian bowed toward Polly. "Madame, McCall, you look beautiful and bountiful."

She blushed, and Adam narrowed his eyes at him.

Ian's eyes lit upon Maggie. "My love. I thought you would be here, and have a most timely gift for you." He glanced at Polly again. "I ran into Henry on the way, and he could not resist a ride in the new wagon."

Henry doffed his cap and bowed to the assembled company. His eyes searched the crowd and found Bethan. She nodded, and without further acknowledgment, went to Elunid's side. He watched her like a thirsty sailor watches the head on a pint of ale.

"Wagon? You brought the wagon here? Could you not have walked?" Ian had brought the wagon just to spite her.

Her husband carried the fresh scent of the outdoors with him, and despite hardly sleeping last night, brightened the room with his vigor. He certainly had the energy to walk about the county all the day long. She could not help but be drawn to his power, for it was like a zephyr after a winter of cold winds.

He kissed her upon the cheek. "If I hadn't come in the wagon, I could not have brought your gift. It arrived on the docks today." He stole a sideways glance at Polly, who watched the scene with great interest. "I wagered you might need it here first." He grabbed her hands. "Come see your gift."

What did the man have in store for her now?

The boys ran out of doors ahead of Maggie and Ian and were oohing and awing over the gypsy wagon.

"I will supervise the children." Bethan rose.

Henry followed her as if in a trance.

Katherine looked longingly at the door.

"Go along, miss," Polly said.

The little girl threw her apron on the table and ran to catch up with her brothers.

Maggie turned to Polly. "Take this time to rest up."

Ian opened the doors to the wagon with a flourish, arms and legs akimbo, eliciting giggles from one and all. "What you are about to see, ladies and gentlemen, has not been seen in this part of the county, nay, world." He wore a pinched, sour face, as if he'd just bit into a bad pickle. "Are you ready?"

"Yes! Yes!"

"Feast your eyes, then." He opened the door to reveal the inside, which Maggie had not yet seen. It was completely covered in red velvet, with ornate gold fixtures on the sides. There was a raised bed at the far end. Upon it two large baskets brimmed with food. He climbed inside and brought out a large object covered in burlap and set it on the ground.

"You brought food." She smiled up at him.

He shrugged. "Many mouths to feed." He came to her, caressing her shoulders lightly.

"It will not go amiss." How could she remain angry at a man who would do such a thing?

He turned to the children. "Care to climb aboard?"

As reverent as little churchgoers, they climbed one by one into the wagon. Ian held his hand out to help Katherine. "Lady Katherine, I do believe you are the fairest eight-year-old in the land." She giggled, blushing spectacularly from her forehead to her neck.

Soon all the children stood in the wagon, gazing in

awe, as if they visited Winchester Cathedral itself.

A spark of warmth kindled within Maggie; as much as she despised the wagon, this would no doubt be the highlight of the children's month. Ian let the children linger there for a while.

"Would you children be so good as to take the comestibles into the house?"

The two oldest children struggled under the weight of the basket. A loaf of bread fell out, and Bethan bent to retrieve it at the same time Henry did.

"*Oof*," Bethan cried, dropping the bread.

This time, Henry placed it squarely in her hands, his large fingers upon her wrists.

"Oho." Ian stood with his head cocked, eyeing Henry. "She's quite bewitched old Henry, hasn't she?"

"She's a charming girl but will eventually go back to Wales. He should not get attached."

"Not a concern of his, just now." He slapped the covered object. "Open it, Maggie."

She pointed to the ram's ballocks on the wagon. "Does it have anything to do with those?"

"No. It requires less care." He grinned, and ceremoniously removed the cloth.

She gasped at the birthing chair. It was made of polished wood and looked much like a regular chair, but with a large hole, u-shaped, where the seat would normally be. It had sturdy arms with ornate carvings for the mother to grip. She had long wanted to have one, for does it not make sense to sit, as the babes must travel downward to emerge?

She embraced him and kissed him on the mouth. "Thank you, husband. I will make good use of this."

"You said you wanted one."

"Thank you," she said again.

"This is what I love about you, my Maggie. You are uncommonly rare. I would gladly buy you jewelry, but you would rather have a gift which helps you serve others."

They returned to the cottage and received a hearty thank you from Polly and Adam.

The baskets stood on the table. "Please enjoy." Ian set out a ham and unwrapped a cloth filled with iced cakes.

Bethan grabbed hold of Katherine's hand and danced her around the room, her long arms and legs and willowy stature accentuating the happy event. "Why, it is like a party, is it not, children?"

Just then, Henry stubbed his toe on the rocking chair.

Ian unloaded a lovely bunch of carrots, some oranges, and three loaves of bread from the overflowing basket. He also unearthed a tin of tea he'd probably picked up on his travels, a bottle of brandy, and some sweetmeats.

Three-year-old Peter pulled on Ian's breeches. "Me mum has two babies in her."

He squatted down at the boy's eye level. "Yes. It is most miraculous, isn't it?"

The boy nodded.

Polly reddened. "Enough, Peter."

Ian winked at him and straightened. "Oh! I almost forgot." He left, and promptly returned with the birthing chair, and proceeded to explain its purpose. Polly eyed it with disbelief.

Adam blanched and retreated outside. "I need to fix something," he mumbled.

"Please enjoy the food," Ian said. "I must take my wife home."

****

"My love, would you like to ride in the back? You could lounge like a queen upon the bed."

"Not a chance." Maggie pressed her lips together.

Exasperating man! She had never been so confused in her entire life. How could she be angry with him when he'd been so kind to the McCalls? But why did he have to purchase this horrible wagon?

Oblivious to her confusion, Ian held the reins, clicked his tongue to get the mare going, and hummed a cheery tune, swinging from high notes to low. Without warning, he belted out a few lines, such as "and that's how maids in sunny France, work their wiles for sweet romance." His sleeves were rolled up on his linen shirt, revealing long, muscled forearms.

He grinned at her, teeth white in his tanned face. "Is it not good to have a wagon? I could not have hauled the food and birthing chair without it."

"A simple cart would have sufficed." She folded her arms and stared straight ahead.

"I do adore it when you're vexed at me, woman. Your displeasure boils your blood, so when I bed you, it is already heated for my pleasure." His mouth quirked up at the corners.

She harrumphed. "If you think you're bedding me tonight, you are mistaken."

"Who said anything about tonight? There's a perfectly good bed in the back. All we need do is park our wagon."

"You must be joking. And it is not *our* wagon. It is *your* wagon."

"What's mine is yours."

"Indeed, it is not."

"You won't know until you try it."

"I said I…"

"I see you need convincing with a song. It came to me immediately upon seeing the wagon for the first time. Here 'tis:

My lover, shall we go this morn
To see the world and be reborn.
We'll travel high, we'll travel low
Exotic climes where peaches grow.
And peaches I will feed you, slip into your mouth
Lick the juice upon your skin and let it travel south."

Like always, his voice, rumbling and intimate, peeled layers of clothing and anger from her. The notes slid into her, and she softened for him, her body tingling. Her resolve not to look his way crumbled.

He took a breath, then:

"To-ooo
Your bosom, your breast, your bosom, your breast
A bosom when it is covered
A breast when it is bare
Your bosom, your breast, your bosom, your breast
Your bosom—the best!"

The laughter burst from her body, involuntary as a sneeze, and she laughed until tears rolled down her face. She grasped his forearm. "You are the most ridiculous man. But thank you for bringing food for the McCalls. And the birthing chair, it is wonderful." She met his gaze. "As I said, no one has ever given me gifts before."

"What a shame, for you are worthy of the finest gifts a man could give."

"You need not say such lofty things. There's no need to court me, for we are already married."

He laughed. "Maggie, all the more reason to court you, for every day you grow more precious to me. You and the child."

What did it serve to stay angry at him?

After they passed under the Landgate, they saw the dark clouds over the water, churning the sea into whitecaps. People were out in abundance, their day of work ending, and refreshments in mind. And of course, the wagon served as entertainment.

"What have you there, apothecary? Are you leaving town and going on the road?" Old Widow Jenkins sat in the shade of a linden tree and cackled.

"See," Maggie muttered under her breath. "We are the laughingstock of the town."

Mrs. Stowe milled about the crowd with papers in her hand, handing them out, while Pete slouched beside her. She pointed at the wagon. "Look at them putting on airs. It is fortunate you possess a more humble nature, dear boy." They made their way down the street.

Maggie wondered what Margaret Stowe was about, but she had other concerns at the moment.

"How do you expect the town to take you seriously, Ian? They come to you for your doctoring as well as herbs."

"Don't fret so much, Maggie. They will grow accustomed to it."

Her face burned crimson, and she lifted her chin. The town had just gotten back to normal after the traumatic events of last year, where superstition and the greed of an evil doctor had split the town apart.

"I can be both performer and doctor, Maggie. If I

entertain, they merely get more for their money."

"Well, there's the big difference between you and me, husband. I need to be taken seriously, in my work."

No, he didn't mind being the entertainment. In fact, he thrived on it, having travelled all over the world, performing for kings, selling his herbs, and gathering new ones to help him with his affliction.

He probably missed his performing days, when he travelled to procure herbs for his brother, and made his way through the countryside of England, Europe, and even the deserts of Arabia, singing for his supper and plying his wares.

"Do you miss performing?"

"The only performing I want to do is in our bed, my love."

Despite her irritation, she could not stop the feeling of pride swelling within her. She eyed his neck, sinewy with muscle, and the length of his tanned broad shoulders, visible through his linen shirt. His buckskin breeches fit snugly on the banded muscles of his thighs. There was an air of increased vitality about him since he came home. All she need do was partake of it and be refreshed. He was hers.

He hummed, the slightly hoarse voice raising the tiny hairs on her arms, and waved to Ed the butcher and his wife.

"What's inside your wagon, Pierce?" Ed hollered.

"New supplies for my shoppe, friend. Cures and treatments, too." He paused for dramatic effect. "And aphrodisiacs to make your wife smile for days."

Ed's wife turned red but giggled just the same.

Ian laughed with abandon. His happiness made her feel all was well, and all would be well, and the life force surging through him flowed through her.

They passed by the Siren Inn. Pete Stowe leaned against the old brick, his mother at his side, mouth twisted with disdain.

"Ahoy, Pete."

Pete scowled in response to Ian's greeting.

"See how he is holding his hand. It is paining him. If only he would come see me, I could probably treat it. He will lose it otherwise."

Mrs. Stowe whispered in Pete's ear.

"What are *you* looking at?" Pete said. "I see you bought a travelling brothel, Pierce."

The crowd buzzed with amusement and anticipation.

Maggie flushed. Pete puffed up as his comment gathered favor. His mother patted his arm encouragingly.

Ed stood in front of him. "If it was, you'd be the first one to pay, Stowe."

The crowd roared.

"Yes, only a man who'd been in league with a murderer and whore-master would say such a thing." Ed cast a look at the shepherdess. "I happen to like it. Time this town had some color, aye? And I'll wager whatever he decides to do with it, will be for the good of the town."

"Hear, hear!"

Pete broke away from his mother's grasp and skulked down the road.

"Where are you going?" his mother cried. "Why can you not stand up to the impudent wastrel? We used to be prominent in this town, and you have made us nothing."

The crowd was too busy admiring the inside of the wagon to hear her, but Maggie stood aside, watching them walk down the road.

"You've done nothing but bring me shame, these long years. God must despise me indeed to deprive me of a worthy son." Mrs. Stowe paused to shake his arm, eliciting a moan.

"Mother! My hand."

"Only you," she hissed. "Every time I walk by the inn, I am reminded of what we lost, and you with no will to do anything about it, except to latch on to those smugglers."

"You enjoyed the fruits of my labor well enough."

She grabbed hold of his ear and pulled it.

"Mother! You know I am unwell."

"Mind over matter, son. We must save ourselves and the town as well."

Maggie wondered what she meant.

Ian touched her cheek with his callused fingertip. "What is it?"

"Oh, nothing we can do anything about."

He nodded. "What a pair. Are you hungry, my sweeting?"

"Very," she said. "When the babe wants to eat, the babe must eat."

They travelled down a narrow close.

"Are we going to fit?" Mayhap he would accidentally damage the paint on this travelling travesty. But it did fit, with nary an inch on either side to spare. They turned toward the docks, to Sarah and Samuel's house.

"I promise I will feed you at the Siren, my dear, as soon as I tuck the horse and carriage in."

After they disposed of the horse and carriage, they walked toward the harbor on the way to the Siren Inn.

"Why is the Stowe family so hostile toward us? Surely they cannot still blame us for what happened to Pete last year. We had nothing to do with Edward Carter's cruelty toward him."

"Greed was his downfall, like so many men," Ian said. "And most times, where there is hate, there is no logic."

"I have the most peculiar sense of unease."

He wrapped his arm around her shoulders. "Let us gaze at the sea like a couple of carefree lovers."

Chapter Fourteen

As they passed the docks, waves hurtled against the pilings, and in the distance, storm clouds gathered, dark with malevolence. The wind had picked up, carrying the smell of rotten fish from a boat caught in a storm in the middle of the channel, and not able to return before the fish rotted. A crowd of people lingered by the boat, commiserating with the newly arrived fisherman.

"Gawd help me, yar never know what she's going to do. Looked fine when I went out, then it started churning and churning like hell's fury."

"Sorry for your misfortune," Ian called.

Josiah Marmont looked up and grinned, displaying a mouth full of rotten teeth resembling tombstones. He reached into his pocket for his snuff box. The fact he had the remains of rotten fish on his hands did not stop him from sticking a bit of snuff into his mouth.

"Wicked storms out there, but good fishing. We'd just netted a mass of cod and headed home, but we could not move toward land, such were the currents. I'm glad to have made it out alive, rotten fish or no."

He tipped his cap respectfully to Maggie as they turned to leave.

Ian said, "I wish you better luck the next time, my friend."

The fisherman grinned. "If I'd wanted a lack-a-day life, I would've been an apothecary."

The wind had picked up as they walked to the Siren Inn, whipping Maggie's cloak around her.

Ian's arm tightened about her waist, and he nestled his nose into her neck. "Oh, Maggie, I missed your scent. Many nights I regretted my leaving, but knew I must."

She could not help leaning into him, stopping for a minute in the greyness of dusk to grasp and kiss him. Who cared if anyone saw? He was home and safe, and could buy anything he liked, even a ridiculous wagon, as long as he was by her side.

The wind pushed at their backs, as if urging them to shelter.

"How quickly the weather—and life—can turn on you," Ian murmured, and ran his hand up and down her back to warm her.

The inn burst with people. Ian held the door for her as they entered the warm and noisy inn. The smell of fish cooking, onions, and ale made Maggie's stomach growl. They made their way through the customers standing around, holding mugs of ale, and talking. Ian received a cheery welcome and no end of ribbing about his wagon. The massive fireplace roared, and the warmth of the room prompted Maggie to take off her cloak. Ian rushed to assist her, his hands lingered on the nape of her neck. Her cold chills in response contrasted with the warm fug of the inn, momentarily making her feel they were alone in the bustling room.

The memories of the evening before, the graveyard, and the story had all but usurped the celebration of their reunion. Maybe tonight there would be no interruptions. She needed time to grasp what made him different from before.

Ian took off his coat, looking around with bright eyes; he so loved a crowd. They found a place near the bar.

Across the room, a couple of windblown sailors sat at a table by the window. Their reek overpowered the myriad of smells in the room. Zelda, one of the town doxies, sat on Pete Stowe's lap, shrieking with laughter.

Stowe yelled into her ear, loud enough for all to hear. "The man is crazy as he ever was, buying a garish wagon like an ill-bred gypsy. Fool. Mayhap he'll do us a favor and disappear in it."

Zelda giggled.

Just then, Josef walked by Stowe's table, rammed into him with a heavy pewter tray, and knocked Zelda off his lap.

Josef narrowed his eyes at Stowe. "Get out."

Stowe slinked off the stool. "Let's take our party to the Shipwreck. They're a mite friendlier over there."

Ian pointed to the corner, where hidden by the polished mahogany bar, Vicar Andrews sat alone, watching Sabine carrying a tray of drinks and comestibles. No wonder he stared. Sabine had plumped up nicely, her face glowing with good health Maggie could not imagine the Siren Inn without the girl now.

Josef rushed in behind the bar, carrying a cask, with a grim look upon his face.

Lena appeared with a tray of dishes in her hands and pointed her head toward Vicar Andrews. "The holy boy spends much time here at the Siren."

"I see." Ian grinned.

They watched as Sabine stood at Vicar Andrew's table, cocked her head, and waited. "You want…something?"

He blushed, wig askew. "Uh."

Everyone who attended church knew when the good vicar got excited about something, he had a problem modulating his voice.

He gawped at her and roared, "Um, yes. A shepherd's pie, please, and fried potatoes."

Sabine started, then repeated the order softly to herself.

Despite the uproar of the place, the crowd grew silent. Every ear tuned in to see what would happen.

Sabine turned to leave.

"Another ale if you please, dear, erm," He blurted, and blushed furiously.

Maggie took pity on him and rose, ignoring her aching legs.

"Vicar, good evening. I quite enjoyed your sermon last Sunday."

"Oh, I didn't see you there at first, Mistress Maggie." He stood, straightened his wig, and bowed.

"Yes, I had just seen the Thompson baby safely into the world. I arrived late, but in time to hear your words of wisdom."

"Yes, a lovely baby with her mother's red hair. One of God's little lambs, welcomed into our fold."

The Lord had some competition for his affections tonight, though. The vicar's eyes wandered once again in Sabine's direction.

Ian sauntered over with Vicar's food and ale. "Your servant, sir."

"Please sit down," Vicar said, an ominous tone to his voice.

"Your friend Josef continues to tell his horrid stories all over town. He came to me this morning, asking me to keep watch with him tonight to make sure his nephew does not emerge from the grave like last night. He instructed me on what to do if he does. For he will, he said, and the consequences will be dire. I tried to talk some reason into him, to no avail."

Ian nodded. "I assure you, Vicar, we have talked to Josef about the foolishness of his stories. I helped him bury his nephew and can make no sense of the body disappearing. But there must be a sensible explanation for it."

"You must get your friend to keep still. I will not have my flock divided by superstition and stories of evil." He suddenly seemed years older. "And there's something else." He reached into his pocket and pulled out a wrinkled piece of parchment. "Have you seen these?" He handed it to Maggie.

It had the title, "Beware the Vampire at the Siren Inn," and a picture of a creature with dark wings and fierce fangs dripping with blood.

"What foolishness," she said.

"Yet people have been bringing me these all day."

"I saw Pete Stowe and his mother passing something out. They are spreading this poison."

"They are determined to discredit Josef and make the most of his grief," Ian said.

"But why?" Maggie asked.

Josef tended to the group of sailors gathered in the corner. One of them leaned his chair against the wall, well into his cups. Under normal circumstances, Josef would be talking to them in his quiet way, showing everyone equal respect by virtue of his listening ears. But tonight, he looked down at his work, face red, hands shaking the tray he held.

"I don't like the looks of Josef," said Ian.

Just then, the sailor who'd leaned against the window bolted upright, spilling his ale. "Tell us the stories of these *vampires*, barkeep. About how they roam the town after sunset, taking the blood of the innocent and returning to their graves." He burst out laughing. "I hear you know one intimately."

His cohorts cheered and guffawed.

Josef shook his head, mouth pressed together, and slid the bowls of chowder on the table.

"Yes." The drunken one poked Josef in the forearm.

Josef clanked the tray down.

"Aye," the man said. "Good time for a story, no matter how far-fetched." He laughed, spraying ale over the table.

Josef grabbed the man's greasy hair, twisted it in his hand, and lifted him off his feet.

"This is no laughing matter," he shouted. "Good people have lost their lives, do you hear? I will teach you to have respect for the dead of my homeland." He shook him. The whites of the sailor's eyes showed as he screamed. His companions stood, fists at the ready.

Ian rushed forward. "How about another round for these valiant men of the sea, Josef?" He deftly removed Josef's hand from the sailor's head, eyeing the rest of his crew with a hard eye. "Your wife is looking for you."

Josef shook himself like a dog doused with water and headed for the kitchen. More than a few customers left their food uneaten and scurried out the door.

Ian towered over the table and stared the men back down in their seats. "I heard there was a motherlode of fish today, and the sea nearly got the better of you. But you prevailed." Ian glanced around and motioned for Sabine to refill their ale. "My friends, raise your mugs for our brave men of the sea!"

A goodly amount of the customers cheered, and the sailors were happy again, crowing about their success.

There was no shortage of talk about Josef's uncharacteristic behavior, and more than a handful of people thought it prudent to go elsewhere.

Ian shook his head. "If our good friend can't find some way to contain himself, he will soon find himself out of customers. But we have a much bigger problem."

"What is it?" Maggie asked.

"Josef is burning up with fever."

Chapter Fifteen

"Pray God Lena does not sicken as well," Maggie said. "While you help him to bed, I will give Sabine a hand."

A while later, all but a few stray sailors had cleared out of the inn. Maggie sat at a table with Sabine when Ian appeared from the private quarters.

"He is resting," he said. "There are no other symptoms besides the high fever, but it is taking a toll on him. There is nothing I can do for him, beyond the willow bark, but I told Lena to send for me should his condition worsen later." He picked up her cloak. "Now I must get you home."

They hurried to the cottage as the rain slashed at them like swords. Ian held Maggie's arm to keep her steady. The wind hastened their journey as they headed uphill toward the shoppe.

They were soaked to the skin when they arrived home. Ian took off her cloak and handed her a piece of linen with which to dry. He peeled off his wet shirt and rushed to build the fire. Despite her shivering, she could not prevent an intake of breath at the sight of his wide shoulders, the muscled strength of his haunches as he squatted by the fire, bringing a glow to the room and to her center. Then, he grabbed the bucket and headed outside.

"Where are you going?"

"I'm fetching water. You will need to warm up."

"I'm not a delicate flower."

"You are to me. Your body is laboring—pardon the pun—to grow a child, and you need your rest."

"And what about you, Ian? You will catch your death of cold."

He stood there for a moment, the strength of him belying her concern. Before she knew it, he had the water ready. He had taken off his breeches, and his thighs glistened with rain.

A shiver ran through her at the sight of him as he moved the washstand closer to the fire.

"So you might wash in comfort," he rumbled.

Water pooled in her mouth as she watched the movement of his thigh muscles under their dusting of dark gold hair. His chest shone with the rain, making the hair gathered there shine in the firelight. His member lay stiff and long against his muscled belly. He had been gone from her nigh on three months, but seemed so different, more powerful, more…

"Turn around, Maggie."

He undid her bodice and untied the ribbon of her shift, draping a linen cloth over her. He knelt before her and removed her boots and stockings. She shivered, but not from the cold.

"Are you warm enough?"

She nodded. "You don't need to wash me. I can wash myself."

"Let me serve you." He leaned over her, a warm cloth in his hand already scented with tuberose soap. He washed her face, long fingers sliding over her forehead, as he hummed a melody she had not heard before, his Adam's apple moving, hoarse voice laced with sweetness, and a kind of innocence, newly born and singing fresh from the soul.

His gaze met hers, hazel flecks in his green eyes shimmering in the firelight's reflection. "Does this please you?"

Her voice rasped, "Yes. How could it not?"

As if a man like him would ever need her approval, but indeed it seemed as if his world depended on it. He paused to put the cloth in warm water, and she looked at his profile, the high cheekbones and long mouth, lips pursed in concentration.

He lowered the sheet to expose her shoulders. "Your skin, Maggie. So soft. How I missed it." He grasped her hands. "I am sorry, Maggie."

"Sorry for what?"

"I was gone so long from you, and I have nothing to show for it, no remedy, no *litio*. All I have is a splintered memory of when the goddess put the cup to my lips, and slowly I emerged from the shattered self I'd become. The *litio* had a sweet, earthy taste, slightly bitter. I remember nothing else." He lowered his eyes, jaw clenched. "I have failed you, for I am still...not what you deserve."

"Look at me," she said. "You had to go, not just for me, but for the people of the town."

"I will never be the perfect man, Maggie."

Rain lashed against the window, and gusts of wind blew down the chimney, dousing the fire before it came to life again. Thunder shook the cottage.

"Let us not talk of it, for you are here now. It is not your fault, Ian. Life is not perfect, or neat and tidy." She reached up and kissed him. "Have you ever seen a child being born? It is messy and primitive. And joyful.

And you, you are like new life to me, Ian."

"Let me care for you, Maggie. Let me anoint you with my love."

Her heart pounded in her throat. He painstakingly washed her breasts, her back, her privities, until she felt reborn. He wrapped the linen around her, as lightning flashed upon his face.

He bent to grasp her foot in his hand, and pressed his thumb from the center of her foot to her toes, a slow, repetitive slide. He set her foot down like a fine porcelain cup, and picked up her other foot, repeating the movements.

She laid her head back on the chair as her womanhood grew moist. Her thighs clenched. "Ah. How do you do this to me? How can you touch my feet and pleasure me this way?"

In answer, he took her hand and led her upstairs into bed.

His eyes glinted like sparks as he held himself over her. "Turn over," he commanded. "I have some unguent to ease your shoulder."

She obeyed, and he gathered her thick, waist-length hair to one side, sinking his face into it. "How I missed the scent of you! It haunted me wherever I went."

He straddled her, knees on either side, and rubbed the ointment into her shoulders, his thumbs pressing into the sorest spot.

"Mmm. It smells good."

"I'm glad you like it. I had it made for you."

"It smells foreign, exotic."

"Wintergreen and eucalyptus." He ran his fingers up her scalp and pressed small circles down her neck.

He lowered himself, resting his loins upon her

bottom. "Am I too heavy for you?"

"No." The rigid length of his cock rested in the cleft of her bottom. She grew moist and could not help but lift herself to encourage it.

"Not yet. Let me take care of you, sweeting. You take care of everyone but yourself."

He applied more of the ointment and worked his fingers down her back, releasing every tired muscle. His palms claimed her buttocks, setting her body on fire. He kissed the side of her face, and she turned her head to kiss him.

"Maggie, when I was away from you, I felt as if the ground moved underneath me and I could not get my footing."

"I felt empty," she whispered. "Fill me, Ian. Fill me up." She rolled over to face him.

He moaned and she guided him into her, rising to meet him. His hands caressed her breasts as he sank himself into her pulsing center. He drew his member out with agonizing slowness, her privities clenched him, but he held himself at her opening, enticing her.

She grabbed his hair and pulled him toward her, rising, rising, and he plunged his hard length into her, until she could feel all of him. She thrust against him, his flames licking her, and when he called her name, pleasure consumed them both, his essence pumping into her to quench the fire.

He kissed her, making tendrils of sensation race over her. "Oh, Maggie. I love you so."

She could not speak, could only lift her lips to his and answer with her center clenching him again. The storm battered the cottage, while she melted against him, hand upon his chest, his heart pounding against her palm, a steady beat protecting her from the storms around them.

Chapter Sixteen

The storm continued to pound the cottage, providing an eerie accompaniment to Ian's music. He sat before the fire, his mind recalling the sights and sounds of recent travel. His fingers plucked the memories from the strings, the melody surging within him.

If he could only be upstairs wrapped in the comfort of Maggie's soft embrace, not fighting his demons with a violin. Nothing to be done about it, but what the good Hindu doctors had taught him. He set the instrument on his lap, willed his feet to stop tapping. He closed his eyes, inhaled slow and steady, heeding his breathing like a mother listens for her babe's steady breathing. He had to listen closely through the raging of the storm outside. And the storm within him too.

He let out his breath: steady as she goes, steady in and out again. Josef's tales of blood and horror snaked through his veins, dry scales scraping through every inch of him, ponderous as a dirge, strange, sinister and menacing, Josef's madness—or was he?

He did Josef no good with his agitation. He was a doctor. He would find what ailed his friend. He lit another candle and perused the Galen tome in search of an answer. His every instinct told him Josef was stricken with more than grief and a mere fever. His aggression was pronounced. And what had caused

Nikolaus' death? He thumbed through the pages, then stopped. No. Hydrophobia was a disease as old as time, but there had been no cases of it in the region for as long as he could remember. No. He would not entertain the notion of such a horrific possibility. Josef would rally round, as he always did. He shut the book, no longer able to concentrate.

His thoughts raced, and suddenly, he was splashed with a memory of Bedlam's doctors, of cold water, of his frustration, for he could not get them to understand his urgency, the need to write the music, the most perfect music, coursing through his veins, seeping through his skin. They liked to hear him sing well enough, the inmates and visitors alike, even the keepers. They loved his dulcet tones and clever rhymes, until they wanted him to stop, but then he could not, no more than Josef could stop the airing of his fears.

Their remedy, to tie him in a chair. He struggled mightily, hit his head when the chair fell over, fists, boots, bruises, blue, and they lowered him, the water rose over him, cold, fetid, the piss of those who came before, and too late he held his breath. His lungs burned, head bursting as he fought against the darkness.

Had they studied it, the doctors? To see how long a man could be submerged without drowning? Certainly, for just as he could hold his breath no longer, they brought him up, threw him back into the cell. Bone deep cold, coursing through his veins, he shivered on the hard floor, his bruised flesh ringing in his ears. The laughter echoed in the corridor, deep discussion.

"Did it work?"

"He's not singing anymore, annoying bastard."

So cold.

Ian picked up his violin and began to play. He would control his affliction as best as he could, with his music, until he found the remedy. God willing, he would discover what ailed his good friend, Josef.

****

Maggie woke a few hours after their lovemaking, to the sound of Ian playing a stringed instrument. The mournful melody sent shivers up her spine. She put on her robe and went downstairs.

He sat on a wooden chair, naked, one leg crossed on his thigh. He held a violin under his chin, the bow in his other hand, sliding across the strings. His hair fell loose around his shoulders. The bare, slender foot resting on the floor beat in rhythm to the strings. His face glistened with sweat.

She came to him, and he stopped playing. He was very pale, with dark circles under his eyes. She embraced him. "You are so cold, my Ian."

He put the violin on the floor and pulled her onto his lap. "And you are warm. I do love the way you look when you are fresh from slumber, all fragrant and flushed, hair tousled, a look of innocence on your face. Oh God, how you comfort me! I do not want to go away again, Maggie."

She took him in her arms to still his bone-deep trembling. He put his head upon her breast like a child, for he had indeed been inside of her tonight. She should have known he still suffered from this thing he called manico-melancolicus.

"I wish I could help you, Ian."

He kissed her. "I am fine. I just cannot sleep, and there's nothing to be done about it. Please go to bed, for it will not help me if you lose sleep on my account."

She lay down on the divan and fell asleep to the sound of the moaning wind accompanying Ian's voice and the plaintive cry of the violin, echoing Josef's sorrow and pain. If only she could take it from them both.

Chapter Seventeen

In the morning, Maggie awoke on the divan to find Ian standing in front of her, staring. He was fully dressed and filthy, the scent of the outdoors on his clothes.

"What are you doing?"

He smiled. "I love to look at you when you sleep, for when you are not at labor, you are not concerned about anyone, you are…you. Mayhap like you were as a child, although I expect you were quite serious."

"Oh believe me. There was nothing playful about my childhood."

"It was a bad storm."

"I slept through it all?"

He handed her a cup of tea. "You sleep the sleep of the innocent, and I am glad of it. Maggie, the streets are a wreck as a result of the storm." His hair had blown out of its tie, and his big knuckles were red and abraded. "Naturally I could not sleep, so I ventured out to help. The homes by the pier were hit hardest."

As he came closer, she sniffed another very unpleasant odor.

"Sorry. Some of the cesspits overflowed. I was helping Henry and young George. They will have their work cut out for them. And there was considerable damage to the docked boats."

"Eat first. I will sit with you."

But he could not hold still, jiggled his feet, tapped his fingers on the table, hummed a tune of some sort, and kept glancing at the door.

"Oh, for God's sake, Ian. Go and be of service. I will get dressed and see how I might be of use."

A short while later, Maggie stepped out to find her world strangely altered. Bits of clear sky appeared amidst wisps of fog, revealing the damage: broken glass from windows, split wood from houses, shingles littered the street. The wind and waves had carried the contents of the ocean on land. Masses of seaweed lay clumped, fish already bloating, dead birds. The tang and stink assaulted her nostrils.

Across the street, part of Ed the butcher's roof had been torn from its holdings. Ed stood on a ladder, cursing.

Ian appeared, shouting, "Here, man. Get down from there."

"He has no business being on a ladder, prone to dizziness as he is," Maggie said. They had not fared too badly on this street. Some of the storefronts closest to the dock were badly damaged.

Captain Jacobs stood in the middle of the street, shaking his head. "Never seen such a thing. Not in sixty years."

Ian helped the chandler place an oilcloth over his window. He was making sport of something, making the chandler smile. When they finished, he patted the man on the back, looked up the street, and spotted Maggie.

"Hello, my beauty!" His voice rang out and garnered smiles and giggles from female onlookers.

He had a way of making things better with his

vigor, as if every problem could be solved.

Martha, the baker's wife, along with her two daughters, had already set up a makeshift table piled with baked goods. The women of the town, young and old, were busy filling the table with comestibles from their own kitchens. Sabine appeared with food and small ale from the Siren Inn, accompanied by young George, Henry's son.

Maggie walked down to the docks. Riggings and sails lay in a tangle in the water. Boats with sails down littered the harbor. *It could've been worse.* Maggie surveyed the good people of the town working together, snatches of song, one about the storm, and the occasional burst of laughter making light work of it.

The worst damage had of course been to the boats in the harbor. Pieces of jagged wood, nets, and casks floated in the water. The robust young lads of the town were swimming and bringing items to shore. It took a strong body indeed to swim in these waters, and withstand the cold.

Jonesy Batters stood at the helm of his boat, holding his arm at the shoulder. Every so often he grimaced with pain.

"Jonesy," she called out. "Go find my husband." She pointed up Market Street. "He'll fix your shoulder."

"Slipped on the deck when I got in." He grinned through his shaggy grey beard. "Had my eye on the torn mast, never seen the likes of it in all the years I been sailing. It came up so sudden-like."

Maggie's own shoulder ached in sympathy.

"You won't be much good for your repair work if you don't see to it."

Ian stood up the street, put his hands around his mouth, and called, "Come on, man! I will fix you up in no time."

"'Tis true." Henry jumped off a boat onto the dock, carrying a mizzen mast in his arms, George picking up the rear. "Just ask his wife, he fixes her up all the time."

Maggie rolled her eyes. Even in times of crisis, men will be bawdy. Come to think of it, women too.

Henry then spotted Maggie. "Begging your pardon, Mistress Maggie."

Just then, Bethan ran toward them, her cap askew, dark hair flying about her shoulders, face red with exertion. Had she run all the way from the cottage?

"Have you seen her?" Bethan gasped.

"Seen who?"

"Elunid! She wandered out this morning, as she does, but never returned. I've looked for her everywhere."

Henry stopped. "Ho, George! Put it down gently, now." He approached Bethan. "I will help you look for her, miss."

"Thank you."

"I'm sorry. I would join you, but we must check on Josef and Lena," Ian said.

Maggie nodded. "Young George has a gift for finding lost things, do you not, lad?"

She patted the boy's head, and he smiled up at her.

Maggie and Ian headed for the Siren Inn to check on Josef and Lena.

"I do hope Henry will be able to find Elunid," Maggie said.

"Poor girl. It is a terrible thing to be so lost."

Chapter Eighteen

Bethan gasped, trying to slow the beating of her heart.

Henry stood in front of her, eyeing her with concern. "Did you run all the way into town, Miss Owen?"

Even though Bethan stood taller than Henry, it in no way robbed her of the reassurance she felt in having his assistance, for he was powerfully built. She put her hand upon the stitch in her side, forcing herself to breathe slowly and evenly.

"Are you certain you can continue?" Henry asked.

"I am fine." She forced herself to stand up straight and tucked her hair back into her cap. "But my sister, she is not. I can feel it."

"Then let us begin." He shaded his eyes with his hand and turned in a slow circle. "Do you have an idea where she might have gone?"

Bethan tried to keep the panic from her voice. Elunid strayed from home, but her pattern was predictable. She'd disappear into the fields and then return in a few hours, usually windblown and dirty, but relatively calm. Never had she wandered so far from home.

"I combed the pastures for nigh on two hours, and the forest outside of town as well."

He stiffened. "I would have you be safe, and it is

169

not safe to be alone out there."

She bristled. "I don't have the luxury of thinking of myself when my sister is missing."

"I understand. If yon George here was missing, I would feel the same."

"I suggest we walk toward the Landgate and skirt the shore there." He eyed her feet. "I see you have sensible shoes."

"Yes." She nodded grimly. "Useful for chasing my sister around."

They began their trek, dodging groups of people cleaning up the streets, Bethan in the middle of the father and son.

"Da," George said. "Are we searching for the woman who looks like this one?" He pointed his head toward Bethan, curly hair flopping in his eyes. "Only she looks sad?"

Good description. "Yes, young George. You are very smart indeed."

"Why does she wander off?"

"George," Henry interrupted. "Mayhap you're asking too personal a question."

They entered an alleyway leading to the Landgate. "No, it's okay." Bethan stepped carefully over tangled netting. "Huh. How could something from a boat end up all the way over here?"

"It was a powerful storm." He held her elbow as they exited the alleyway and headed for the marsh.

"At least it isn't dark out." Bethan broke herself away from his grasp, striding ahead on her long legs. "But if I know her, she has left her cloak somewhere."

They reached the shore and walked along the bank.

George ran ahead, peering at the water. "Do ye

think she went for a swim? The older boys were swimming by the docks."

"No, lad."

Pray God she did not get into the water. Bethan shivered.

George danced around in front of them, eyes alight with excitement, as if they played a game of hide and seek.

"Eyes on me, George." Henry waited until the boy paid heed. "I want you to search the cliff side. Go toward the caves. Look and listen for Mistress Elunid, but do not go into the caves."

The caves were nestled in the side of the cliff, a popular spot for smugglers and thieves to hide their stolen wares. They searched the marsh, calling for her.

"She has no awareness of what she does, where she goes. It is up to me to keep her safe." A shortness of breath plagued her as it always did when she suffered distress. It squeezed her lungs and made her feel as if she breathed through a reed.

Henry put a hand upon her shoulder for one brief moment. "We will find her, Mistress Bethan. Although George cannot recognize his letters, he is like a bloodhound at finding lost things."

The man had a quiet strength about him, a solid, comforting presence, making it easier for her to slow her breathing, as they searched high and low, George peering in the semi-darkness at the base of the cliffs.

The wind blew from the marshes as they walked for what seemed miles. Bethan's throat ached from calling her sister. She paused to wipe the sweat from her forehead, though it had become increasingly cool.

George lingered by the mouth of a cave. At the

same time, Bethan stiffened. Her sister's anguish raged over her like a squall.

"She must be near. I feel her." Elunid's suffering mounted upon her chest. She struggled for air.

Henry grasped her hand. "Mistress, we will find her. Remove all else from your mind, and focus on the sound of your breathing, air in, air out. Yes, easy."

George stood at the entrance to a cave up ahead, waving his arms and shouting. They hastened to reach him, and the cries echoed from within the cave.

"Elunid!"

They reached the mouth of the cave. Henry put his arm out to stop Bethan from going farther.

"We must make sure no one is there with her." He drew his knife and disappeared into the mouth of the cave, turning sharply to the right. "Elunid. Your sister is here. Is there anyone with you?"

"No. Get thee behind me, Satan."

Her keening echoed in the cave, raising the tiny hairs on Bethan's spine. She rushed into the darkness. Just inside, Elunid crouched, one hand in the air making the motions of sewing, the other holding an imaginary piece of cloth. They shook violently.

"Elunid." Bethan kneeled in front of her and gently took her hands.

Elunid flinched and shrunk away from her. "Do not take me. I have tried, *am* trying." Her hoarse voice cut into the darkness. "I must try," she screamed. "You know I am trying, but I cannot find the right color to please you most. Do not make me hurt so. I will do as you ask."

Bethan tried to dodge her flailing arms and winced as her sister's sharp nails raked her face. "Elunid,"

Bethan put her hands upon her sister's face. "It's me, little dove."

She spoke in their special language, the one they'd used as young children. "*Sligh-mannon, Meecheh.*" It always served to calm her, but if it didn't, what would she do?

She sang it over and over, soft as a mother's caress, prayed it would stop the shaking, the screaming, until the light of recognition returned to Elunid's eyes. "Come, little dove. You are so cold. Let's get you home."

Elunid did not cease her screaming but held her hands out to Bethan.

"Stand up, sweeting." Bethan put her hand on the top of Elunid's head to guard it from getting bumped on the way out.

As they emerged into daylight, Elunid's legs suddenly buckled. Bethan struggled to hold her as Henry rushed forward and gathered her up in his arms. She took her cloak off and draped it over Elunid.

"But Miss," George cried. "Now *you* will be cold.'

"George, help me get my cloak off," Henry called.

The boy soon had the cloak free and put it over Bethan's shoulders.

"Thank you, George. You are very kind."

A gust of wind pushed them from behind as they climbed the steep path from the beach. Soon they were walking on the well-worn path toward town. Elunid struggled in Henry's arms, long legs and arms thrashing. A guttural scream tore from deep within her. Garbled curses, vulgar and malevolent, shattered the air.

The abject fear in her sister's eyes pummeled

Bethan like fists. In her mind she cowered, but no, she could not cower. No one else could care for Elunid and her demons. She braced herself against it, straightened her back, and quickened her pace.

"She is frightening when she's in this state. The townspeople will think she's possessed," she shouted over her sister's screaming.

With little effort, Henry reached her side. "Mistress Bethan." His deep voice resonated within her, and her panic stilled. Though her responsibility for Elunid was hers alone, and she did not know this man, his quiet strength reassured her, and for a moment it seemed he shared her burden.

"The town is not without pity. Besides, why anticipate trouble when you have enough of it right now?" He grinned. What manner of man could find humor in such a dire situation? How easily he carried Elunid, despite her struggling.

"I don't know how I'd have gotten her home, the kind of shape she's in," Bethan said. "If not for you, I would have had to leave her to get help. So I thank you."

He nodded. "Those words you uttered. What language was it?"

She brightened. "Since we were babies, Elunid and I have had our own language. We were the only ones who could understand it. We used it for our own amusement, and to keep secrets. Mother put a stop to it soon enough, but both of us remember. It helps to calm Bethan sometimes."

George sidled next to his dad. "Don't worry, miss." He spoke to Elunid. "Sometimes I get frightened too, and my da makes me feel better."

At the sound of the boy's voice, Elunid stilled.

"You're a good lad, George." Henry smiled at his son as they turned down the lane to the cottage.

Adam approached them from the other direction. "My God! I've combed the countryside for you!"

They rushed into the cottage, and with great dispatch Bethan got Elunid into bed and placed warm bricks wrapped in flannel at her feet. Thankfully, she'd ceased her raving and lay still as death under the layers of blankets. The children were uncharacteristically silent. Any fool would know it wasn't good for them, seeing Elunid like this. But what could she do?

One thing at a time. "She needs sustenance, but she needs to rest first. And I must clean her up. She's filthy and will not be able to rest unless she's clean."

"Bethan," Adam called. "She *is* resting. She doesn't care. Leave her be and come have a bit of whiskey to warm you."

She paid her brother-in-law no heed. Elunid hadn't had so severe an episode in a long time. What brought it on? She poured some water into the basin and brought it over to the bedside, taking Elunid's pale arm out. "Look. Filthy."

Polly waddled over. "Bethan, you are exhausted."

She shook her head. "There is much I can't control. But I will not let her lie here filthy."

Polly pushed a glass into her hand. "Rest for a minute. Come over by the fire and sit."

Like her niece and nephews, when her older sister spoke in such a way, Bethan obeyed.

Henry and Adam stood over by the fire. Polly led Bethan to the rocking chair. "Sit."

"You're the one should be sitting."

"Hush."

"I travelled to Scotland last year to see my family." Adam gestured with the glass. "Brought this back with me. It's from the Orkneys. I've been saving it for an occasion like this." He raised his glass. "To our good friend Henry."

Henry brought the glass to his lips. His eyes over the rim of the glass matched the whiskey's amber hue. "You'd have done the same for me." He caught her staring at him and smiled. The whiskey glistened on his full lips. Such full lips. No. She must tend to Elunid.

She took a sip of the whiskey, felt the warm glow hit her stomach, and set it down. She could finish it later, but Elunid should not be lying in filth. Her legs ached as she stood over her sister, and in no time at all finished cleaning her up as best she could. A bath would be better, but not when she was insensible.

When she stepped outside to toss the dirty water, Henry and George joined her. They stood in awkward silence.

"Wait," she said. "I will get your cloak." She ran into the cottage and soon returned. She handed it to him. "I cannot express how grateful I am for your assistance today."

He opened his mouth, closed it.

"Yes?"

"I was wondering if perhaps you might be agreeable to…"

She waited, watched his mouth, found herself closing the distance between them. Stopped. How could she be feeling this magnet pull toward him, a stranger, and a…oh God. A night soil man. He had rescued Elunid, had rescued her as well. But the man handled shite. And even if the thought didn't make her shudder, there was no room in life for her own happiness.

She backed away from him. "Again, I thank you."

He inclined his head. "Anytime I can be of service, Mistress Bethan." His eyes held a knowing look, as if he read her thoughts. "Please take a care for yourself."

"Thank you for your kindness, George."

"Anytime *I* can be of service."

The lad's perfect imitation of his father was so apt, she had to bite her lip not to smile. "It is good to know," she said gravely.

"Come, my boy. Let us go to the Siren Inn and see about dinner. I'm sure Lena and Josef could use a hand."

She stood and watched them walk away, waited until she couldn't see them. What was he going to ask her? A walk, perhaps? Tea? It was implausible, for she had duties to attend to, even if she wanted to, which she didn't. She straightened the skirts of her dress, smoothed her hair, and went inside to see to her sister.

Chapter Nineteen

At dusk, Ian escorted Maggie to the Siren Inn. There was nothing more they could do until the light of day. Most of the town was gathered there, commiserating and grieving the loss of life and property.

Ian sat Maggie down and fetched her some ale.

"Will you not sit here with me and have a bite, Ian?"

His Maggie did not understand the impossibility of sitting still when the inn was so alive with stories of the storm and destruction, their adventures, and their survival. The experience of shared grief had brought the town together like nothing else did, and it did much to comfort him.

Once again, Henry and George kept themselves busy, delivering food and clearing off tables in Josef's stead. Ian had just checked on the innkeeper. The fever seemed to be lessening, and he rested well, but was in no way well enough to work. Ian joined Lena in the kitchen.

She shot him a thankful glance. "My Josef is feeling better, *ya*?"

"Yes, his fever *seems* to have abated. Best not speak too soon."

"*Gott sei Dank.*" She lifted a pot of oyster stew out of the hearth.

"Here, Lena. Let me be of use."

She should not be lifting such heavy things in her condition, particularly when she had lost a child. But she was stubborn, like his Maggie.

He returned to the taproom with the soup to find Pete Stowe had come in with a few friends. Who knew why he returned here when his reception was less than cordial? Perhaps he hoped he would one day get a rise out of Josef and Ian. The former constable had been taking a gulp of ale, and upon seeing Ian, slammed his mug on the table, splashing his tablemate, and earning a cuff on the ears. He scowled and picked it up again.

"Hey, Pierce. Where's our innkeeper? Good of him to be lolling about when his poor wife is slaving away."

Ian stopped. "Where were you today? I didn't see you, working."

Stowe held his bad hand in the air. Yellow matter seeped out of the bloody bandage. "I am unable. I have an injury obtained while in the service of this town."

"Service to the town?" Captain Jacobs yelled. "In service to your own needs, maybe."

The room as a whole laughed, particularly old Harold, who'd had a wooden leg since '29, and tirelessly cleared debris all day. "Would your mum not let you off her teat, lad?"

The room exploded with laughter.

Stowe pushed off the table with both hands, forgetting his injury. The color faded from his face.

Ian rushed to sit him back down and lowered his voice. "Come see me tomorrow and get your hand taken care of."

"The day I see a lunatic for doctoring is the day I'm desperate indeed."

Ian shook his head. "You look desperate enough."
The dolt would lose his hand if he didn't get it attended
to. His mother's ineffective nursing would not do the
trick.

"Ian," Maggie called. "The stew is getting cold."

"Listen to your wife, man! I'm starving," Ed the
butcher said.

"Sorry." He then made a show of passing the stew
around, serving Maggie first, and stopping to kiss her
soundly.

She rewarded him by displaying a lovely pink
blush, which made him think of the flush on her bare
skin when he'd driven her to pleasure and beyond. He
soon returned with hot bread. Despite the din of the
room and the commotion, his beloved had fallen asleep
with her head upon the table.

He roused Maggie. "I will walk you home, love."

She nodded. "It is late. But you need not
accompany me."

"Save your breath, sweeting. The fog is thick and
treacherous." He took her arm.

****

"You act as if I have never walked in the dark or
the fog alone," she muttered. But truth be told, it had
not taken her long to get used to the sensitivity of his
fingers again, as if he knew exactly how hard or soft to
please her most, with the mere touch of his hand, any
hour of the day.

"I will do it just the same," His tone brooked no
argument. "Give me your basket."

She had to admit Ian was right. As she stepped out
the door, she felt encased in cotton.

"Be careful, love." The warmth of his hand through

her cloak made her feel secure, warming her heart as well.

As they set out toward the cottage, she could barely see. He took her arm as they walked downhill and guided her over the uneven and slippery cobbles. The sounds of people going about their nightly rituals echoed in the air. Muffled sounds rose from the shipyard, the pounding of hammers and the clang of a ship's bell accompanied Ian's humming.

Suddenly, something panted and snarled behind her, blew its fetid breath and a reek of blood and death upon her neck. With inhuman strength, the panting creature knocked her to the cobbles, wrenching her away from Ian's hold.

Chapter Twenty

"Maggie!" Ian picked her off the ground and held her in his arms. "Are you hurt?"

Her heart pounded in her throat. She gasped for breath. "No, I just got the wind knocked from me."

In truth, a white hot pain shot through her shoulder, the same one injured by Edward Carter. For a moment her vision grew black around the edges, and she forced herself to breathe deeply. It hurt when she inhaled, but otherwise the pain was manageable. And what was the man doing, carrying her?

"Put me down."

He ignored her. "No, my lady. You are obviously injured."

"Stubborn man."

"When it comes to your welfare, yes. Your face is wet." He wiped it with a handkerchief. "I am sorry, Maggie. I was taken unawares."

"It was not your fault." Why did the man take everything on himself? "What manner of thing was it? I don't know if it was man or beast." She still had trouble catching her breath.

"Just be still, love." He held his hand on her heart. "Your heart is beating like a gong."

"A gong?"

"Never mind."

"You can put me down now," she said as they

entered a narrow close.

"No."

She shuddered.

"What is it?"

"It was heavy, and stank of death." She trembled, chills racing down her back.

"Shhh," he crooned. "It was probably just a stray dog, confused by the fog."

"It did not feel like a dog." It was something else, something more sinister. But what?

A short while later, Ian examined Maggie's shoulder. "Look at the swelling." His labored breathing raised the fine hairs on her back.

"All I need is a good night's sleep. And there's no need to get upset, Ian."

"I know. But I do not like to see you in pain." He had taken off her bodice and untied her shift so it fell over the swell of her breasts. He laid a warm compress on her injured shoulder.

"Ah! It feels wonderful."

"I have some lady's mantle already infusing for the bruises and something to help you sleep."

He put the cup into her hands. "Drink this. I'm sure your shoulder isn't broken or displaced, but I assure you it is going to hurt for a few days."

"Ian, whatever knocked me down did not seem like a dog. What if it *was* a supernatural creature? It would not be the first time we witnessed the supernatural, would it?"

Suddenly the cool mist of the fog surrounded her, acrid fear invaded her senses. She began to shake.

"Maggie." His voice echoed from a long distance. Arms wrapped around her.

"You have suffered a shock and are now only feeling it. It is over, love. You are safe."

A glass against her lips. "Take a sip. Brandy."

Her eyes teared as the brandy licked flames down her throat, making her eyes burn, but her shivering slowed.

He helped her upstairs. "Look at me, Maggie. It is over." He slowly removed her skirt, her stockings, and skimmed his fingers over her body by the light of the candle.

"Do you hurt anywhere else?" His breath rustled like a zephyr on her neck as he removed her shift. He took down her hair and brushed it, the rhythmic, steady strokes calming her.

He carried her to bed and tucked her in. "I will return soon. I must go to Lena's to see how they fare. I won't be late."

She drifted off, for one brief moment wondering why he did not make love with her, when he clearly had a need.

****

Ian made his way to the Siren Inn. His aching cockstand would plague him until the punishment fit the crime. He did not deserve the reward of her passion, for he had not protected her from injury.

He should have been vigilant when walking her home this evening. Instead he had probably been listening to a tune in his head, stacking harmonies like wooden blocks. He had let the beast knock her down; she could have hit her head, broken her neck, and it would have been his fault. So for tonight, he would suffer his cockstand as penance. He turned his burning face into the cold gust of wind from the Channel.

He was alone, his footfalls on stone, the wind whistling through cracks in old cottages, waves against the cliffs. He inhaled the kelp and salt tang, and let the sea wind entice him away to a time when loving one woman was as inconceivable as the face of God.

He had crossed the sea to be free from the prickling of his skin, the buzzing of his blood, the songs pounding like hammers in his head. He could not escape, for every inch of skin sang with the touch of the morning air upon his face, made him cry with joy and pain. No matter how far he'd sailed he could not escape his affliction. The docks on the edge of the earth offered women soft and bountiful, and he had thought mayhap the cascade of pleasure and pumping of his seed would drain the poison from him.

So he became a celebrant of all women, worshipped their bodies and begged for their blessings. He lauded their soft flesh with hand and cock and the hard weight of his body, learned countless ways to pleasure them. Make it last, young Ian. Make it last, for the longer you do, the longer you might stave off the crash of cymbals in your head. But a song soured, the raging waves screamed at him, and he ran aground.

Ian turned from the sea. All he wanted now was the warm embrace of his Maggie, though he did not deserve it.

When he arrived at the inn, it seemed most of the respectable folks had gone to their beds, and those still there were well into their cups, especially Pete Stowe. He slumped at the table, head in his hands. A group of fishermen joined him, jostling him about.

"Take a care. I'm wounded."

They ignored him.

One of them said, "We've had a mild winter, we have. The storm came out of nowhere. I've never seen such a thing before."

"It's yon innkeeper," Stowe said. "He brought evil back into this town with his talk of the undead."

"Hold on." Ian would make sure everyone heard him. "How dare you malign your host, making such accusations?"

He had their attention now, but it did no good. Everyone knew fishermen were the most superstitious beings on earth.

"I heard from Josef's own lips the boy emerged from the dead." One of the fishermen raised his mug to get Sabine's attention.

The good folk of King's Harbour stirred themselves up like sea foam.

From across the room, a man yelled, "Never seen anything like the way the storm came up. Like Satan stirred the sea with his own hands. I survived it, I should know."

The room fell silent. Ian guessed they spent a moment visualizing the devil stirring the ocean, forked tail bristling with evil. Wasn't hard to imagine.

The man's companion said, "One minute it was mild, and we headed home with no more on our minds than the warm, open thighs of our wives. The next minute we held on like Beelzebub himself chased us."

"I did not think I would make it here alive. Lost all me nets, I did. Would have set me up pretty. The trip was cursed, and it's Josef's fault."

Henry joined Ian, his countenance stocky and forbidding. "Go ye home, and sleep off your foolishness."

The weathered fisherman scowled. "See here, we have a right to finish our drink in peace without getting run out of here. We did a good day's work, we did."

"Aye, aye!"

"Henry, there will be no convincing these men tonight," Ian whispered. "They are too drunk, and when superstition gets ahold of men, it taints their blood like poison."

Henry nodded. "I'd best put on some fish. Perhaps more food will settle them down."

Ian breathed deeply, expelling the miasma of fear from his lungs. He must do something, but what? Perhaps if he distracted them. They were brave men, men of the sea. The melody already swam in his veins; he had but to dream up the words.

He cleared his throat. "I have a song for you tonight, gents."

"Aye, let's hear it," they cheered.

Ian began:

"I know some lusty seamen, they drink with me tonight.

They are the bravest of their kind-aye- morning, noon, and night.

Their muscles, they are fearsome, their cocks-well-even more."

Cheers of "hear, hear" filled the room. Ian took a swallow of ale.

"They fight while breakers rock their boat
While horny as a billy goat,
And when they dock,
Beware the cock, ye lasses!
They turn from open seas and they head for open thighs,

Warm and ready, open thighs, white, delightsome is
their prize
To all you heroes, this applies.
Warm and willing, open thighs."

"Aye, aye." A burly seaman stood up, mug raised. "To willing women!"

"Aye, aye!"

"Those warm thighs await you," Ian called.

It was nigh on closing time, thank God. He must return to the cottage to see how Maggie fared. Hopefully, she still slept as he'd left her. The crowd dispersed with haste, one thing on their mind, Ian guessed. Sometimes a few well-placed lines never went amiss, and recalled what was important. The last line elicited a chorus of parting comments:

"It has been too long. She is waiting for me, to be sure."

"Not what I heard."

Laughs all round.

"Shut yer gob, bastard."

"What about me? Are there women to be had in this town?"

"Of course, young dolt."

Finally, the last customer left the building.

"Well played." Henry grinned and slapped him on the back. "How do you come up with those tunes, lad?"

"I haven't the slightest idea." Or the slightest idea how to stop them.

Ian and Henry wasted no time helping Lena and Sabine clean up.

"Lena, I will check on Josef in the morning."

"You are good friends," she said. "Thank you for your help tonight."

Ian closed the door and lifted his face to the heavy fog. Perhaps the fresh air would tamp down the malice and confusion imbedded in his skin like splinters. People could so soon forget the goodness of their fellow kind. His well-placed song served as a distraction, but superstition and fear trailed his town like a beast of prey.

His footsteps echoed as he made his way to the cottage. The rhythm brought to mind a song learned long ago, a steady beat sinking into his skin, pounding through his veins, a rhythm from hell, pounding through the dirt floor, rattling the chains, a pulse of cold setting his joints to aching.

Poor soul down the corridor, clanging his irons together, chanting, more moan than song, moan song, beyond anguish, as if to say, I am still here, I am human-almost. I breathe, I have a soul. He longed to call out his soul. But his mouth would not open, his muscles gripped in rictus. The cold, heavy boots echoed toward him, and he slid into the corner, where the shallow breathing of his companion gave him some small measure of comfort.

Ian stood, the fog swirling around him, and breathed deeply to expel the memories of Bedlam. He let the moisture of the fog bathe his face. When he felt calmer, he headed for the cottage.

But he could not expel the malice of the men in the inn. If he could but climb into the warmth of their marriage bed and nestle into Maggie's warm thighs, and give himself up to sleep. But he would only awaken her with his restlessness and spread his poison to her.

Ian poured a glass of brandy. He would better occupy himself with trying to identify the strange disease Nikolaus died from, and Josef now suffered from, he suspected. But he could only think of Maggie, who glowed like the moon when she rose above him in passion. The words for her song surged within him. "You are the moon rising above me, love me."

The search for Maggie's song began to quiet the noise rioting within him: fear, anger, discordance. If he could but find the words for Maggie's song, mayhap he would never have to leave again. He reviewed Josef's symptoms. The fever had abated, but in its place Josef was confused, agitated, and aggressive. It was like no disease he'd ever seen. He rushed into the parlor and retrieved the other books he had gathered in his travels. They confirmed what he most feared, and with every bit of strength he possessed, he bid himself stay calm.

****

Later, Maggie came downstairs, eyes heavy with sleep. "The Holy Sister spoke to me in a dream. She said I must save the baby. Julian of Norwich is so strong within me, especially since I've been with child."

"You are the instrument with which she performs her miracles."

He poured her a cup of tea, and handed it to her, wrapped his long fingers around hers to steady her grip.

"Why me?"

"Because of the love and dedication you have for your women, and your self-sacrifice. Because you are the finest woman I have ever met."

Her eyes, welling with tears, looked like a tide pool at dawn. It seemed their babe made her more emotional. He quite liked it, this softer side to his Maggie Moon.

"It must be young Becky Myer's baby, the one

having trouble suckling. He's the only newborn."

"You want to leave now."

"Yes, she tells me to make haste, to save the baby."

He fetched their cloaks.

"I will not even bother trying to convince you to stay here, though I've walked in fog my whole life without mishap, until…"

"Until last night, and I was standing right beside you." He gently palpated her shoulder. "How does it feel?"

"It is fine. At any rate, I've no time to worry about it."

He wrapped her cloak around her and handed her a roll with cheese. "You urge your mothers to eat, and so must you."

"Thank you." She reached up to kiss him, a palm on his jaw. He closed his eyes to better enjoy the feel of her soft hand upon the rough texture of his stubble.

She removed her hand. "We must go."

"Let's away then, sweeting."

Upon arriving at young Becky's home, Maggie was surprised and relieved to find her propped up in bed, nursing with success.

On the way home, Ian took her arm. "You are holding your shoulder at an odd angle. It is hurting you."

"Don't fuss over me, husband."

"We will put a compress on it when we get home."

"I don't have time to sit about with compresses on my shoulder."

"You will make time, Maggie mine. I will not have you suffer pain."

Maggie sighed. There was no sense arguing with

him. "Ian, if not Becky's child, who is in distress?"

No sooner had they returned to the cottage than Lena burst through the door, red-faced and panting.

"Ian, Maggie! You must help me."

"Lena, what are you doing here? What's amiss?"

She held her belly with both hands, her face tear-streaked and red. "Josef is gone."

Chapter Twenty-One

Maggie hurried to Lena's side. "Lena, you walked over in this fog, alone? You know there is still much wreckage in the streets. And there are people who have lost much and are bitter about it."

"I didn't think. I came to you because you are his friend."

Maggie helped her over to the divan.

"He left before dawn." Lena's chest rose and fell rapidly, one hand embracing her belly.

"Lena, where is your cloak, dear?" Ian placed a quilt over her shoulders.

"You mustn't worry. Perhaps Josef had an errand to run and did not want to wake you?" As soon as the words emerged from her mouth, Maggie knew how foolish they sounded. "I will get you some tea."

"No." She made to rise. "There is no time. We must find him. He has been gone for hours, and where did he go? He was not himself."

"Lena, did he hurt you?"

"No." Her lips quivered. "But he frightened me. He was so angry. He tore the bedcovers with his bare hands. What have I done to anger him so?"

Ian sat down beside her on the divan. He looked so pale. What ailed him? Surely Josef would return soon.

He grasped her hands. "Lena, you did nothing to anger him. He is sick."

A fine sheen covered Lena's pale forehead. "There is something else."

Maggie handed her a cup of tea. "Here it is, nice and sweet the way you like it. Just rest for a moment, Lena."

Lena's hands shook so badly she could not hold her cup. Maggie held it to her lips. Lena pushed the cup away. "No, I must tell you. I know not what it means, but Josef had..." She blushed. "What do you English call it, a cockstand?"

Maggie and Ian exchanged glances. Not an uncommon thing.

"It hurt him. He held it and it pained him so, and he looked at me as if he wanted me, but would not let me touch him."

"We will find Josef." Ian clasped Lena's hands in his. "More than likely he was just feeling ill and did not want to wake you."

Suddenly, Lena paled and clutched her stomach.

"Are you having pains, Lena?"

"Yes," she grunted. "My womb is pressing on me."

"Have your waters ruptured?"

"I don't know. I've had a trickling, but I thought I pissed myself."

She was more than likely in labor. Ideally, she would deliver at home. But it was too late. At any rate, Samuel's horse was well known for his fright of fog, and who knew how Ian's old nag faired in this weather? Better they should make her comfortable here, and send word to Sabine her mistress was in labor.

It seemed Ian had read her mind, for he walked outside the door, and whistled for an errand boy.

Maggie joined him. The lad was so encased in fog

she could barely see him.

"Care to earn some coin, Johnny?" Ian reached into his pocket and gave him a shilling and an orange.

The boy's eyes grew. "For certain, sir."

After Ian's instructions, he raced off. They heard the pattering echo of his footsteps through the fog.

"Let's get you comfortable on the divan, Lena." There was no argument from Lena, for she was too busy casting up her accounts. Maggie had never seen a delivering mother with morning sickness, not in her training or the eight years she'd been a midwife. Lena's humors were surely unbalanced, and she was already weak.

"My poor friend," Maggie murmured. "It will be all right."

But inwardly she wondered if the baby had been harmed by Lena's overexertion. Every good midwife knew witnessing frightening events could affect the baby. She shook her head; she would not let Lena have another stillborn.

Ian rushed behind the counter and returned with a cup. "Here, Lena, this is a tonic and should help you feel better."

"It doesn't matter about me. We must get Josef. Bring him home safe."

"I will fetch Samuel, and we will go together and look for him," Ian said.

Just then, Mrs. Stowe came in, her face rigid, lips pressed with distain.

"Mrs. Stowe, how can I help you today?" Ian smiled, ever civil, but the woman eyed him with the utmost disgust. There was a bump on the outside door, and Maggie saw Pete's profile as he leant against the window. He had the grey pallor of someone in dire pain.

"Why do you not have your son come in? My husband is skilled in treating wounds."

"He will not touch my boy."

"He looks very ill," Maggie said. Would the woman rather see her son suffer than have a competent doctor treat him?

"I can take care of my son."

Maggie struggled to school her face against revulsion, for the memory of the underground dungeon and the screams of a tortured man rose in her gorge.

Maggie handed Lena a warm cloth to wash her face.

"I need some willow bark." Mary Stowe anxiously glanced out the window.

"Mrs. Stowe." Ian folded his arms on the counter. "The willow bark may relieve his pain somewhat, but it will not treat the pustulence invading his hand. It will spread, and likely has already."

"You know nothing." She snatched the packet of medicine out of his hand and threw the coin on the table with a look of such malice Ian stepped back.

She stalked to the doorway of the parlor and scowled at Lena. "Your husband has been seen all over town this morning, indecent, moaning and shouting epitaphs at anyone who will listen."

Lena eyed her between strands of hair, leaned over, and vomited again.

Mrs. Stowe grimaced and made haste out the door.

Ian tapped a staccato rhythm on the counter. "Pay her no mind, Lena. She is only happy when causing others unhappiness. She has never forgiven Josef for winning her husband's love and respect, or her son for not possessing Josef's work ethic."

He began humming one of Lena's favorite songs.

Lena smiled weakly. "*Gott im Himmel,* you have butchered the tune."

Her vomiting abated momentarily, and Maggie urged her to take some broth. "Try, one spoonful at a time, slowly." She tucked a quilt around her. Mayhap she could rest a bit. After Maggie built up the fire, she was gratified Lena's eyes had closed.

The door opened again and Samuel, Sarah, and Ruthie filed in.

Samuel wiped his face with a handkerchief, which came away black with soot from the forge. "Pierce." He smiled at Ian. "So you've returned from your travels, eh? Why is it when you're gone, all is tranquil, and when you return, chaos returns?"

Ian grinned and shrugged.

Sarah shook her head at her husband. "We are not here to harass Ian."

"My dear sister-in-law. Are you feeling quite the thing?" Ian asked.

"Nothing a good night's sleep won't heal," Sarah said, smiling. "Thank you for your concern, Ian. It's why we're here. Do you have a sleeping draught safe enough for little Grace to take?"

"The imp does not sleep more than two hours a night," Samuel rumbled.

"How interesting," Ian said. "Nor do I. Can't say I know right off-hand, but I will think on it and find something harmless for her."

"We have heard the most foul rumors about Josef today," Sarah said.

Maggie held her finger to her lips and pointed to the parlor. "Lena's here. I am fairly certain her travails have begun, though her pains are far apart yet."

Sarah's brows rose. "It is early, but not dangerously so, depending on the size of the babe."

"Yes." Maggie gathered supplies for the hours to come. "I had hoped her sickness would abate, and I could get some food into her to strengthen her."

Sarah nodded.

While Ian treated Ruthie to a handful of sweetmeats, Sarah went over to the divan.

"Lena is sleeping."

"Good. This is the best thing for her." Maggie put a pillow under her feet.

"Where's little Grace?"

"Ah, we dropped her off at Joannie's for a time. She enjoys playing with the children, particularly the twins, who are but a year older than she. You know Joannie, the more children around her, the happier she is."

Last year, Joannie had served as wet-nurse for little Grace when Sarah was unable to care for her.

Sarah nodded, her blue eyes turned inward, staring into the fire for a moment, as if she were alone. This happened sometimes with her sister. She would always be a bit altered, for after all, she'd been buried alive. Maggie shuddered.

Then Sarah started and sat by the fireplace in the rocking chair. "Ruthie, come sit here with me. It is not often we have time to spend together without your little sister distracting us."

Ruthie beamed and skipped over to her mother.

Ian slapped his forehead, eliciting a cascade of

giggles from Ruthie.

"Look what I brought back for you, Ruthie!" He handed her a book of fairy tales and bowed. "For you, madame. As always, I am utterly at your service."

Ruthie's delight did much to cheer Maggie. The little girl was truly becoming a beauty with her pale skin, a hint of apricots in her cheeks, light blue eyes, and glossy, dark curls. She settled in her mother's lap with gusto.

Ian returned to the parlor, carrying a pail of water. "You will need this, I expect."

"I am glad you are here today, sister." Maggie hugged her.

Indeed she was, for anything could happen with a birthing, and if anything happened to Lena, she would never forgive herself.

Ian kissed the top of Maggie's head. His hands trembled. "Samuel and I will do our utmost to find Josef."

Just then, Lena stirred and bowed in pain.

Maggie approached her, doing her best to exhibit a calm and comforting demeanor, though she did not feel so.

"Come, Ruthie." Sarah led Ruthie by the hand out to the shoppe. "You can tend the shoppe until Uncle Ian returns. There will not be many customers in this kind of weather, and you may call for me if need be. Read your fairy tales."

Maggie couldn't help but smile at the ecstatic look on Ruthie's face. "Yes, Mother."

Sarah quickly made a pallet on the floor and ran upstairs to gather the spare pillows and bedding from Maggie's bed.

Maggie knelt by Lena and took her hand. "You will be holding your babe in your arms soon, Lena."

"It is too soon."

"Not necessarily. Last I checked you, everything seemed fine. So, we will not worry." She helped Lena sit up and handed her a cup of white wine boiled with mugwort. "Just a sip. It will fortify you for the trials ahead."

Lena's skin was sallow, and the cup teetered in her hand. Maggie put her hand around her friend's, and helped her hold it steady. "Take a drink, sweeting."

Before long another pain folded Lena into herself. The pain seemed severe for being so early in labor, but there was only one way to tell. She must not let the friendship she had with Lena cloud her judgment. But seeing her friend already suffering, with the added weight of not knowing the whereabouts of her husband, was enough to weaken the strongest woman.

She must be professional. "Lena, let's get you settled in front of the fire, and I will examine you to see how far along you are."

Lena nodded, her face pinched, eyes fixed on Maggie's.

Maggie and Sarah soon had their friend settled in front of the fire. Maggie anointed her hand with almond oil and inserted two fingers within Lena's privy passage to gauge her readiness to deliver. "Lena, you are already more than halfway ready. With every pain, your passage widens and makes way for your child."

Sarah held a cup to Lena's lips. Lena gagged and turned her head away.

Maggie and Sarah exchanged glances.

"Sarah. Fetch an egg, beat it, and mix it with two

drams of almond oil. We will need to pour it into her privy passage when she is ready to push."

"She has already broken her waters, then?"

"Yes, it must have happened hours ago."

A few hours passed, and the intensity and strength of the labor pains increased. When the pains abated momentarily, Lena sank back onto the pillow and all but fainted.

Maggie hurriedly checked her progress. "It is almost time for you to push. A few more pains, and you will be ready."

Sarah wiped the sweat from Lena's pale forehead. She held Lena's hand. "You will meet your babe today. Remember, this will soon be over."

Sarah propped Lena's hips up." Lena, we must give you something to replace the waters you have already lost, to ease the way for the babe."

Lena opened one eye. "Will it take the pain away?"

Maggie snorted. "If only." She slowly poured the mixture into Lena's privy passage, and as soon as she finished, Lena had another contraction. "Where is my Josef?" Lena's hoarse faint voice echoed in the silent room. "I want Josef."

"Samuel and Ian will find Josef. Your job is to deliver this babe." How could they find anyone in the thick fog? And where would Josef have gone?

Another pain assaulted Lena, and Maggie's womb tightened in sympathy. Lena had reached the stage in labor where the delivering mother became the pain consuming her, the baby's head engaged in a passage so small it seemed impassible.

"I need to push."

"Pant like a dog, Lena. You mustn't push just yet.

Good girl. You are very brave."

After the contraction, Lena grew so still, Maggie thought she'd fainted.

"Lena."

She opened her eyes to a slit. Maggie breathed a sigh of relief. "Take a bit of wine."

Lena turned her head and vomited, then moaned as another pain began.

"I see the head, a fine mass of hair," Maggie said.

Lena grunted.

"With the next contraction, you can push."

Sarah kneeled behind Lena and helped her lean forward with the next contraction.

Lena moaned.

"Take a deep breath, and push. Push from deep within yourself."

Lena gasped a deep breath in and bore down.

"Good, good." The head had emerged, but with the end of the contraction, receded.

"Soon you will have your child in your arms, dear Lena," Sarah soothed. "Close your eyes now, and rest." She wiped her face with a cool cloth.

A contraction upon her again, Lena held her breath and pushed, and the babe's head emerged. But the babe was a deep, dusky blue. Maggie put her finger in its mouth and pulled out phlegm, in hopes of clearing the airway.

"Oh God, take it from me, take it!" Lena screamed, as the babe's shoulders began to emerge.

Maggie could do nothing for the baby until it emerged completely. Fear stiffened her fingers as she waited for Lena's next pain. She prayed from deep within herself. *Please help me. Help me save the child.*

"It is almost over," Maggie said. "The babe has a nice head of dark hair, like Josef."

She would not tell Lena the babe was blue, the same color as the stillborn she'd delivered before. She prayed with every fiber of her body as she cradled the babe's head with one hand, and the other splayed at the privy passage opening.

"Push, Lena." Sarah had met Maggie's panicked gaze.

With a huge, ragged breath and the fierce cry of a warrior, Lena bore down.

Maggie braced the slick little head and turned the shoulders to ease their passage. She raced to catch the slippery body as it slid out.

Maggie turned the babe on its side and cleared a plug of mucus out of his mouth with her index finger.

"It's not crying," Lena whispered.

Maggie pushed her fear away and rubbed the babe, none too gently, with the blanket. She held the babe downward, tapped it between the shoulder blades. *Please, my lady. Help me.* Still, the babe lay cold, lifeless. No. This could not happen to Lena. Not again.

She felt a surge of power flow through her, covered her mouth over the babe's mouth and nose, and breathed. No. She waited. Breathed again and yet again.

The babe gasped. His chest rose, and he took a breath, and soon the blue turned to red. He opened his eyes and cried lustily.

Thank you, Holy Sister.

She quickly wiped the blood and white matter off Lena's babe, loosely wrapped him in a blanket, and handed him to Lena. "It's a boy, dear Lena."

"My sweet boy," Lena crooned hoarsely. She

opened the blanket and ran her hands over his little body, felt his toes, and fingers. "You are perfect."

Dear Lena was right. Though small, he was strong, judging by the volume of his cry.

"I must have him back for a short time, Lena. I promise it won't be long."

She cut the cord, cleaned him more thoroughly, and swaddled him in a warm blanket.

Sarah helped Lena put the child to her breast, and she soon had him suckling. Her face glowed with pride. "My sweet boy." She winced as he clamped his jaw down upon her tender nipple.

"Lena, I must deliver the afterburden. You will feel some cramping."

But her friend only had eyes for her babe and did not take notice.

Sarah fetched some warm water and pushed Maggie out of the way. "Let me clean her up. Catch your breath. And well done, sister." Her eyes searched Maggie's face.

Maggie glanced at Lena. "I was afraid she would lose the babe," she whispered.

Sarah smoothed the hair from her sister's face. "But she did not, for you revived it."

Sarah efficiently cleaned Lena and pulled the covers around her.

"I had help from the Holy Sister. She warned me, and now I understand."

Ruthie popped her head into the doorway. "Is the babe born? Not a long birth, was it?"

Sarah laughed. "You know too much, child. Would you like to see him?"

"Oh yes!"

"Maggie, you look done in. Sit down and put your feet up, for you must think of your own babe."

Maggie obeyed and plopped down in the divan with a contented sigh, and enjoyed watching Lena nurse her new babe.

"My Josef must meet his son. He will be so proud."

Maggie schooled her expression. Where had he gone? And what of his odd, combative behavior?

Sarah held her arms out for the baby. "Lena, we must get some food into you." She smiled. "I notice you are not vomiting."

Lena grinned. "I am hungry, *ja*." She kissed the babe on the forehead and handed him to Sarah, who put him in a wooden crate lined with a soft quilt. He had pinked up nicely and had a dribble of milk on one side of his slack little mouth.

"We will feed you some chicken broth with an egg beaten into it to see how you do."

Ruthie handed Lena the bowl. Sarah sat in the rocking chair with the babe and began to feed him a caudle made of sugar, milk, and gruel, using a pap boat, which had a linen-covered opening through which the child sucked. He scowled, a look so like Josef's.

"Come on, wee boy," Sarah crooned. "It is good for you. Then I will bathe you and swaddle you, and you can go back to your mother."

"He is his father's son." Maggie laughed, then winced, for her shoulder throbbed and burned like hot coals. Suddenly even the teacup seemed too heavy.

Ian arrived shortly after Sarah had placed the babe back in Lena's arms. His eyes widened at the sight of Lena in her makeshift bed. "What's this?" His sincere look of shock made Maggie laugh again, and she involuntarily clutched her shoulder.

"What's the matter, Maggie?"

"My shoulder. From the fall."

He knitted his brows. "I will tend to it tonight." He kissed her and approached Lena, kneeled beside her. "Well done, Lena!"

She parted the blanket to properly display her prize, her round cheeks glowing with pride.

"He is beautiful."

Just then, the babe screwed up his face and cried.

"Oh ho, I did not mean to offend, your highness." He placed a kiss on the top of Lena's head. "He will rule the roost, will he not, good Lena?"

Lena chuckled. "*Ja*, I expect so." A shadow fell over her face. "Where is my Josef?"

Ian's face fell. "I'm sorry, Lena. We have not found him yet." He met Maggie's worried gaze. Self-reproach darkened his eyes.

Lena sat up. "I must go home. Josef will go there first when he returns."

Maggie hesitated. "I would rather you not travel just yet, Lena. You had a fairly easy birth, but it is better if you rest."

Lena gave her the gimlet eye. "You should have your baby and then tell me if it was *easy*." She put the babe to her breast again with the ease of an experienced mother. Some midwives were against women nursing before their milk came in. But Maggie could not see the harm in letting the babe suckle for the next two days, and it helped cement the bond between mother and child. It seemed the early nursing made the womb contract, which helped the mother better recover from the birth.

Lena would rest better in her own bed. "Lena, I'm going to examine you and make sure you are not bleeding excessively. Then we will see, though I'd prefer you to spend the night."

Ian stood. "I can take her in the wagon. It is good I acquired it, is it not?"

Though his face was haggard and pale, his eyes glowed like embers. "You must now admit it was a sage purchase."

"No." She set her jaw.

He came to her and whispered in her ear, his breath tickling the fine hairs on her neck. "There is no shame in admitting when you're wrong, Maggie mine. I will not fault you for it." He brushed his lips down her neck.

She pushed him away. "Annoying man. Let me see how she fares."

"I'll go ready the wagon," Ian said.

Maggie did a quick check of Lena's privities. "You seem fine. Do you think you're strong enough?"

"*Ja*, of course I am strong enough, for my Josef." Lena sat up. "He may have need of me when he returns."

Dread filled Maggie as she took the baby, swaddled him, and laid him in the wooden crate. She helped Lena up, sat her in the divan, and wrapped her warmest cloak around her. "Are you feeling light-headed at all?"

Her friend shook her head. "No, but I am ravenous. I hope Sabine has made some chowder."

"You must go straight to bed when you get home."

"I will. Sabine can take care of the customers."

They soon set off for the short ride to the inn. Maggie sat with Lena in the back, holding the babe, whose muffled cries from the depths of the blanket sounded indignant.

"Wee lad's got a temper."

Lena rested her head against the side of the wagon. "He will have to learn to control it as I did."

Ian drove slowly to avoid jarring Lena and the babe, no doubt. It gave Maggie more time to look at the opulent red velvet interior. She shook her head. Like she'd said before, they could have borrowed a wagon.

Before long, Ian and Maggie had Lena settled in bed. Sabine immediately fetched her a steaming bowl of chowder and a thick slice of buttered bread.

Maggie and Ian set off for home at dusk, Ian's arm encircling her. Maggie flinched.

"I must tend to your shoulder immediately."

She nodded. "What manner of thing knocked me down last night?"

Chapter Twenty-Two

As soon as they arrived home, Ian built up the fire and poured Maggie a measure of brandy. He had taken off her bodice, and untied her shift so it fell over the swell of her breasts.

"Shite blossoms! The swelling."

She jumped. "What ails you?"

"This needed to be tended to straight away." His labored breath raised the fine hairs on her back.

"Well, getting angry does not help."

He leaned over and laid his cheek against hers. "I'm sorry. I am angry at myself for letting it happen."

"Ian, it is not your fault, nor is it your fault Josef is missing."

The fire hissed in the silent room.

Ian said, "In our youth, he looked after me, no matter my condition. And I can do naught for him now. Samuel and I could see nothing in the fog. Where could he have gone?"

Ian lifted the compress off.

"Oh God," she gasped.

"I'm sorry. Am I hurting you?"

"Yes. No. Put it back on."

He popped his head around with an exaggerated look of confusion. She laughed, which made her shoulder throb.

"I mean, it hurts, but it feels good."

"Yes," he rumbled. "Like a love bite."

"Um, yes, I suppose."

He anointed his hands with almond oil and placed them on top of her head. He spread his fingers and began to massage her, slowly working his way down to her neck. "You need rest, or this shoulder will not heal."

"But what if I'm needed?"

"Should any woman need delivering, your sister will have to do it. Or I will."

She laughed. As he ministered to her, she stared at the fire, and her vision blurred. Where was Josef? Lena needed him. His son needed him. She closed her eyes and gave herself up to his skilled fingers, let them carry her, drifting, to a place with no pain.

"I will put you to bed."

He helped her upstairs. "Look at me, Maggie. The day is over. You have paid a price for it, and I am sorry." He removed her clothing and helped her into bed.

"Is there anything else I can do for you?"

"I don't know." She cried in great spasms, holding her shoulder as pain and bone deep exhaustion wracked her inside and out.

He held her and let her cry. The light touch of his fingers and roughness of the calluses awakened her skin. He kissed her.

"Love me, Ian."

"But you're in pain."

"I want to go to sleep with the feel of you inside me."

He caressed the insides of her thighs in long slow strokes. "Tell me if I'm hurting you."

"Only when you stop."

His wicked laugh sent a liquid rush to her center. He kissed her breasts, laid his head gently on her rounded belly.

"You are dressed."

"Yes."

"Take off your clothes."

"No, I think not."

He held her breast with one hand, covered her privities with his other palm. Her breath quickened at the rough feel of his shirtfront against her belly. One long finger circled her pleasure bud, slow and torturous, one finger plunging into her warm wet center. She arched against him, spasms of pleasure coursing through her.

"Oh, Maggie," he whispered. "I do love to see you glow when I have brought you joy."

She cleared her throat. "But what about you?"

"Tonight is for your enjoyment. It is enough for me to make you moan."

He helped her on with her night rail and tucked her in. "I will go see how Lena fares and make myself useful at the inn. I won't be long."

She struggled to keep her eyes open. "Thank you…for your service."

He laughed. "You are welcome."

He kissed the top of her nose and tucked the covers up around her neck.

She drifted off, with one last lingering thought: why did he not seek his own release? Had he lost his desire for her?

****

Ian grinned with satisfaction, for he had left his

wife limp and warm with pleasure, and drifting off to sleep, free of pain.

He had done all he could for Maggie. Rest would mend her body, but he could do nothing for Josef. Dread rose in his gorge, as the symptoms revealed what he had suspected. It was a disease as old as time itself, and there was no cure for Josef's illness.

There had been no cases of hydrophobia in this region for years, but it mattered not. He remembered the nasty bruise and bite Josef had on his side when he helped him clean up for Lena. From Josef's description, his nephew had exhibited the same symptoms, the fever, the animal-like behavior, the madness. Had Josef's nephew bitten him? He must have.

Every fiber of his being railed against the realization: Josef was dying of hydrophobia. He could no longer deny it. He must find Josef and tell him he was dying, for there was no cure. He fought the bone deep trembling with deep breaths; he must tell Josef, for otherwise he would not go with him to a place of safety. He and Henry could secure him out of town, tie him up. They would have to watch him die.

Gentle Josef would not want to harm anyone, least of all Lena. He must protect the townspeople from Josef. He must remain calm, pretend nothing was amiss, and above all, keep his affliction at bay. He could not find his friend in the dark, so he might as well help Lena.

He arrived at the Siren Inn, where an impressive crowd gathered despite the late hour. He could barely edge his way to the bar, where Sabine stood with a row of mugs in front of her.

"Sabine, my dear! How are Lena and the babe?"

She set the mugs of ale and bowls on a tray. "She and baby sleep." She grinned, displaying a set of dimples on each side of her mouth. "She eat much food."

"Any sign of Josef?"

"No." Her large almond eyes welled with tears.

"Wench. Where is our food?" A sailor yelled from a table in the corner. "And if you've anything else to offer, I'm happy to oblige you." He looked to his comrades for approval. They guffawed and pulled him back down to sit.

Sabine blew a strand of hair out of her face and shot the sailors a flinty-eyed look.

Ian put his hand over hers. "Do not worry, Sabine. I will find Josef. And after I see Lena, I'll help you with your customers."

"Thank you." She handed him a mug brimming with ale and wiped her hands on her apron. She paused to smile at old Widow Jenkins, who handed her an empty bowl.

"*Xie 'xie*."

"If ye say so." She eyed Sabine with distrust.

"Oh. More stew?" She smiled.

The old woman nodded again, jowls shaking. The dear old crone could sure stow the food away. Ian bowed and took her bowl. "I will carry it for you." He placed his hand upon her gnarled one. "Tell me, dear lady, what is the secret to your timeless beauty?"

She giggled and smacked his hand. "The secret be not taking bullshit from knaves like you. Go away." The cock of her head and her smile belied her words.

He laughed, for he could no longer ignore the rush of white heat like flames licking through his veins. To amuse someone was another way to stave off the signs of his affliction, for 'twas better to be the butt of a joke than lose control. He helped her onto the stool. "You are still quite nimble, miss." He wagged his eyebrows.

"Go on with you." She hit him with her spoon.

Sabine headed over to the sailors, her tray heavy-laden. For such a slip of a girl, she was strong.

He headed for the private quarters and knocked on Lena's door. Upon her answer, he quietly walked in and stood beside the bed. "How are you feeling?"

She glanced up from the babe, eyes alight. "Did you find my Josef?"

"No, Lena. Not yet." Should he tell her the nature of Josef's terrible illness? No. Mayhap she would never have to know what a horrible death he would suffer.

"My poor Josef. Oh God." Her face crumpled. "What am I to do? Where could he be?"

"I'm sorry, Lena. I don't know." Perhaps he'd been spotted by one of the townspeople? He would ask around. "I will search for him tonight. I have in mind a place I did not check this morning."

She sobbed, a shaking hand shielding the babe from the rain of tears. She shook her head. "God knows what is happening to him."

"Lena, I will do my utmost to find him. But now you must think of your child—Josef's child." There was a cup of tea on the bedside table. He reached into his jacket and pulled out a packet of herbs. "I have some herbs to ease the discomfort newly delivered mothers suffer."

She thanked him.

He wiped her tears with a clean handkerchief. "You will do Josef no good by neglecting yourself."

She sipped the liquid. "Thank you, good friend."

"I will stay and help Sabine through the worst of the crowd, and then go search for Josef again."

"Thank you."

Mayhap Lena would never know the agony her husband would suffer.

He vowed to find Josef. What kind of a man was he if he could not protect the people he loved?

****

Several mugs of ale and plates of fried fish later, Ian's old performing troupe entered singing. They were the last people he wanted to see tonight. He would not be pulled into their old association, traveling around the country, singing for their supper, dining with kings one day, cutthroats the next. He did not want the memories of self-indulgence, momentary pleasures of the latest conquest, the rush of pleasure a temporary remedy for his affliction.

The crowd grew silent and parted for the Wayfaring Wastrels. They stared with open-mouthed curiosity at Charlotte, who preened in response.

Reginald hailed for a drink. "So, there you are, Ian. What, you resorting to manual labor?"

"Just helping out a friend tonight." He lifted a barrel of pickles onto the bar and felt Charlotte's eyes burn a hole through his shirt.

"You seem to have grown into a man since last I saw you, my pet. Although there was nothing wrong with you at all back then. No indeed." Suddenly she stood right in front of him, her breasts jutting against his chest. He stepped backward.

"Ooh," Sabine squeaked.

He had trodden on her toes. "I'm so sorry, Sabine,

my dear." She had her baby on one slim hip and a mug of beer for Reginald.

Reginald eyed her up and down. A smile ripe with calculation lit his face.

She backed up. She'd no doubt seen the look before as a former prostitute. "I put baby down." She escaped into the living quarters of the house.

Ian grabbed Reginald by his necktie. "Do not even consider approaching the girl. She is off limits."

Reginald backed up. "Ho! No cause for alarm, my friend. A man can look, can't he?"

"No," Ian said.

Vicar Andrews was in the throes of a coughing fit. Perhaps he'd overheard the conversation. His guileless hazel eyes followed Sabine until she disappeared. Poor hopeless lad.

During his reverie, Charlotte had taken advantage of his distracted state to adhere to him like a lemming. She ran her hand down his upper arm. "Yes, you have changed, Ian."

He took her hand from his arm and stepped away. "Charlotte, I have changed in many ways. Most significantly, I am married and deeply besotted with my wife. The past is over."

She pouted. "A lady can try."

He bowed. "Well, madame, I'm not sure 'lady' is the word I'd use to best describe you." Thankfully, Reginald popped his head on her shoulder, and she swatted him with her fan.

"Besides," Ian said. "You have Reggie at your beck and call."

"He's so very boring after all these years. Are you sure I cannot tempt you? You're a staid, provincial boy now?"

"Most definitely," he said.

She leaned over the counter, affording him a view of her perfect, round breasts. He backed away and shook his head. "No, Charlotte."

"I can't see your great love lasting." Reginald surveyed the room.

"You can be as cynical as you like, Reggie. But some day you will fall in love and forsake all others."

"I am already in love." Reggie grabbed Charlotte's tiny hand and kissed it. "But she is a most fickle creature."

Ian rolled his eyes. "Quite busy here. And I imagine you will be departing soon for greener pastures."

Reginald eyed Sabine, who had bent over to retrieve a fallen plate. "No, I believe we will bide here a while. King's Harbour, despite being provincial, is a congenial place."

Charlotte's open-mouthed stare was quite unattractive. "You want to stay *here*?"

He shrugged. "If you won't have me, I must look elsewhere. You may go on your merry way, if you wish."

"You would break up the Wandering Wastrels?"

His dark eyes flashed like a pirate's sword. "I would do anything for true love."

Her high-pitched giggle made Ian's head ache. "You would never leave me."

"Don't be too sure, Charlotte. I'm going to stay in this congenial town awhile."

She slapped Reggie on the arm and turned to Ian. "At least sing with us. I have missed your golden

217

tongue, Ian." She winked and turned with a swish.

They sallied forth to find a table, thank Zeus.

He filled three mugs and carried them over to Ed the butcher and his two friends.

Ed tipped his head in the direction of Reginald and company. "Some friends of yours?"

"They used to be, in another lifetime," Ian said.

"Yon strumpet seems to be quite fond of you."

"Charlotte is fond of most men, actually. But I assure you, I am not fond of her."

Ed nodded. "Do you have any oyster stew?"

"I'll check the kitchen." With great relief to have the conversation at an end, he made a hasty retreat.

By the time he deposited the stew and bread at Ed's table, the visiting performers had begun singing. He couldn't help mouthing the words silently. Ah, it'd been ages since he'd sung it. "Ever the Doting Suitor" was the kind of melody that made even the nonmusical whistle it for days after.

"Come, Ian. Join us, for just one song!"

What could one song hurt?

"Ever the doting suitor, ever the faithful man…"

The crowd clapped their hands and beat them upon the table, singing the chorus. Charlotte moved to link her arms with him, and in self-defense, he grabbed the nimble Widow Jenkins sitting nearby, making her squeal as he wheeled her around. He knew Charlotte; she had more wiles than Cleopatra.

Ah, but it felt good to sing in harmony again! To sing one song, when all the songs in his head fought for dominance. It calmed him—for the moment, at least.

"More, more!" The crowd groaned as Ian broke apart from the group.

"I am sorry," he said. "But I have a warm and willing wife waiting for me at home, and she gets fractious if I deny her."

They roared and clapped him out the door. He stepped out into the night air and slowly turned, first toward the ocean. The white caps shone with the moon's light, beckoning him like sea maidens. It had only taken one song, but the memory of those dissolute times sank into his skin. No. He would not go there again.

With intense concentration, he practiced his breathing ritual. Where would he go if he was Josef, frightened, sick, and needing to feel safe? Where had they gone as children, when Josef hid to recover from Mrs. Stowe's beatings?

The stars glowed stark against the black sky, reminding him of the desert, the fragrant, willing women, limbs, mouths, endless pleasures. No. He must concentrate on the task at hand. For Josef and Lena, for Maggie.

Think, man! As a child, Josef had learned how to blend into a setting; it explained his quiet, taciturn nature. But he had been a changed man since he married Lena. A good woman could transform a man.

He headed up Siren Street toward the Landgate. He desperately wanted Maggie's warm bed, to slide in beside her and sink into her warmth and protection, but he would go to her bed more worthy if he could find Lena's husband.

When they were children, they used to escape to an old abandoned cottage in the forest. Perhaps he hid there. But Josef was nowhere to be found. God only knew what kind of shape he was in now. Ian pricked his ears up at the sound of a dog howling, and the hair on the back of his neck rose.

He would check the cave on the cliffs and make his way home by the water's edge. They used to hide in the caves as children, pretending to be pirates. Josef had saved him from drowning there once. He smiled. Despite his small size, Josef was strong as a bull and an impressive swimmer.

But the sun rose upon Ian's failure. He had nothing to show for the night but a lingering melody and a feeling of deep unease.

****

Early the next morning, a crowd gathered right inside the Landgate. They surrounded something, and Ian ventured closer to see what had transpired.

"Ruthie," Sarah's voice rang unusually loud. "Do not touch it."

A large brown dog lay against the stone wall, swollen tongue hanging out of its mouth, eyes black with death.

"Oh, Mother! No!"

"Poor girl," Sarah whispered, as Ian joined her. "She has such a tender heart. I wonder how she will survive in this world."

Ian nodded. "Yet you have done fine, have you not?"

Ruthie backed away from the dog as a sailor arrived. He turned the stiff body over with his boot. A gaping hole had been ripped out of the dog's stomach, and the entrails lay against the blood-matted hair.

"Mother of God," Ian exclaimed. "What kind of butchery is this?"

"The dog's been ripped open," the sailor said.

"Looks like the work of the innkeeper, Josef."

Another man, reeking of gin, backed away. "One of the night creatures, transformed into a dog."

"Come now." Ian stepped forward as the crowd backed away, fear etched on their faces. "I know this dog, saw him playing in the water the other day."

"He's the devil's own," a woman cried.

Sarah led Ruthie away.

"But what about the poor dog?" Ruthie said.

Sarah put her arm around her as she cried.

Did this dog run Maggie over yesterday? Surely not, for what had knocked her over must have been stronger.

"It's a sign of evil," Captain Jenkins cried.

Shouts rang out from down the street. Josef ran into the crowd, breeches torn and filthy, his hair matted and dirt-filled. The crowd backed away.

"It is him," he screamed, guttural and primitive. "My Nikolaus. He has transformed. I saw him last night." His throat worked convulsively. He seemed to be having trouble swallowing. "What has happened to him?"

"Josef, you must come with me. Let's get you away from here."

Ian's friend did not seem to hear him. He ran to the dog, kneeled beside him, laid his head on his bloody, matted fur. "I have searched for you, but I could not find you. I could not protect you. Oh, Nikolaus, what have they done to you?"

"The man's been taken over by the devil, by the vampires he brought with him. He is one of them now, cost me my boat."

Ian reached down to help Josef up. "You are

frightening these good people. Come away."

Josef turned to Ian, bared his teeth in a bloodied face.

Ian backed away. Josef sat on his haunches, eyed the crowd, and suddenly leapt up, hands dripping with blood. He ran toward the Landgate. The crowd stood motionless, then began to speak at once in a cacophony of fear.

"We must bar the doors tonight."

"He will be out there, looking for blood."

"What has our town done to deserve this?"

"We are cursed, and it is the innkeeper's fault."

Ian straightened to his full height. "Good people. Josef's behavior is the result of illness. Use your reason, I implore you."

He followed after Josef, to the grove of trees where his nephew had been buried. He grabbed him by the arm.

Josef flung his head toward him, growling, teeth bared, eyes red with rage.

"Josef, my good friend. Please, let me help you. For Lena's sake."

A dim light of recognition passed over his face. He became Josef again. "My Lena?"

"You are going to die. There is no cure, but I will make you as comfortable as I can."

Josef's eyes filled. He did understand him, then. "I want my Lena. The child."

Ian fought for control. "I'm sorry, friend."

"My Lena," he cried. He tore at his hair, spittle frothing from his bloody mouth.

"You would keep her safe?"

Josef nodded, blood dripping from his face.

"You must come with me. We will go where you cannot harm anyone." He reached for him.

"No." Josef snarled, the light of recognition gone. He knocked him to the ground, and disappeared.

He could not cure Josef's descent into madness and death, but if he could find him, he could perhaps prevent the gentle man from harming someone else. His aggression would only worsen. Where could he take him if he could find him? Henry and Samuel would help. Perhaps they could tie him down, keep him isolated, ease him into death, if possible. Oh God. Not this gentle man.

Josef could not be free to roam the town. Once the townspeople found out he had the dreaded hydrophobia, there would be panic. No one must know; better they think he was a monster than know of his disease. Should he tell Maggie, Lena? What good could it do?

He would not wish this death on his worst enemy. He closed his eyes and breathed deeply to staunch the flow of pain gushing like blood through his mind. Not his good friend.

****

Josef ran. Could not see. Only black. Red. Blood, blood of Nikolaus. He pulled the words from the part of him still human. The wind slammed against his face, his throat closed and he gasped for breath.

His Nikolaus. Tried to help the boy, but failed. Could not swallow, but must bite, warm flesh, teeth sinking in sinew. How could he tell his sister her son was dead? No, for soon he would not care. Lena. His love for Lena, the last bit of his soul sliced away with bloody talons, tooth and claw.

Chapter Twenty-Three

Maggie sat in her Sunday clothes, nursing a cup of tea. Where had Ian gone? Widow Jenkins had already visited her, telling her all about his activities at the Siren Inn, his singing, flirting. Perhaps the appeal of an old flame's bed was too tempting to withstand.

She was so beautiful, this Charlotte, like a China doll, and no doubt practiced in the arts of love. And she was just Maggie—a midwife, plain and serviceable. With so many aches and pains this morning, she might as well be an old crone. Last night, when he gave her such pleasure, why did he not take his? Did he not desire her? Had he met another woman in his travels who soured his desire for her?

She warmed up her tea and added an extra dash of sugar. Mayhap it would sweeten her disposition. The door opened to his characteristic humming.

He came straight to her and embraced her, not letting go. "Maggie."

"You're soaked through! Where have you been all night?" Would he tell her the truth? "Old Widow Jenkins was just in, on her way to church, looking for some chamomile tea for her grandson."

"Church! I had forgotten."

"Yes, I'm sure you had." She pulled away from him.

"Maggie, what is wrong?"

"You were out all night, and I did not know where you were." She sounded churlish even to her own ears.

"I am sorry. I was helping Lena, and…"

"Yes, and singing. I heard. I hope you enjoyed your reunion."

"What? No Maggie. You think I would break our marriage vows to be with her?"

"I may be a plain ordinary midwife, but I saw the look passing between the two of you. What am I to think?"

His eyes burned into hers like fire's blue flame. "You would think me so shallow? When every touch, every look you give me makes life flow through my veins? I stayed at the inn to help Sabine with the crowd and walked outside of town, looking for Josef. It had nothing to do with Charlotte."

He took both of her stiff hands in his. "You do not understand the depth of my feelings for you, Maggie. *Plain* and *ordinary* are words I would never use to describe you. The word 'beautiful' shames me as a wordsmith, so I will not use it." He kissed her. "I will take you upstairs and show you what I mean."

She sighed. "But for one thing: it is Sunday. Did you not hear the church bells? I cannot miss church when I'm able to go, husband. As a midwife I am supposed to be pious." She did not feel very pious at the moment, watching him as he unbuttoned his shirt, rubbed a linen towel upon the muscular planes of his chest, eyeing her as if she sat naked before him.

"I know. I will accompany you, for I do respect your calling."

Confusing man. One minute he did not seem to want her, and the next minute it seemed he would ravish her on the spot. She shook her head.

"What, my love?" He had stripped down completely now and bent to dry his legs. He took an inordinate time drying off his cockstand, watching her.

Warmth pooled in her privities, and she could not help but stare, for it had a life of its own.

"You see," he said, with the devil's own grin. "It only has *eye* for you."

"You are impossible." She did not bother fighting her own grin. "We are going to be late, if you are going."

"Of course I'll accompany you. I won't be long." He bounded up the stairs, and her center turned liquid at the flexing of his buttocks and his muscled back.

By the time she'd splashed the heat off her face at the basin, he returned looking refreshed, but sober. He told her about Josef and the dog.

"What manner of disease would cause a man to act so irrationally?"

And then he told her about his diagnosis of hydrophobia, a disease she'd never seen. They stood in the middle of the apothecary shoppe, the comfort of his arms her only anchor. What would Lena do without her Josef? How would she tell her friend her husband would die a horrible death?

"Come, Maggie." Ian took her hand and led her out the door. "We must go to church and pray. What else can we do?"

He took her arm as they walked down the street. "By the by, you look lovely today, Maggie."

"Thank you," she replied.

Darkness pooled below his eyes, and a quiet desperation lined his face. She understood; he was trying to achieve a bit of normalcy. No one must know of Josef's fate.

There was no shortage of comments regarding Ian's night at the Siren Inn. Apparently, looking for Josef wasn't the only thing he did last night.

"Pierce, some fine singing with the China Doll last night. Don't know when I've enjoyed myself more," the chandler called out as he waited at the door for his wife. "Every Sunday she says she'll be right out. Every Sunday I wait. It's enough to make a man insane."

Ian grinned. "My Maggie. Always punctual. You'd rather poke a stick in your eye than be late."

She harrumphed.

The baker, walking arm in arm with wife Martha, greeted them. "Mistress Maggie, you should have seen your husband last night. Put on quite a show he did, with the fancy singing woman. Their voices blended together just so."

Walking behind Martha and her husband, their daughter turned to her sister Bess. "I heard tell they did more than sing."

They both giggled, eyeing Ian.

Martha turned around and gave them the gimlet eye. "Shut up, Isadora, before I slap you silly. I am shocked at you both. You know I don't abide by idle gossip."

A laugh bubbled up from Maggie's throat. She coughed to cover it.

"You will not malign our good friends in this way," Martha continued. "If you can't keep a civil tongue in your head, you'd best be mute."

Both girls reddened, and Martha shook her head. "I'm sorry, Maggie. They just repeat what they hear, the little chits. Please don't concern yourself with the talk, old friend. There's always jaw-wagging about one thing or another. I will box those girls' ears when I get them home, for they're old enough to know better."

Unease cramped Maggie's stomach as they climbed the steps to the chapel. When they found their seat in the polished wooden pew, there was no shortage of looks aimed in their direction, some curious, some blatantly malicious.

Ian whispered, "I'm sorry to have caused you embarrassment, Maggie. It is never my intention."

"Yes, but somehow you always manage to do it. First, the wagon…"

Vicar Andrews appeared and the service began.

Maggie leaned into Ian, her agitation momentarily forgotten with the solid feel of his hand tucked in her arm, and the peace of the ritual helping to calm her anxiety.

As was his habit, the vicar surveyed his congregation, casting his eye on each one present.

"My good people, Christ entreated us to not react with fear, but with understanding, even to those who have transgressed and are lost. Fear has invaded our town, and we must ask for God's assistance. Let us pray."

As they knelt, the familiar peace of tradition swept over her upon hearing Vicar's gentle, yet commanding voice.

They rose from prayer, and Vicar began his sermon.

The silence shattered upon a scratching at the door.

A man screamed, hoarse and guttural, "Help me! Help me, God!"

Chapter Twenty-Four

The door swung open, and a ragged figure covered in blood staggered into the church. "Help me!"

Bloodshot eyes burned through the black hair fallen in its face. The figure swung its head around, teeth bared. Sweet Jesus. Josef.

"Help me." He tried to swallow but choked, saliva dripping from his mouth. He clutched his throat. "Please, Ian." He held raw, blood-soaked hands out to him.

Ian reached him before the rising congregation. "We will help you."

"Kill me, friend."

Ian clutched his blood-spattered coat. "No, Josef. Come with me."

With colossal strength, Josef shook Ian off. "Not human."

Maggie cried out, "Josef!"

Josef jerked in spasms and collapsed to the floor, teeth bared.

At first, Ian had not been aware of the onlookers forming a circle around his friend, the men in front with fists out, some holding knives. The women hid their children in their cloaks. The chorus of alarm and panic pounded in Ian's ears like drums of war.

"Look at how he shakes. The devil's inside him."

"He is sick." Ian stood in front of him.

"He is a monster. He is possessed."

"No, leave him. Retreat and give him room. He came to us for help." Ian spoke with all the authority he could muster.

"Get yourselves away from here." Maggie herded the women and children to the back of the church.

Josef stared, eyes black and luminous.

Ignoring the clamor of the crowd, Ian asked. "Josef, what happened?"

Josef struggled to swallow. Sweat poured from his face, mixing with blood and pooling on the stone floor around him. His feet were bare and bloody, and blue with cold. "He came to me. My nephew. As a beast, not a man." His chest rose and fell as he gasped for air.

"Be still, Josef." They would kill him right here if he did not cease.

"No, it is true."

The crowd gasped, and Josef seized, head lifting off the floor, teeth bared, hands contracted into claws.

"We must kill him, before he spreads his evil!" As one, the men approached.

The vicar fought his way through the crowd. "No. There will be no weapons drawn in God's house."

Henry stood with Ian, his son beside him, confusion marring his handsome face.

"Good people. You know this good man is not of the devil."

Sounds of dissension echoed around the high rafters.

"I know I am but a humble night soil man," Henry continued. "But under the laws of man and God, the devil cannot come into our sanctuary. You know it is so. Is that not right, Vicar?"

Vicar straightened to his full height and made his way through the crowd. His voice rang with authority.

"He is right. Satan cannot enter here. You must trust your maker to see you safe."

"But people have died," someone said.

"He is sick," Ian shouted.

"Look at him, he's covered in blood. We know what he said about the vampires, how the devil commissions them to take blood, for his sake."

"No," Ian said. "I implore you, good people. Still your panic. Have compassion. Do you see he is not hurting anyone?"

"He needs our help," Vicar said.

A few of the men backed away, but Pete Stowe, with two burly men, approached, and catching Ian unawares, forced themselves through and began to drag Josef out by his blue, cold feet.

"No," Ian shouted, and blocked the door with Henry's help. "Is there not anyone who will help me?"

Henry stood with Ian, powerful body daring anyone to approach. "Has this poor man not served the town well, offering hospitality and charity to you all?"

"He needs quiet and care, not violence," Ian added.

There was a lull for a brief moment as some in the crowd nodded. "Aye, it's true."

His fierce Maggie broke through the crowd, swinging at Pete Stowe. "Get away from him. He's done nothing."

Suddenly, convulsions shook Josef's body. He bared his teeth, a white substance foaming from his mouth.

"Who will stand with this good man?" Vicar asked, eyes blazing with authority.

The number with Ian and Henry grew. Pete Stowe and his friends backed away.

"Peace be with you," Vicar said. "Pray with me, my flock. We must pray for him, and for this town."

Josef's lips bared in a savage grin, groans issued from his mouth. His eyes flickered shut, open and shut again, as the convulsions shook him.

He stilled.

"No!" Maggie sobbed.

The crowd grew silent. Ian leaned down, bent over his friend's chest, and checked for a pulse at his wrist. "He is gone."

"Silence, everyone! Vicar shouted. "We must pray for this poor man."

The rabble of panicked townspeople overpowered the vicar's prayer.

Pete Stowe interrupted the vicar's entreaty. "You pray for a monster?"

A collective gasp went up among the crowd at his blasphemy.

"Better you should pray for *us*, for there is much to fear in this town." Pete Stowe and his friends shoved their way out the door.

Henry exchanged a glance with Ian and left to follow Stowe.

The whispers of doubt spread round the room.

"He's right. We are all in danger."

"Dead livestock, dogs torn to pieces, it was him!"

"Have you ever seen such a horrible thing?"

"Who will be next?"

Ian searched the eyes of his neighbors, noting Mrs. Stowe's hurried retreat out the door. "I beseech you, good people. We must cling to logic. You have always known Josef to be a good man. There is no evil here, only illness. He was the best of men."

"Go home now," Vicar called. "Go home and pray for this good man. Do not let fear rule you, but trust in God."

The chapel soon was empty, and Maggie's sobs echoed on the high ceiling. Ian glanced up and stared at the stain glass window's depiction of Jesus healing the sick. It cast a blue light upon Maggie holding Josef's limp hand.

"Poor Josef," she sobbed. "What will your Lena do?"

"Maggie. We need to get you home. It is not good for you to be on the cold floor."

He helped her up. She was like ice, and he made an effort to keep his voice calm. "We must bury him soon."

Henry returned. "I will help the vicar prepare the body while you see Maggie home."

"Come, Maggie." Ian put his arm around her. As he helped her down the steps, her legs gave way.

Ian rushed to gather her in his arms. She took a deep breath, opened her eyes. "I am fine. I just…"

"I will carry you home."

"Ian, we must go to Lena's and tell her of Josef's death."

"I will do it, Maggie."

"No, I must be with her."

"Maggie." Obstinate woman.

"Carry me if you must, but carry me to Lena's. She needs me. I am not having pains; it is not the babe."

"I *will* carry you, and you will sit once we arrive."

She nodded and leaned her head against his chest.

233

He made haste to the Siren Inn.

"Put me down. I can walk now." Her eyes glinted steely grey, and she had life in her voice again. Her trembling stilled, and he felt her deep measured breaths as she fought to gain control. His fierce warrior. He set her aright, and they embraced, drawing strength from one another. "We will go slowly. If you need to rest, we'll stop."

There were no questions from bystanders as they neared the inn. Everyone already knew what had happened. As Maggie and Ian came within sight of the Siren Inn, they stopped and stared as Mrs. Stowe exited, a smug smile upon her face. No. It was obvious what she was about; she had rushed to the inn to give Lena the news before anyone else could.

Maggie stiffened. "Mrs. Stowe!"

The woman turned.

"Why would you do such a thing? Why would you draw pleasure from a fellow woman's pain?"

"It is no less than she deserves, what he deserves."

"You are an evil creature." Maggie's nostrils flared, and she took a step toward Pete's mother, fists clenched.

Never had he seen her so incensed.

"They have done nothing to you but offer their kindness and hospitality to your son."

"He took the inn away from my Pete. It was rightfully his."

"It was your son who thought so little of it he would wager it away in a game of chance."

"Maggie," Ian said quietly. "You cannot change her views, or change her. Save your strength."

"Stay away from her, do you hear me?" Maggie's

voice shook.

"You will get what you deserve." Mrs. Stowe turned away and walked down the street.

They quickened their pace to the door, and hurried in.

Chapter Twenty-Five

Maggie and Ian rushed past the tables and into Lena's private quarters. A baby's cry echoed through the quiet room. Maggie stopped and swallowed down the bile of Mrs. Stowe's hate. She fought for control. For Lena to learn of her Josef's death from the bitter mouth of Mrs. Stowe was beyond unfair. But her anger would not help Lena. Ian laid his hand upon her head like a loving father, and a blessing of comfort and protection flowed through her.

Sabine answered the door, red-eyed and trembling. Ian took her child from her arms. Maggie embraced her and strode to Lena's bed. Lena lay propped upon the pillows, eyes blank with shock. The baby screamed in its cradle. Sabine picked him up, rocking him and crooning in her native language.

Lena lifted her head. "It cannot be true. My Josef cannot be dead."

Maggie approached her. "Oh, Lena. I am sorry. He's gone." She wrapped her arms around her, smoothing the hair out of her eyes.

She lifted her head. "She said Josef was like a monster when he died. She said Satan had him in his grasp. Tell me it is not true. He cannot be gone."

Ian stood at the foot of the bed. "He was sick."

"Why would she say such things about my Josef? He was a good man, a gentle man." She shook her head.

"He cannot be gone. No, it is not true." She cried in great gasping sobs and curled into a ball.

Maggie could only pat her back and stare helplessly. Why did God choose to make his good children suffer? The babe's wailing increased in volume.

"Lena, you must feed your son."

"No, I cannot."

Maggie could barely hear her. She tried to ignore the twinge of guilt as she said, "*Josef's* son is calling to you." Lena should have the right to mourn her beloved husband. But she could not, for she must carry on.

"I will fix her a calming tisane." Ian quietly left the room with Sabine's babe.

Lena struggled to sit up. Maggie adjusted the pillows behind her and washed her face with a warm cloth. Lena's hands shook as she bared her breast for the babe. "Give him to me." She held out her arms and put him to her breast.

"My little Josef," she whispered, and quietly wept.

Sabine stood by the door, sorrow etched upon her face, making her look years older.

"You have a long road ahead of you, Sabine. Take the time while we're here to sit, rest, and eat. You need your strength."

She nodded. "I bring stew for us. Mother Lena needs to eat."

"Thank you, Sabine."

Ian returned with a cup of tea. "This will not take away the pain, but it may help you rest and perhaps sleep a bit."

Maggie took the baby from Lena and put him in the cradle.

Ian eyed Maggie. "You promised you would sit." He glared at her until she sat in the straight back chair in the corner.

Sabine soon returned with a tray, and the four of them ate in silence.

Lena's eyes drooped as the calming tisane began to take effect.

"How are you feeling?" Maggie took the bowl from her.

She closed her eyes, tears seeping down her pale cheeks. "My Josef, he is gone."

"Yes." There was nothing more she could say.

Lena grasped her hand. "Do not leave me, Maggie."

"I won't." She must do something for her friend. "Oh, your poor hands are so chapped and dry." She took some almond oil from her basket and massaged Lena's work-worn hands.

"*Ach*," she whispered. "Feels so good."

Maggie watched Lena's eyelids droop. How would her friend withstand the loss of Josef, and indeed, have the strength to carry on? How would she keep the inn going?

"So tired," Lena murmured.

"Yes, rest is the best thing you can do for your babe."

Ian laid a hand on Maggie's shoulder and led her to the door. "I must get back to the church and help ready Josef. It's the least I could do."

"Ian. You must not blame yourself. No one could know what would happen."

He kissed her. "But if I had tried harder…"

"I know, my love."

"I will come back for you when we're finished."

How was Lena to hold onto her fatherless babe, in a world of grief and heartache?

Sabine stood by Lena's bedside.

Lena opened her eyes. "Are there customers?"

Sabine shook her head. "I." She poked her chest. "I take care of things."

Her lips quivered, and tears rolled down her smooth olive skin. She squared her shoulders. "Mother Lena, I can brew. I can cook. *You* will rest."

Lena reached for her hand. "My dear girl. My daughter."

She gestured Sabine to get on the bed, and when the young girl looked questioningly at Maggie, she nodded.

Lena turned on her side and pulled Sabine to her.

A short time later, Maggie pulled the covers over them and crept from the room.

****

When Maggie emerged from Lena's rooms, she was relieved to see a mere scattering of loyal friends and customers, among them Henry and George, the baker and his wife, Martha, and a somber Vicar Andrews.

"How is Mistress Sabine?" Vicar asked. "I don't see her anywhere." He took a sip of his brandy. "Josef was like a father to her."

"Yes, he was fond of her and loved the baby like a grandfather." She sat beside him.

Ian arrived. He bent to kiss her forehead.

"You make a fetching barmaid." He waggled his eyebrows.

How he could think such things in her bedraggled

state, she'd never know. Her body ached from the fall the day before, making her feel old as a crone.

Ian nodded to Vicar. "Thank you for your kind service to my friend."

"It is what I am called to do," Vicar said. "I'm sorry there is no question of burial at the church kirkyard, despite my belief Josef was devoid of evil. I would hate to lose my position here." He lowered his voice. "After last year, when the town was stricken with fear and superstition, and my superior got word of it, my job was in danger."

"I had no idea," Ian exclaimed.

"I will leave the secret with you," he said. "For I suspect you know how to keep one."

Just then, Vicar became distracted by Sabine's entrance. She smoothed her hands over her apron, looking the better for a few hours' rest. When she saw the Vicar struggling comically to rise, she didn't smile, exactly, but the dimples on each side of her mouth deepened. She nodded at him, and he blushed, but his hazel eyes shone at the attention.

"Erm, my condolences, Mistress Sabine."

"Thank you. I must go to kitchen."

"My regards," Vicar said, at her retreating form. He sighed.

Henry came out of the kitchen, wiped his sweating face on his apron. "I've been shucking oysters," he said. "Got a pot of stew on the stove and some fish frying."

"I did not know you were so handy in the kitchen," Maggie said.

"I lost my cook last year and have not replaced her."

He wiped his eyes with his apron. "I can't believe I

will not see Josef again."

"Regarding the funeral tomorrow," Ian said. "Why do we not use my wagon? Lena will insist upon going, as unfit as she is, and she can ride in it to save her strength."

Vicar nodded, gulping the remainder of his brandy down. "If it helps the dear woman, then it is worth it."

"I half expect Josef to come trudging in here with a barrel full of drink, a surly look on his countenance." Henry chuckled.

"I remember when he got drunk and dropped the barrel of rum." Maggie smiled. "I thought Lena would whip his hide." She could not prevent a giggle from escaping. "It smelled like rum in here for days."

For a moment, they enjoyed the memory of their quiet, but kind friend. A few people began filing in, perhaps for mutual company and remembrances of Josef.

Henry clapped Ian on the back, causing him to spit out a mouthful of his winter ale. "Go home, man. Tend to your wife."

"I couldn't agree more."

"I'm not tired," Henry said. "We have no rounds tonight, so George and I will stay here, to watch over the place."

At this, Vicar shot Henry a look and stood. "I must go home and prepare for tomorrow."

"Get some sleep," Ian said. "You have done a hard day's work."

Ian helped Maggie with her cloak. "There's another one who sleeps the sleep of the innocent, I wager."

Maggie smiled. Even in the depths of sorrow and

exhaustion, he could bring her a glimmer of joy, of hope, of a future free of strife, for however long it lasted.

A short while later, Maggie sat in front of a roaring fire. Ian stood before her, awaiting her approval. She stared, open-mouthed. He should have looked silly, in this below the knee-length silk nightgown. But he looked resplendent. He bowed, and through the opening of the robe she glimpsed a muscular thigh covered with light brown curls.

"What are you wearing?"

"It's called a banyan. Do you like it?"

"Yes." She surprised even herself. "I do."

His pleasure was apparent underneath his robe, where his manhood celebrated the success of pleasing his wife. "Men in the Orient wear this type of robe during the day as well. It is their custom."

Her breasts tingled at the intensity of his gaze. "Come, husband. Sit down with me. Tell me the story of where you got this banyan." Was it so wrong of them to retreat into the comfort of their love?

She slipped open his robe, enjoyed the smooth feel of the silk on her fingers, and the hot skin of his powerful shoulders. He closed his eyes, and she stared at the pulse beating in his throat. Her center tightened at his power, and he put his hands in her hair and kissed her, the heat of him making her gasp in his mouth.

The cottage shook with the pounding of the door. "Let me in, Pierce!"

"Damn him," Ian growled. "It's Reginald."

"A little help, please! The bastard's heavy."

Maggie pushed him off and tightened her robe, her ardor cooling like sheets on the line. She stood in the doorway to the shoppe.

Ian opened the door. Reginald half carried, half dragged Pete Stowe across the floor, and Ian rushed to help him into a chair. He leaned against the wall, eyes half open, mouth twisted in pain. His red, festered hand, swollen to twice its size, lay against his torn, mud-soaked linen shirt.

"I found this poor sot lying in the alley. Don't say I never gave you anything, friend. The man reeks, by the way."

Stowe opened his eyes for a moment, then his head lolled back against the wall.

Ian rushed up to examine him. "Good God, Stowe. You should have let me treat this hand. You're burning up with fever."

Reginald bowed to Maggie. "Good evening, madame. So sorry to disturb you." His hooded eyes roved over her attire.

"Yes, um." A most nauseating smell permeated the air. Sickeningly sweet, and foul. Maggie opened the window.

"I must take my leave, Pierce."

"No you don't, Reggie. Make yourself useful for once and bring me the straight-backed chair from the parlor. We will need to tie him." He sniffed. "I smell opium. He's been trying to dull the pain, no doubt."

The two men soon had him settled. Ian gave him a dose of willow bark for pain and fever, and tied his suppurating hand to the wide chair arm.

Ian shook him. "Pete, wake up. If there's a chance to save this hand, I must lance it, and release the purulence."

"Lance?"

The willow bark seemed to revive him a bit. His pupils were huge. He shook with fever and fear. "Oh God."

"We must do this. It's the only way, and indeed I do not know if I can save your hand."

"But…"

"There's no sense belaboring it now, but I could have prevented this."

Maggie saw the effort it took him to hold his temper. He stood very still for a moment, breathing deeply, as she had seen him do before, and the trembling in his hands stilled.

"Are you ready?" Ian grasped a lancet. "Reggie, hold him."

With a deft hand, Ian sliced a three-inch long incision into the space between his missing thumb and index finger.

Pete screamed, legs scraping against the floor and moving the chair forward.

"Reggie, hold him still, I said. I have a knife in my hand."

Maggie held a hand over her mouth against the putrid smell and shut the window. They'd have the neighbors waking up if they didn't watch out.

The poison began to flow in a yellow river out of Pete's hand. Ian rinsed it with hot water, while Reggie gagged. At the sound, Maggie responded in kind.

Ian glanced up. "Maggie? Okay, sweeting?"

She nodded. When had she gotten so squeamish? "I will make some tea."

He smiled. "Yes, I think it's best."

Her timing was fortuitous, as she overheard Ian saying, "I must lance it again, Stowe. I'm sorry."

"No doubt you're enjoying it, hurting me."

This garnered a stifled laugh from Reggie.

"I am not your enemy, Pete, and never have been. I will fetch you some brandy before we start again."

Ian strode into the parlor, his gown flowing behind him. He poured some brandy and soaked a clean rag in the herbs simmering beside the fire. "Messy business. You look a little green around the gills. Here." He poured her some of the golden liquid. "Sit down." And he was gone again, taking the brandy with him.

Relieved, she plopped down on the divan and sipped her brandy.

"Here, man. Swallow this, and I will put another poultice on your wound."

"Ah! Yes," Pete mumbled.

"You know I am only trying to help you, right?"

"Uh huh. Damn fine brandy."

"Obviously, by my actions, I mean you no harm. In lieu of payment, I would ask you some questions." A pause. "The hand is draining, but we must cut again."

Reggie groaned.

"Go pour yourself a glass, Reggie, you great big girl."

"Now then." Ian's tone softened, as if he talked to a young boy. "Will you answer my questions as best you can, Pete?"

"More brandy?"

"Answers first, brandy after. What do you know about the disappearance of the body of Nikolaus, Josef's nephew?"

"N-nothing."

"Did you move the body, Pete?"

"I said it was wrong."

"Answer me."

"It's wrong."

Ian removed the poultice. "It's draining the poison, but not enough."

"He's fainted," Reginald said unnecessarily.

"Damn," Ian said. "Pete! Wake up. I must lance the hand again."

He cringed. "Don't hurt me."

"I'm sorry. Reggie, hold him. Put down the glass, you imbecile."

"Shut up."

Stowe giggled and then belched.

"Let me just say, this is not how I imagined I'd be spending the evening," Ian drawled.

"Oh, by the by, old friend. I like your attire. I remember it from our travels together. Quite the fetching outfit with the apron."

"Yes, ha ha. Let's get this done, and you can be on your way."

"Ready, Pete?"

The poor man screamed.

"Yes, there's the spot."

"Holy hell." Reginald gasped.

"Reggie, don't you dare faint on me. There, now. It's draining as it should. How is it feeling, Pete? Any better?"

"A bit. The cut hurts, but there's less pressure."

"I'm finished now. I am going to wrap a poultice of boiled brown seaweed on it and bandage it up. Then—listen to me. You must use this poultice three times a day, and change the bandage frequently. Come see me in two days. Comply, or you will likely lose your hand. Do you understand?"

Maggie heard Ian's footsteps, the opening and shutting of drawers. "Take these poultices with you. Do you want to bide here awhile and rest?"

"No, I must go home. Mother will be wondering where I am. Mayhap."

Ian washed his hands and face at the basin. "After I dress, we'll take him home, Reggie."

"Why don't you take him home, and I'll stay and keep your wife safe and warm." Reggie sidled next to Maggie, hand hovering above her shoulder.

Before she could blink, Ian grabbed Reggie by his cravat and slammed him against the wall. "Keep a safe distance from my wife," he rasped. "Now, do as I say and help me take him home. And then I can return to my beloved and continue what we started." He released Reggie and whispered in Maggie's ear. "Go upstairs, sweeting. I will return soon." His hoarse voice resonated deep within her belly.

They were soon out the door, Pete between them, poor bastard. She climbed the stairs to their bedchamber, where Ian had left a candle burning for her. Despite her fatigue, she craved the touch of his fingers upon her, his lips reverent upon her breasts. She climbed into bed, curled on her side, and fell promptly asleep.

Later, Ian's breath tickled the hairs on the back of her neck. "Ah, Maggie," he murmured. "May I wake you? I long to be one with you, to sink myself into your bounty."

She nestled her bottom against him in assent. He reached his long arms around her and lifted up her nightgown, his fingers sliding up her legs, and she begged of him, hurry, and he paid her no heed when he reached her secret place and slowly slid his fingers into her warm, slick center. His manhood bulged against her buttocks.

In one swift movement, he turned her on her back, rose above her, and sank himself into her. She tightened around him, enclosing him in her warmth. Flames licked her passage, carrying her up and over the edge when she heard his cry.

"Oh, Maggie, you soothe me so. And bring me such pleasure. But did I pleasure you?"

She quivered with helpless laughter. He knew. But he wanted to hear it.

"You enlighten me, Ian."

His kiss upon her lips was the last thing she remembered before she fell asleep. Later, she reached out for him to entwine her limbs with his but found his side of the bed cold.

Chapter Twenty-Six

The strings of Ian's lute echoed through the cottage, plaintive and urgent, grasping at Maggie's heart. His husky baritone joined the lute, keening without words, and spread its dark wings to shelter her from the night's sorrow.

Later, when dawn began to lighten the sky, she listened for him, but the cottage lay silent and empty. Why must he go? He said she was everything to him, but why could he not abide with her for even one short night? Surely he found her lacking, how she went to bed with the chickens and ached like an old woman. This Charlotte was a night owl like him. Did she ever sleep? Even as the thoughts ground into her, she cursed her doubts. Had he not just made love to her as if she was the only woman who existed? But God knew he had the vigor of two men. Perhaps he needed more. Perhaps he got tired of singing alone.

As she lay in bed, a prickling of foreboding spread over her. *Something's amiss.* The prickling spread throughout her body. She sat up, reeling as if she'd been thrown spinning into the air. A smell of incense permeated the room. A voice resounded through her body, like an echo, gentle yet urgent.

The holy nun.

"What is it you want?"

"She is doubly blessed, midwife, but in distress."

The pains sliced deep within her belly. Doubly blessed. She must go to Polly McCall. And she felt the warmth of approval from the holy nun.

She gathered her materials in haste and walked toward the Landgate as the sky began to lighten. No birdsong as yet, but the faint sound of singing from the Shipwreck Inn, Ian's voice heard above the rest. She had guessed correctly where he preferred his company, singing with the butterflies instead of home with the moth. No matter. She gathered her cloak around her, shivering.

She had not taken time to break her fast, not when the holy nun urged her to take action. The roads outside the Landgate were littered with potholes full of water from the rain last night. She made her way over the bridge, picking her way carefully over the soft spot.

When Ian returned, he would not know where she was. She couldn't help a momentary flash of satisfaction; mayhap he would know how she felt. But more important were the urgings of the nun.

As she turned down the lane, the figure of Adam McCall raced toward her, the smaller figures of the oldest boys behind him. "I was just coming to fetch you. How did you know? It's time."

She bowed her head in thanksgiving and prayed God and the holy nun would bless Polly, the babes, and her hands in service.

The door to the cottage hung wide open. Bethan, Polly's sister knelt with the youngest child in one arm. She had her other hand upon Katherine's head. "I promise you, darling, your mother will be fine."

"But two babies! Two!" Little Katherine cried.

"She has done this many times. Now, enjoy this

bright morning and play some games with your brothers. Mayhap you'll have some sisters born today."

The sheepdog licked Katherine's face, and a wrestling match ensued with the other two boys joining in.

"How extraordinary!" Bethan smiled down at Maggie. "You're here."

Maggie's moral dilemma lasted only a few minutes: normally, a maiden would not be privy to the secrets of the birthing chamber, but she needed an extra pair of hands.

"Where's Elunid?" Maggie asked.

"She is…" Bethan jerked her head toward the field. "She took herself off before dawn and hasn't been seen from since. There will be no budging her."

"She must be cold," Maggie said.

"She doesn't seem to feel it," Bethan said.

"Bethan, I need your help birthing the babies. Can you do it?"

She nodded. "Yes, I believe so. I think I might like bringing new life into the world, although I have never done so. They are so fresh and untouched, free of troubles." A wistful look made her appear years older.

"Well, then. Let's be about it."

"I will engage the children in an activity." Bethan clapped her hands and the little ones came running.

Polly grabbed Maggie's hand and whispered, "Something is wrong. I can feel it. This doesn't feel like the others."

"Has your water broken?"

She smiled. "Yes, like a dam. Elunid took to the fields upon seeing it."

Bethan snorted. "The children thought she pissed

herself. They had a jolly laugh about it."

"How does it feel different, Polly?"

The pains, they're more intense."

Maggie soaked a cloth in the essence of lavender she'd brought in her bag and laid it gently upon the woman's brow.

Just then, another pain doubled her over. Maggie lowered the blanket and put her hands upon her stomach, feeling the tightness of the womb. A limb kicked her palm. Good, at least one of the babes still moved.

When Polly's pain abated, Maggie said, "Polly, would you like to use the birthing chair? Some women find it to be helpful."

Polly smirked. "As you can see, Katherine saw fit to decorate it. Does it not look festive?"

Maggie hadn't noticed upon entering. She chuckled. "Maybe next time."

"Ha ha." Polly smiled, and then a fresh pain came on.

"That's right, Polly. Slow, deep breaths. This will not last forever."

"Cold comfort," Polly gasped.

When the contraction was over, Polly repeated, "Something is wrong."

"I am going to take a look, dearie. But remember, you have never given birth to twins before."

"I pray I never will again."

Polly's brave attempt at humor buoyed Maggie. This was no inexperienced mother. But could anyone ever be prepared for the trial awaiting them? Would she when the time came?

The sound of the children playing with their father

outside put the slightest of smiles on Polly's face, as Maggie applied the almond oil to her hands and pulled up Polly's skirts, noting the bloody show. She gently inserted two fingers into her birthing passage.

Bethan stood at Maggie's side. "What should I do?"

"I will need you later, but for now just try and make her comfortable."

Bethan nodded.

She turned back to her patient. "Polly, you will be happy to hear you are almost ready for the babes to emerge. Your pains are doing a fine job of opening you up to receive your children." She soothed the woman's hair back from her flushed face.

"I cannot wait until you deliver your first, Mistress Maggie. I wonder what you'll be saying then." Polly's mouth quirked on one side.

"I hope you will be there to help me, dear Polly."

Bethan snorted in amusement. "Are you comfortable, sister?"

"Do I look like I am *comfortable?*" She cast Bethan a withered look.

"Here, take a sip of this." Bethan held the wine to her lips.

Polly nodded gratefully. Just then another pain hit, and the remaining bloody fluid of the membrane sac soaked Maggie. "There's the other one. Well done. It will help speed things along."

She did not need to tell Polly to lie back and rest between pains. They were increasing in frequency, and Polly needed every minute to rebuild her strength from the last ordeal.

Maggie prayed for a safe delivery.

Holy Mother, please do not forsake me. I do not understand your ways, but I have felt your presence, and pray you be with me, here and now.

She checked her materials, noting Bethan's bright interest. She had already laid them out: a sharp knife for cutting the cord, a clean string for tying it, and linen, to wrap the babies in. Polly groaned as her womb shifted dramatically. In all her days of delivering babes, Maggie had never seen anything so massive.

"I'm going to check you again, sweeting. It will not be long now."

There was no answer, and for a moment she thought Polly had fainted, so still she'd become. But Polly had instinctively turned inward, communicating with her babes in the secret language of a delivering mother.

As quickly as she could, before another pain came crashing down, Maggie inserted her fingers. Dear God, a foot. Breech. This would explain the excessive pain and Polly's instinctive feeling of something amiss.

"It's time to start pushing with the next contraction, Polly. Your passage is open. Do you feel it?"

"Ugh," she moaned.

"Bethan, put a pillow under her back so she can lean forward."

Bethan obeyed and held the wine to Polly's lips.

"Polly." She met her gaze. "One of the babies is coming out foot first." She hated breech births. "I must try to help the babe out. It will have to happen when you are pushing." A barely perceptible nod.

She returned to the foot of the bed and steeled herself for what was to come. With the next pain, she stuck her hand in and felt a tiny foot. "Don't push yet,

Polly."

The foot moved down, but then with the lessening of the contraction, it receded again. She could not pull on the foot. It was too late to try to turn the baby, and so she must guide the baby out, without pulling.

She removed her hand and urged Polly to close her eyes and rest. "It will be over soon, Polly. You will soon be holding your babies in your arms." She hoped so.

She asked Bethan to fetch the chicken broth mixed with the yolk of the poached egg that she had brought from home. When Bethan returned to her sister's bedside, another pain began. "It will be over soon."

"I am going to die, this time."

Maggie wiped the sweat off Polly's face with a cool rag. "No, you're not. Polly, you are carrying twins. One of your babies is coming foot first. Do not worry. I know what to do. Now breathe."

In hopes the baby would shift as the throes came upon Polly, Maggie laid her flat, then elevated her thighs with a straw-filled pillow. She made sure her head was lower than her body. Perhaps the shift in her position would encourage the babies to move.

"Polly, do not push. If you get the urge, pant."

Fortunately, she did not have the urge as yet. Maggie anointed her hands with almond oil, and with a firm touch, slowly massaged Polly's misshapen belly. She slid her hands down its huge slope to encourage the passage of the babes.

Polly writhed in pain with the force of another contraction.

Maggie felt the babies writhe as well. "Come, little ones."

Polly's belly shifted and rolled. "Sweet Jesus," she moaned.

The contraction lessened, the belly softened. Bethan gave Polly a bit of chicken broth with the poached egg beaten into it.

"Just a sip, Polly."

Polly nodded her thanks and got the glassy look of mothers in this stage of their ordeal, as another round of pains battered her. It was almost time.

"I must push," Polly groaned.

As if by instinct, Bethan helped her lean forward. "Hold my hands, Polly. Hurt me if you like."

Maggie put more almond oil on her hands and reached into the birth passage as Polly's pains increased. She knew what she must do, and she spoke aloud, in part to calm herself, and also to calm Polly. "After your next pains, I am going to try to put the babe's legs together, so he may come out, easier. I want you to pant like a dog. Do not push."

She reached her hand into the passage and felt the little foot, while searching for the other foot with her index and middle finger. She found it and also felt the cord. She gently placed the legs together, and reached higher for the arms, which luckily were at the babe's sides. The uterus clenched around her hand and she wondered vaguely if her hand was broken.

'Okay, Polly." She removed her hand as another contraction began.

"Take a deep breath, Polly, and push. Hold it and push."

In the midst of the contraction, the bottoms of the babe's feet, purple and tiny, emerged for a brief moment. Polly screamed.

"Well done, sweeting. I saw both feet. Very good. Now, rest for a moment, for it won't be long."

At least there was no heavy bleeding, only the natural amount when a woman gave birth. "Here," Bethan said. "Take another drink. It will fortify you."

"Shut your face," Polly said.

"Pay her no mind." Maggie glanced at Bethan. "Women often say things they don't mean at this time."

"She can tell me whatever she wants, poor dear. I never want to bear a child."

Maggie laughed. "I felt as you do, once."

Adam must have taken the children for a walk. Wise. They did not need to hear their mother's screams as she pushed through another contraction.

"Well done." The legs had receded again. The next contraction needed to be strong, so she could grasp the legs and slowly guide them out.

"Polly, with the next contraction, you must push with all your might."

Polly moaned, guttural and primitive.

"Okay, push with all the strength you have."

The legs were out, and Maggie struggled to grasp them. They were slippery.

"I must push again. Oh God, I cannot do it. It's ripping me in two!" Polly moaned.

At this time, a woman summons strength like a soldier summons courage on the battlefield. She does what must be done.

"Not long, Polly. And I see his sex. It's a boy."

If he lived, for he was not breathing now.

A low, animal-like sound came from Polly, prickling Maggie's skin. With one last push, the buttocks emerged.

"Almost done, Polly."

Bethan whispered, "Sweet Sister," as another pain came upon Polly.

She pushed, grunting.

Maggie prayed with all her might as she gently guided the babe out. Thank God the arms were crossed upon his little belly. Soon she delivered the shoulders, rotating them to help ease Polly's pain, and mayhap prevent tearing. Polly moaned. With a few more contractions, the babe emerged. She rubbed his chest vigorously, then the babe's chest rose and fell, and his color changed from blue, to purple, to a mottled red. She tied the navel string, cut it, and swaddled him, rejoicing to hear his lusty cry.

Thank you, Holy Sister.

"Bethan."

Without hesitation, Bethan took the baby and placed him on Polly's breast. Polly revived, and made those indistinct noises all mothers make upon seeing their child for the first time.

"Take some refresher, Polly. You will need it."

"Well done, dear sister. You are brave indeed." Bethan held the drink up to Polly's mouth.

Polly's quiet communion with her babe was cut short as a new contraction hardened her belly, and Bethan snatched the baby up and put him in the cradle nearby.

"Sweet Jesus. I don't have the strength," Polly moaned.

"This will be easier, Polly. Your passage is already prepared, has already stretched. And the baby is coming headfirst. Thank God."

Bethan wiped the sweat from her sister's face with

the lavender-soaked cloth. "I promise I will never torment you again."

Polly grunted. "So you say." She grimaced as another pain came on.

"I see the head," Maggie exclaimed. "Full of dark hair! Do you feel you must push?"

"Yes."

Bethan braced her back, and with a few more pushes, the babe's head eased out. Maggie gently rotated the shoulders as they emerged. Polly cried one last time as a little girl slipped out like an otter, emitting a tiny cry.

This time, after she clamped the cord, Maggie handed the girl to her mother, and delivered both afterburdens. She examined them and found them intact.

Polly encircled the child, arms shaking with fatigue. Although she was very pale and weak, her eyes shone with exultation.

She smiled down at her daughter. "Sweet girl." She put the babe to her breast. "She has not taken hold yet." She glanced up at Maggie.

With great haste, Maggie examined Polly's privities for tears and cleaned her up, with Bethan looking on. The girl was certainly not squeamish.

She smiled at Polly. "She is probably just tired, having to wait for her brother to make his way out."

Polly smiled and bent her head to her task again. "Ah, there she goes."

"Katherine will be overjoyed to find she has a sister," Bethan said over the lusty baby boy's cries. She picked him up and sang to him in her Welsh tongue.

"Let him cry a little," Maggie said. "It is good for

him." She let herself breathe a sigh of relief. The babes were small and needed some fat on their bones, but they were whole and healthy.

Polly was tired but had suffered no apparent ill effects from the birth. Maggie lay a warm cloth soaked in seaweed and lavender on Polly's privities, and soon had her tucked in with both babies at breast.

"I will go fetch your husband."

Bethan smoothed the hair out of Polly's face. "I am so proud of you, sister. Look at these two beautiful children." She fluffed the pillow under her head and gave her another sip of the fortifying liquid.

Adam rushed to his wife's side and kissed her. "My Polly. Are you all right? Oh God."

She nodded. "Katherine will be so pleased. She finally has a sister."

He gazed at the two babies. "A boy and a girl? Oh, my queen." His tears fell upon her face as he kissed her.

Bethan and Maggie stepped outside to give them a moment together.

Bethan's face glowed, as if the sun shone on her alone. "How...extraordinary. I never knew what women went through, but after seeing my sister, I am awed. I would aspire to be a midwife as skilled as you, Mistress Maggie. It's quite a feeling to bring a new life into the world, is it not?"

"It is indeed." Mayhap it was Bethan's calling.

"You did well today, Bethan. You were cool-headed and seemed to know what to do instinctively."

Perhaps she could use an apprentice. She wondered how long the twins were staying in town.

Katherine was the first to run into the house. They followed her in.

"Mother!" She stood in awe, not approaching at first.

"Come here, my girl."

"You're so pale, Mama."

"I'm fine. Come here to me." With Adam behind her bracing the babies, Polly took her firstborn into her arms for a wordless moment.

"Katherine," her mother said, "you have a sister."

Joy flushed the girl's cheeks. "Which one? They look alike."

Her father chuckled. "Don't they? The one on the right, the smaller one."

Katherine kissed her upon her cheek. Instinctively, the child turned her head toward her. Katherine giggled. "She kissed me back! Oh, we will be the best of friends!"

She bussed the other babe's cheek. "I love you too, little brother."

The two little boys ran into the cottage, eyeing the babes with a mix of trepidation and excitement. They kissed their mother's cheek and stared open-mouthed at their new brother and sister latched onto their mother's breasts. The youngest one, hoisted up by his big sister, tried to clamber on the bed. He cried for his mother, objecting to the usurpers of his place of honor. Adam grabbed him and patted him on the back, murmuring soft words of endearment.

Maggie's heart soared at the joy and wonder in their faces as they celebrated the miracle of their new family members. She took Bethan aside and told her she or Sarah would return tomorrow to check on them. She shut the door on the happy family.

Holy Sister, thank you for your presence, which

strengthened and sustained me.

She stretched her arms above her head, wincing at the pain in her shoulder, and flexed the fingers of her right hand. A sense of pride and exultation washed the fatigue from her body. She was a skilled midwife, gaining in experience and ability with every birth. But she tamped down her pride, remembering she was not alone today. The power of the holy nun had coursed through her, steadying her mind and her hands.

She had half expected Ian to arrive at the McCall's as he had before. Surely he would guess where she was? It was late afternoon, and the sun was out, although it was cold. No matter. The walk would do her good. Maybe he decided to go to London with his old troupe. He had perhaps gotten tired of his plain, hard-working Maggie.

Chapter Twenty-Seven

Bethan watched Maggie go. Never had she felt so elated. She had helped deliver a baby—two! Some of it was most shocking, and there was a sense of unreality about it still. She thought about her privities, which she'd only looked at once and received a tongue-lashing from her mother for her efforts. How did the giant head of a child go through the small passage, and not split a woman in two? But she saw it with her own eyes, the abject suffering, pain upon pain, but how fierce her sister was. Ah, the joy of it!

She had always liked Maggie, but now her admiration knew no bounds. How did she know what to do? The midwife had remained calm, even with the unexpected complication, and possessed a strength and kindness for her mothers. She would aspire to be like her. The weak sun seemed brighter, the scent of the air sweeter this afternoon. She would be a midwife, just watch her. Lord knows she had plenty of practice at taking care of someone.

Mother would certainly disapprove. No matter. A giggle escaped her. It wasn't as if she saw her more than two times a year, for Mother could not tolerate Elunid's presence and would do anything to rid herself of her.

Just as quickly, her elation cooled. Where was Elunid?

She heard them before she saw them. A deep bass joined a tenor in harmony, a lilting, cheery tune. There were no words, only the tune. It sounded familiar; what was it? Ah! Composer Henry Purcell, one of her favorites. "Trumpet Tune." How curious.

Henry came into view, with young George, and...Elunid? She held young George's arm, and he gazed up at her. He sang *to* her, and she regarded him with a small smile on her face. How singularly amazing!

She watched the three of them for a moment. Henry's black hair curled tightly against his head, one errant lock on his forehead. He wore a white linen shirt, open at the neck. His shirt was so worn she could make out the dark circles of his nipples-oh! Never had she seen so intimate a part of a man's body, except her father, once. The weak sun alone could not have made her so warm.

She shook her head in hopes of clearing her confusion. How did a lowly night soil man come to know about a seventeenth century composer?

Henry spotted her and smiled, teeth white in his tanned face. "Greetings, Miss Bethan. We found yon sister." He cocked his head toward Elunid. "She was on the road headed into town, so we brought her back."

How had they managed it? Few people could get Elunid to do *anything*. "Thank you. Polly delivered her twins, a boy and a girl."

"How wonderful. Please give them my regards. I will not impose upon them at this special time."

She must tell someone. "I helped deliver them. I am going to be a midwife." It felt good to say it aloud.

He gawked at her, then regained his composure.

"How extraordinary it must have been."

"Yes," she said. How boastful of her. She took her sister by the arm. "Elunid! What am I to do with you?"

She might as well have not addressed her, for Elunid continued to listen to George's singing, the sweet clear notes flowing from him like a wellspring.

Henry touched Bethan's sleeve, motioning her aside. She sniffed. Not a hint of shite smell on him. She checked for it in his fingernails. She could not abide the sight of dirty nails, an all too common occurrence. His nails were clean and trimmed. He smelled of hay, mint, and something unfamiliar, perhaps just *him.* She stood so close to him she could feel the warmth radiating from his body, the sun lighting his eyes the color of butterscotch.

Her throat had gone dry, and she had trouble catching her breath. Why did he stand so close to her, half-dressed like a savage? Although she was taller, it did not seem so. With his muscular chest, and the bands of muscles in his arms, he made her feel, well, feminine. A rare occurrence indeed. As Mother said, "You're tall as a man, Bethan. Taller. How is my great big oaf of a girl ever going to find a husband?"

She wagered he could carry her if he had a mind to. He'd carried Elunid. Mayhap she would like to be carried sometime, to be cared for. Her face burned. How selfish she was. Time to return to her duties.

She backed away from Henry. "How ever did you get her to come with you?"

Henry shrugged, the muscles in his shoulders flexing under his thin shirt.

She swallowed.

"I'm not sure. Mayhap she remembered us from

last time, somehow." He glanced back at the two figures. "My George often has a knack for saving lost animals and souls." He smiled.

"I thank you." She touched his arm without thinking. It was so warm, and the rough hairs tickled her palm. Her heart plummeted to her stomach, the same feeling she got while standing at the tallest point of the lighthouse and looking down. He met her gaze, his smile fading. She jerked her hand away and strode over to George and Elunid.

It was good timing, for Elunid's hands began to move feverishly in the motions of sewing. She looked down at her hands. "Not done."

"Thank you for bringing her home, George." Bethan had to speak loudly to carry over the boy's singing.

He stopped. "She is my friend. She likes to hear me sing."

"Yes." She smiled. "And no wonder, for you have a beautiful voice."

He eyed his shoes. "Thank you, Mistress Bethan."

She took Elunid's arm. "Come, sister," she crooned. "You have a new nephew and niece. We must brush the dirt off you. And then you must wash." As if in a trance, Elunid followed Bethan into the house.

"Again," Bethan said. "I thank you for returning her safely."

Henry bowed. "It is my pleasure to be of service to you, Mistress Bethan."

As she led Elunid inside, she felt his eyes upon her back.

Chapter Twenty-Eight

Maggie shook her head. No. She would not let her petty resentments overshadow the joyful success of birthing two healthy babies. She pulled her shoulders back, wincing, and headed on the path toward home.

She walked onto the bridge and lifted her eyes to the heavens.

"Holy Nun, I do not understand your ways, why you let some women die during childbirth and another is doubly blessed. Why have you chosen me? Thank you."

All at once, the bridge gave way under her feet, and she tumbled down into darkness. Her arms and legs flailed in the air, and she dropped with a thud, the air leaving her lungs. She had landed with one leg under the other and a sharp, knife-slice of pain seared up her leg.

She tried to rise from the hard, rocky ground, but could not. She held her stomach, felt it tighten. Oh God, do not let her lose the baby. It was pitch dark and dank. She lifted her head off the ground, fighting a wave of dizziness. She spat dirt from her mouth and pulled out a rock imbedded in her cheek. Clods of dirt fell from the narrow opening above.

Her eyes adjusted to the light. She was in a cave, small, irregularly shaped, with bundles filled with something along the edges. Smugglers? There were the remains of a fire; if only she had a flint. The dank cold soaked into her bones. She flexed her foot. She could move it, but just barely.

She kneeled, her vision spinning. The rocky surface of the floor bit into her knees. Where was her bag? Who would ever know what became of her? She lay there for a moment, gasping, leaned over, and vomited.

Fighting her dizziness, she turned around. A cold draft hit her. Something, someone, watched.

Maggie, calm yourself.

She breathed through her nose gingerly, for every time she took a breath, her side hurt. Underneath the dank smell of the cave, a sweet, foul odor dominated. The smell of death. She closed her eyes, fighting the chill of panic. No one knew she was here, not even Ian. The McCall family no doubt assumed she was on her way home.

Why did Ian not come for her? If he had returned to open up shoppe, wouldn't he know she was gone? How stupid could she be, not leaving word?

She was trapped. She could put a bit of weight on her leg, but when she tried to walk, dizziness overcame her. She crawled to the side of the cave, so at least she could rest her back against it. She shivered. Her foot swelled within her boot, and she bent to untie the laces.

To her right was a narrow opening where the cave continued. Resounding within its depths, came a sound like a chorus of children clicking their tongues on the roofs of their mouth. Children with red eyes. Bats. She screamed, her terror echoing through the cave.

An army of bats flew toward her. She crouched down, covered her head against the sound of flapping wings, as they flew past her and out the opening above.

Later, she awoke lying on her side. She could see from the narrow opening that night was falling. She must have been unconscious for a while. Soon she could barely see her fingers in front of her. Her foot throbbed to the beat of her heart and she struggled to catch her breath. Drew a breath, pain radiating up her leg. Her cheek stung where the rock had been. *At least I can feel pain. I'm not dead yet.*

The incessant chirping of the bats crawled into her ears; she could not think. Water dripped somewhere deep within the cave. Too bad she could not drink it.

Ian. She would never again see the smile light his face, see his delight in the smallest of things. She would never be able to lay his head against her breast to comfort him, feel the warmth of his long arms around her and the heat of his lips upon hers.

She would die here, for she was injured and could not even help herself. She had not her midwife bag, and no means of relieving the pain in her leg. It felt as if it had been severed with a dull knife, and indeed had swollen to twice its size. She closed her eyes and prayed. If not for herself, then for Ian and the child. Did he search for her?

What would he do without her to center and comfort him? Or perhaps he would not miss her? *Stop it.* She would not just give up and submit to the pain and the cold. She would catch her breath despite the way her heart beat in her mouth and rushed in her ears.

She crawled to the bundles in the corner. Perhaps the smugglers had left food, water. With shaking hands, she opened the bundle and found a bottle of wine, a jar of marmalade. A smooth, round stone. She grasped it in her hand. It seemed warm against the cold air. She would laugh at her silliness if it did not hurt so much.

She opened the stopper on the wine and took a blessed swallow. She coughed, her ribs on fire. It was brandy, not wine, and it burned its way down her throat, but when it hit her stomach, it warmed her and reminded her she had not eaten in several hours. But after a few more swallows she did not care. If she died, she would not die sober.

She laid her head down on the bundle and closed her eyes. How long would it be before someone found her? Would she be bare bones, or merely reek of death? Would Ian cover his nose and make someone else carry her home? Or would they bury her then and there? If she had the chance to love him again, she would not waste their time in petty jealousy.

Her eyes had adjusted somewhat to the darkness. The sweet, sickening odor had not abated, and she saw a bundle of clothing across the cave, against the other wall. At first she thought it a bundle of supplies, but no. It was a dead body, the body of Josef's nephew, Nikolaus.

Chapter Twenty-Nine

Last night, Ian had merely gone out to catch some air, perhaps to sing awhile with his old cohorts. But more than anything, he wished to join his Maggie in their warm bed, but his veins sang with the grief of all he had lost. He would not infect their marriage bed with his darkness, with the clashing tunes warring in his head, burning the backs of his eyes with their fire.

He took himself in memory back to Varanasi, where the masters taught him to breathe, to fill himself with air and expel what plagued him. But breathing could not still his frenzy, the apparition of bloody Josef flashing in his mind like lightning. He would seek the company of others, ones who didn't mind his darkness, who only wanted to be entertained by his madness.

He did not return to the cottage until morning. He entered with misgiving. She would be angry with him, and who could blame her? He walked about, calling for her, but the cottage was empty. Why would she leave without telling him where she'd gone? Where else could she be but in service of a mother, unless she had grown weary of his disappearances and ever-changing moods? Mayhap she was at her sister's. No need to panic. She would be making her rounds, seeing to the needs of her mothers and babies.

Before he could leave the cottage to find her, Widow Jenkins hobbled in. Her kneecaps were so swollen with rheumatism she could scarcely walk. She kept him busy with one ailment or another.

"I saw your wife walking out the Landgate this morning, over to Polly McCall's place no doubt."

"Oh, you saw her?"

"Do you not know where your own wife is, man?"

The old woman shook her head. She had cause to be disgusted.

It was late afternoon when he arrived with the wagon at the Siren Inn to fetch Lena and Sabine for the funeral, and Maggie was not there.

He could not go to the McCall's now, for he must witness the burial of his friend, escort Lena and Sabine so they might say goodbye. Vicar gave Josef the respect he deserved, and in no way did the hastiness of this burial belittle the memory of Josef.

"Josef was a good man. In his quiet and generous way, he served the people of King's Harbour, offering his hearth, his food, and ale. We will commend him to God's spirit and pray for him."

Most of the town had come to the inn to pay their respects and share their memories of Josef, but Maggie was not there.

"Don't fret, man. It takes forever for babies to be born. And Adam would not let her leave in the dark. Surely she will spend the night." Henry slapped him on the back.

"You're right." Maggie might be stubborn, but she had plenty of common sense.

Ian felt a measure of relief and at Henry's urging, assisted him with serving the mourners. Shortly thereafter, young Billy Myers ran in with his index finger nearly severed. Ian carried him back to the cottage, and it took the better part of the night to sew him up.

Before dawn, with an increasing sense of unease, he rode out the Landgate toward the McCall's cottage.

His mind raced. Perhaps she was finished with him. He would not blame her. He had sensed confusion in those grey eyes, a doubtfulness he had tried to dispel. When they'd gotten married precipitously last year, he had warned her he would be near impossible to live with. Perhaps finally she realized she deserved a whole man.

Stubborn woman. He had told her before not to go to the McCall's alone, three miles on bad roads and who knew who lurked there. She must have left before light yesterday, or the chandler's wife would have seen her. She was always sweeping her storefront at dawn. But where had he been when Maggie needed him? Trying to sing his affliction away, and not succeeding.

He forced himself to slow down. It would do no one good if the horse became lame or a wheel broke off. He swallowed his worry. No doubt she was safe and sound, and could still be delivering the babes. She would be tired, and the wagon would be faster. He could get her home and rub her shoulder, give her the care she needed.

He parked the wagon near a patch of grass for the mare and walked down the road to McCall's house.

He knocked on the door. Little footsteps ran to answer it and grunting ensued at the effort of opening the door.

"Hello there," he smiled. Surely she was here.

"We have two babies," the little boy said, making a face. "They scream a lot."

"Adam, let Mr. Pierce in," Adam McCall called.

He entered into a peaceful family scene. Polly nursed one of the babes, the boy, their sister said. The other children sat at breakfast.

He looked around for Maggie.

"Mr. Pierce, we didn't expect you here, so early."

"Where is my wife?"

"She left yesterday, late afternoon."

Oh God. Where could she be?

"She was on her way home," Adam said. "I will help you search for her."

"I'll go toward town, and you search the surrounding woods."

Adam nodded, and they set off.

A cold dread washed through his veins. What had happened? It was well known the smugglers used the caves for hiding their stash, and much mischief could be wrought beyond the eyes of the law out in the countryside. Where could she be?

She would have taken much the same path home. There was only one way to go back. He should have been with her. If anything had happened to her, it was his fault.

Thankfully he had a lantern in the wagon, for the sun had not risen yet. He had parked the wagon before the bridge, and had not crossed it when he came, nor even looked in that direction.

Perhaps she was in town, perhaps she had gotten called away straight from delivering the twins. It was like her not to think of herself. He started across the bridge without lighting the lantern, and then he saw it, her midwife basket.

Had she been accosted? No trace of a struggle upon

the ground, and robbers would have taken the bag. She carried opium in it. If anyone hurt her…his foot slid, and he saw it in the dim morning light. The narrow hole, from which seeped a dank cold.

A faint moaning echoed from underground. He got on his belly and called to her. "Maggie, it's me. I will get you out."

A weak, barely audible moan in answer.

"Are you hurt?" Dolt. If she was not hurt, she would be answering him in her clear, sweet voice. "Maggie, can you hear me?"

She was in a cave, and the only way to reach it was to go to the cliffs and travel through the cave tunnels.

"Maggie, I am going to the cliffs. I know there is a cave, a tunnel that will lead me to you. Do you understand?"

How badly was she hurt? He heard a faint croak, a raspy sound. "Hold on, Maggie. Can you hear me?"

Nothing.

Ian ran through the woods. He knew this cave, how to get there. He followed the river to the sea cliffs, climbed the rock wall, and crossed the tiny stretch of beach, nearly impossible to reach except by sea. The tide would soon be coming in. He must get her out. There was no other way. He must hurry, for God forbid she could have lost the babe and might be bleeding.

He found the mouth of the cave, travelled by feel, by memory, through the narrow passageway, through the tunnels. He called to her. Her voice had sounded so weak. No answer.

The bats swarmed around him. He brushed them away from his face and chest, and willed himself to ignore them. The pungent scent of bat guano and the dank cold sank into his skin. God, she had been down here all night. A cold sweat formed upon his brows. One of the little bastards latched onto his hand, and he brushed it off on his breeches.

****

She heard him. His voice echoed through the darkness, and she tried to rise, but a sharp pain in her leg sucked the breath from her mouth.

She called upon the holy nun. "Please help me, help our child. I promise I will do my best to honor my calling. Let me see Ian one more time, feel his fingers on my skin, his heart beat next to mine." She closed her eyes against the dizziness. No. She must stay awake.

Then live. Draw breath. Find your voice and call to him.

His footsteps. *Thank you, Holy Sister.*

"Ian," she croaked. She willed her eyes to stay open, resisted the urge to sink into a world free of pain.

"Maggie."

She opened her eyes. "Ian," she whispered. "You're here."

"You're safe, Maggie. I will get you out of here."

"I can't walk."

He took off his cloak and picked her up. "You don't have to."

A groan escaped from her lips.

"I'm sorry, my love."

"There's treasure here, Ian. And a dead man." She pointed across the cave.

He stiffened against her. "I will send the constable out to take the body, for I must get you home. God, you're so cold. I will have you in a warm bath before you know it." He tucked the cloak around her. He headed for the mouth of the cave, toward the clicking sound of the bats, high-pitched and demanding. "Put your arms around my neck."

She shuddered. He held her with one arm and walked into the darkness. There was just enough room in the tunnel for them to walk through. She sensed, rather than saw, the walls closing in on them, dank and cold. Water dripped on the woolen cloak, and she screamed as bats butted against her.

"We are almost out, sweeting."

What about Ian? Surely the bats assaulted him as well. She gave herself up to the wave of dizziness, succumbed to her terror, and fainted. She awakened when he carried her up the steep path from the beach.

"I'm sorry to cause you so much pain."

"Ian. You saved my life. You found me."

They reached the wagon, and she passed out again. When she woke up, she found herself lying on the divan in front of a roaring fire, wrapped in a quilt.

Ian bent over her. "You're awake."

It hurt to inhale. There was a linen bandage wrapped around her middle.

"Here." He held a cup to her lips. "Drink. Something for the pain."

"I don't feel horrible."

"You are still in shock. I'm afraid you'll be sore tomorrow, and more so the next day."

She groaned. "There is much to do."

He smoothed the hair from her face. "Are you warm enough?"

"Yes. It feels so good to be home, warm, and with you. Ian, I didn't think I would see you again."

He embraced her, and she reveled in the feel of his

warm breath upon her neck.

"You must eat, Maggie."

"I think the babe is unharmed," she said. "I have had no cramping, and I feel a...certainty within me telling me all is well."

"And you've had no bleeding. It's nothing short of a miracle, considering how far you fell. You do, however, have a broken rib, and a very sprained and possibly broken ankle. So you, madame, will be resting for quite some time." He held her face in his hands, gently palpating the sore spot on her cheek. "I cleaned it out as best I could. I'm surprised it didn't wake you, but I'm glad you were spared the pain."

He went to the fire and brought back a bowl of soup, spooned it into her, and bid her to lie down again. He took off her bandage. "I'm going to put some warm compresses made with vinegar and marigold leaves, to draw the swelling out."

She gasped. "My foot is twice its size! No wonder it hurts."

"It will be more swollen tomorrow."

"I'd rather not think about it right now."

She laid her head back on the armrest and closed her eyes. "It is not the same foot as my bad foot, so I will limp on both. Mayhap it won't look like limping at all now." She chuckled, then winced.

He smiled, and despite her fatigue, she saw the drawn look on his face, and his bloodshot eyes. "Maggie, my love. Thank God I found you."

"Yes," she said. "I wanted only to see you again before I died."

"Well, you're not going to die."

"Are you sure? I feel quite wretched," she croaked.

"You need water." He lifted up her head and put the cup to her mouth. She slurped greedily.

"By the way, you reek of brandy." He smiled and sniffed again. "And marmalade. Please tell me you weren't drunk when you fell *into* the cave. I think you must have been, to consume those two items together."

"It was the only thing to drink *or* eat, you jackass." She closed her eyes and longed to escape the pain with sleep.

Ian carried her upstairs and dressed her in a woolen night rail. He placed warm bricks wrapped in flannel to warm the bed.

"Feels good." She moaned and grabbed his hand. "Oh, Ian. I love you."

"Maggie, I'm sorry I wasn't there."

"It is not your fault. I was tired and didn't heed where I was going. God, Ian! The dead body."

"I am fairly certain who dug up the grave and put poor Nikolaus there, though I don't have proof. But none of it matters right now."

She nodded, wincing.

"I am sorry for leaving you for those long months, but I did it for us, to be whole for you."

"I know. Believe me, Ian. I will take you as you are, whole or otherwise. The rest we shall settle later."

He tucked her in.

"Stay here with me, Ian. I don't want to be alone."

"Of course." He slipped into the sheets and put his arms around her.

"I fell into darkness," she murmured. "And you brought me out. I wish I could do the same for you."

"You do, Maggie, as much as a mortal can. My affliction is a powerful thing."

In the morning, she woke to a chorus of voices downstairs. It wasn't long before the whole town had learned what had happened, and the good people of King's Harbour brought food, drink, and a healthy dose of curiosity to the cottage.

Martha, the baker's wife, sat by Maggie's bedside. "Did you hear? The constable and his men carried the body of Josef's nephew into town. He was not a monster after all."

"That is what I've been trying to tell you." Ian was right; she hurt all over today. Even raising her eyebrows made her face throb.

"Who would do such a thing? Why hide a body?" Martha shook her head, jowls shaking.

"Someone who would like to make Josef look bad," Maggie said.

Ian came up with a breakfast tray, fresh gingerbread compliments of Martha. "Enough ear wagging, ladies. And Maggie mine, don't even consider getting out of bed today." He scowled at her. "You must rest, for your body has taken a shock. My guess is you hurt all over."

She nodded.

"You're lucky you didn't break your neck when you fell. You will likely feel worse tomorrow."

"Thank you."

"I will brook no nonsense from you." He kissed her forehead and smoothed the hair back from her face.

She felt considerably better the next day, and even better the next. By the end of the week she hobbled around with the help of a cane. Their story was a popular topic of conversation in the town.

"It is the stuff of romance, how the gallant and

powerful Ian saved you." He sat beside her on the divan.

She'd just returned from a slow and ponderous journey to see her sister, and it had tired her out more than she anticipated.

"I told you we should have taken the wagon home."

She poked him. "What happened to your hand?"

"I don't know. It's nothing to be concerned about."

But it looked angry and swollen, and there was a little bite mark on his palm.

"Oh, I remember now. One of those winged rats bit me in the cave tunnel."

She shuddered. The incessant clicking of the bats still invaded her dreams.

Later that night, he rubbed it. "It is tingling in the most peculiar way."

"You need a poultice for it," she said practically.

"Don't fret about it." He picked up a purple and white rock from the mantelpiece, the size of a walnut. "This was enclosed in your hand when I brought you home."

"I found it in one of the bundles whilst I was foraging for food. It gave me an odd sort of comfort during the night, warming me a little in the cold."

****

The next morning, as he poured her tea, she noticed he poured it with his other hand.

He saw her glance. "My hand is a bit sore, and still twitches. Did it yesterday, while I was pouring medicine for Widow Jenkins. Most embarrassing."

"I was not aware you had the ability to be embarrassed."

He didn't look quite right. She felt his forehead. "Ian, you are fevered. You must rest."

"No, I am fine. I will take some willow bark, and all will be well. It is just a little ague. I will ignore it, like any self-respecting man."

"Like any stubborn man, you mean."

In the evening, a sense of unease fell like a shadow over her when she did not hear him play his music.

Chapter Thirty

She awoke the next morning, shocked to find him still abed. He lay with his hands over his chest, the wound from the bat bite red and angry. She laid her hand upon his head; he burned with fever. He started, opened his eyes. Green pools of emptiness stared back at her.

For three days and nights, she ministered to him as he lay abed with fever. She tried everything in her power to bring it down, to no avail. She could only try to spoon broth into him, wash him down with cool cloths, and pray. The sight of him, unmoving and quiet, hollowed her out inside.

But on the fourth morning when she climbed the stairs, he sat up in bed, pale, but cool to the touch.

"I am ravenous," he said. "Feed me, wench."

She blinked, then embraced him. "Thank God! My love, you were so sick. Nothing would break the fever. I thought you were going to…"

With surprising strength, he pulled her down beside him. "I could not leave you, Maggie. My heart wouldn't let me."

It was as if he'd never been ill, other than the injury on his hand, upon which she wrapped a poultice.

Later that morning, reassured Ian was well again, Maggie limped her way over to check on Lena. Henry stood on a ladder and nodded at her as she entered. At first she did not see Bethan, who sat hunkered down at a corner table, a bowl of pottage with cream steaming in front of her. She gaped at Henry, her spoon in midair.

Maggie's stomach growled. It seemed the babe needed a second breakfast.

Bethan started. "Oh. Good morning, Mistress Maggie. Sit down. I will fetch you a bowl."

Maggie nodded her thanks. Bethan certainly seemed at home. "Bethan, what brings you to the inn so early in the day?"

"Adam arranged for us to live here now. Elunid frightened the children, and they did not have the space. I will help Lena and Sabine with the babes, and wait upon customers as needed."

Henry dropped the hammer, climbed down, and retrieved it. "Ladies." He nodded and went out the door.

Bethan avoided her eyes. How curious.

"What of Elunid?"

The young woman shrugged her slim shoulders. "Elunid is seldom…present. She can be absent anywhere." She grinned. "I am hoping you will require my assistance with any deliveries in the future. I have never felt so alive, so at one with God before." She blushed. "I must sound ridiculous."

Maggie touched Bethan's arm. "No, I understand completely and would love to take you on as my apprentice when you are able."

Bethan hugged her. "Thank you!"

It was not Maggie's habit to pry, but indeed she was curious about the strange behavior of both Bethan and Henry, and she must admit it served as a distraction from her own troubles. Now was as good a time as any to find out.

"Bethan, I sensed something awkward between you and Henry. Is everything okay? I only ask because I've noticed you seem to get along well together."

Bethan looked toward the door, opened her mouth, closed it again.

"I understand it is hard to talk about these things. But sometimes it helps."

She wrung her hands, confusion clouding her eyes. "I saw him this morning."

"Yes? Saw him what?"

"Shoveling shite."

"And?" What was the girl about?

Bethan grasped Maggie's hands. "Don't you see? He shovels shite for a living. How can I..." She squeezed her eyes shut, opened them again. "How can I be *enamored*—of a man with such a lowly and dirty occupation?" She shuddered. "But mayhap I am."

It took every bit of willpower for Maggie not to laugh.

"I'm enamored of him?" Bethan grew very still.

"You find him attractive."

"Yes." The girl's pupils grew huge. "Oh yes."

"You enjoy being with him."

"Very much so."

"Then tell me why you've become so awkward together."

Bethan folded her hands upon the table. "This morning I rose early. I stepped outside, and I saw him. Saw him emptying cesspools."

"And?"

"And he greeted me. He greeted me, and I ignored him in the rudest manner possible, for his occupation disgusts me."

"So now he is hurt."

She nodded. "Maggie, what am I going to do?"

Maggie patted her hand. "These things have a way of working out."

"He shovels shite for a living." She wrinkled her nose.

"Yes, I know. Eat your pottage, Bethan, for I suspect you'll need your strength. I'll fetch my own."

After she finished her victuals, Maggie checked on Lena.

The new widow did as well as could be expected, thanks to her friends and the spiritual counsel of Vicar Andrews.

Maggie examined Lena and the babe. "All is well. You must rest more."

Lena smiled, though it did not reach her eyes. "And you must go home and tend to your husband."

"Yes. He is feeling better, but he is not himself. I fear his affliction may be worsening, and the melancholy part of it is surfacing. He is irritable, touchy. And I can do nothing for him."

Lena patted her arm. "Perhaps he is just tired from his illness."

"I doubt it."

Her fears were confirmed during the night. His side of the bed lay empty. He walked about downstairs, but played no music.

She came down. "Ian, what is wrong?"

He shook his head, voice rough-edged with annoyance. "Go back to bed. I cannot sleep, as usual."

He had lost weight during his illness, his cheekbones stark against the light of a single candle.

"Where is your instrument?" She laid her hand

upon his neck. "Why do you not play your music?"

He flinched. "It hurts my ears." He spoke in a flat tone, as if it didn't matter.

"Hurts your ears?"

"Did you not hear what I said?"

She nodded. She must not be offended by his mood. Surely it was a result of his affliction. "I am sorry for it."

"I'd be better off if you would stop cosseting me and return to bed."

She drew back. She did not like this side of him, not at all.

****

Ian snuffed out the candle and sat in the dark. Maggie's steady breathing gave him a small measure of comfort. Her sleep would buy her time, a time to remember when her life was not filled with horror. For there was no mistaking his own diagnosis of hydrophobia. It was only a matter of time.

Tonight he would indulge himself listening to her sleep sounds. Would comfort himself with the night's rhythms: the beat of a drum from the Shipwreck Hotel, the clanging of a ship's bell on the Channel, two lovers whispering at the top of the street. Perhaps his hearing was more keen because of the absence of his music. The melodies had left him, left his body, veins, and brain. His songs washed away with the tide, lost at sea.

Chapter Thirty-One

The next day, Maggie awoke, expecting to hear the usual morning sounds of Ian preparing her tea, humming, whistling some cheerful morning tune. Then she remembered. How long would this change of Ian's moods last? He could not help it. But perhaps he did not tell her the whole truth. Had he grown tired of this life, of her? Perhaps Lena was right, and he still recovered from the illness. To be sure, the wound from the bat remained red and swollen.

She should be ashamed of herself, expecting to be waited on like a dainty duchess, like the songstress Charlotte. She shoved her needs aside. What could she do for him? For when she tried to help him, he pushed her away. She dressed and found the parlor and shoppe empty.

She was having her tea and a plate of kippers when Ian arrived.

He darted his eyes at her, then away. He raised his head again, nostrils flaring. "What in God's name is that smell?"

"What do you think?"

He held his hand to his mouth and ran to the basin. "Get them out of here, Maggie." And he vomited.

What was she to do with him? She tried to hold a cool cloth to the back of his neck, but he pushed her away. Perhaps he'd had too much to drink last night.

For his clothing and person was in great disarray, as if he'd hastily dressed.

"I know not what to do for you, Ian."

"I'm sorry." He slumped into the rocking chair. "I went to see the constable, and suggested he talk to Mrs. Stowe and Pete about the snatching of Nikolaus' body, and how it ended up in the cave. I'm certain they distributed the poisonous pamphlets and would not be surprised if they mutilated the poor dog."

Would the light in his eyes ever return? She would give anything to see him smile.

"Ian, something is wrong. Please tell me. Let me help you."

"There is nothing you can do."

"If you are having one of your bouts, you can tell me. I love you through it all, good and bad."

He laughed without humor. "Bouts? I fear it may be much more serious than that."

Perhaps he did not love her anymore.

****

Later, after she had returned from visiting one of her mothers, Maggie picked up the purple and white stone she'd found in the cave and rubbed it, for it seemed to calm her when she was distressed. She could forget her troubles with Ian during a work-filled day. But she could not bear to return to the empty cottage, to the absence of Ian's presence, whether he was there or not. Damn him for invading her heart, her body, and then leaving her empty. She poured herself a brandy, sank upon the divan, and fell asleep.

She awoke with a start to Ian's lips upon her neck.

"There you are, my lovely!"

"Lord, Ian. You gave me quite a scare." Instead of

his trademark insincere apology, he kneeled in front of her, placed his hands on each side of her face, and kissed her soundly. He undid her cap and threw it on the floor.

"What has come over you?"

"You, Maggie!" He grinned.

She had so wanted to see his smile again, but how could he change his moods so quickly?

He grabbed her hand and placed it over his engorged member.

"Oh!"

Out of all his cockstands, this was the most magnificent. She gulped.

"You must relieve me of this agony, my love, and only you can satiate me."

"Only me?"

"Do you doubt it?" His eyes burned into hers.

"No," she whispered. "I only want to understand you."

He carried her upstairs and undressed her with rough ardor, coaxed her onto the bed.

"I'm sorry, my love. I have not the words to make you understand."

As he ministered to her with the tenderness of his fingers, and the sincere service of his body, she could think of nothing else but the warmth of her privities, the hard strength of his cock hot and stiff against her. She gasped as he thrust into her once, hard and fast. And then he withdrew slowly, inched himself into her again, and drew back until she begged him to come inside. He plunged his member deep into her center and stopped.

She opened her eyes. "What is wrong?"

He kissed her, his lips warm, supple. "I would offer

you all the pleasure I can give you, Maggie. Do you feel the strength of my passion for you?"

His cock slid into her passage slowly, encircled it, until the magnitude of his thick erection enflamed her. He drove deeper, her muscles squeezed around him, and his power swept through her. She cried out, pain upon pleasure.

"Look at me, Maggie."

She barely heard him over the pounding of her heart, and the throbbing of his member within her, sending new tendrils of heat through her limbs.

"Maggie, never doubt my love for you. No matter what happens, you hold my heart captive."

She squeezed around him in response as he rode dominion over her. He came in crashing waves, cried out as if in agony, and lay still. A few minutes later, he put his arm under her neck, nestled his face in the hollow of her shoulder.

He lay quietly, matched his breathing with hers. He did not hum or wriggle his feet. She thought perhaps he'd gone to sleep, but his cock rose to life again, and he pulled her on top of him.

"Maggie, I must have you again."

Their gazes locked. Desperation swam in his green depths.

"Ian, what is wrong? Please tell me. I don't understand."

"Just love me."

"Yes." She grasped his member and slid onto him, gasping. He filled her, body and soul, and she tumbled into weightless rapture.

Again they lay quietly, and again, as soon as she'd caught her breath, his cock had regained its strength.

He rose from the bed. "I am sorry. You must no doubt be tired of me by now. I cannot rid myself of this cockstand."

"I still want you, Ian." She cleared her throat. "But I am sore."

"Each time you were so…ready for me."

She blushed. "Yes, I'm a wanton. I had no idea I would still love it, even during pregnancy."

He bounded downstairs and brought her some warm water with which to wash. "Let me help you." He sat cross-legged, a warm cloth in his hands.

"You're dripping water on the bed." She smiled. "No matter."

He cleaned her tenderly and thoroughly. She took the cloth from him, soaped his member, and ministered to him with her hands.

"Thank you, my Maggie." He pulled the covers to her neck. "You must nap. You are still recovering from your fall, and then had to take care of me."

"Will you not rest with me?" She knew the answer would be no from the way he paced the room.

"No, I must move. Mayhap a long walk would help my little friend here settle down." He looked down at his bulging breeches.

Her limbs trembled with weakness from their activities. "I feel like a slattern, but I believe I could doze off."

"You must indulge yourself sometimes, Maggie. I will be back in time for tea."

Chapter Thirty-Two

Ian stepped out into the fog and adjusted his breeches. He should leave now, before he frightened her. No matter how often he made love to her, he wanted more. But this was different, and only served to confirm his worst fears.

And there was naught he could do about it. When he and Henry buried poor Josef, he had been both alarmed and impressed by his friend's persistent cockstand. So when Ian awoke with the same condition, he could deny it no longer. It was more than his affliction. It was a symptom of the same thing that had killed Josef and his nephew.

No matter how much he wanted to, he could no longer deny the symptoms: the hypersensitivity to sound, taste, smell. An endless erection. The fear of water. He should leave her now, before his Maggie had to witness the agony of his death.

He covered his face against the fog. It prickled on his skin like needles, and the sound of the surf hurt his ears to bursting. A high-pitched hum threatened to split his head open. He walked without direction, seeking silence.

Where was he? Had he climbed up the hill past the church to the other side, and toward the Landgate? Doors slammed, voices clashed inside the cottage, a woman's voice raised in anger, a man's voice raised in defiance, a slurry of sounds and the flash of a lantern. His throat ached with thirst, and perhaps if he visited a quiet alehouse, the one on the edge of town?

Yes, the Landgate, and the Landgate alehouse right beside it. He entered, and squinted against the fire's glow. It burned into his skin. Perhaps the other customers would assume he was merely mad, as usual. He was mad, for certain. Mad dog, madman.

Good. The townspeople seemed to accept him, as long as he didn't provoke anyone. He had never killed a man but the rush of heat and desire to hear the smack of flesh on flesh rose from deep within, and he tamped it down with every bit of strength he possessed.

Greetings all round. He tried to respond but found his mouth too dry. He could only mumble, "A pint, please."

The alewife gave him a funny look. "Not feeling quite the thing, are you?"

When she placed the mug upon the table, he flinched at the sound.

"Looks like Pierce is having one of his fits."

They waved to him, smiling for pity's sake. They should not pity him, for he could plaster the wall with their guts had he the desire. And oh, he did desire. He brought the cup to his lips but could not drink it. He set it away from him, for the thought of drinking made his throat constrict.

Some men came over, ready for a song.

He must leave or he would hurt them. The wound on his hand tingled, and his fists did too. He would dearly love to slam his fist into the pity on their face.

"Sing us a song, Pierce."

"No, not just now." His words sounded garbled to

his ears.

"Aw, come on."

He tried to swallow so he might respond. They could not know how close they were to having their faces pummeled. He turned away as their voices engulfed him, flying into his ears like spears, ears like spears. He smiled, but no melody came. He gasped and stumbled out the door.

The fog had cleared, but it was colder now, and he shivered. Tried to swallow, knew he must get home to Maggie, his light, and mayhap she could save him. He passed by Reginald. Friend of his? He couldn't remember. And that slip of a girl, did he not swive her once? He tried to keep his distance; they hailed him and he kept walking. Footsteps, then Reginald approached him, put his flaming fingers on his shoulder.

He turned and grabbed his chin. "Don't touch me. Let me on my way."

The baby girl voice—not a woman, a girl and it made his ears itch. "Looks like my man needs an experienced woman to tame him. I'll have a go at it again."

Saw Reginald rub his chin. "No, I think it's best we leave him to his wife, Charlie."

"You know I hate it when you call me Charlie."

Her whine split his ears open. He growled and rushed past them.

"My God, Pierce! What ails you, man?"

"Maggie, I need Maggie."

The cottage was blessedly quiet, the only sound her breathing in sleep, but it filled the room with peace. For a moment he stilled himself enough to undress and climb into bed with her. He must get himself away, but let him have this one last night with her.

****

She awoke with a start when his cold arms wrapped around her. She turned without thinking to embrace him. "You're cold as sea water," she said.

"Help me, Maggie."

He kissed her, so hard it bruised her lips.

"Ian...you must..."

"Love me." He mounted her.

Hearing his desperation, she opened her legs and let him enter.

She fell asleep after, and he must have too, because he lay too still, his breathing shallow.

The moon cast a luminous light in the bedroom. She ran her eyes over the length of his body, on its side, turned away from her, and the long length of his muscular legs, the bulge of his upper arm, his legs bent and feet together.

She put a hand on his shoulder in tenderness. He sat up, turned a skeletal face to her, eyes empty in their sockets, teeth bared.

"Ian!"

Not Ian. A monster.

He writhed away from her, crouched on the floor. Through clenched teeth, he said, "Help me, Maggie!"

Her vision blurred. She fought against her fear. He was doomed, like Josef.

Chapter Thirty-Three

He could not swallow. Saliva frothed at his mouth, and she wiped it away. What must she do? He gasped for air, his eyes splintered like broken glass. Somehow she had gotten him back on the bed. It shook with his spasms. She heard the wagon wheels of Henry and ran down the stairs and outside.

"Henry, Ian is ill. Say nothing to anyone. But please help me."

He nodded.

"We need to tie him up. It's all I know to do, so he will not hurt himself—or us."

He turned to George. "Come, lad. We must help a friend." He grabbed rope out of the wagon, and they hastened up to the bedroom.

Ian stood on all fours, gnawed the leg of the table. No. An animal. Not her Ian. "Oh God, why is he doing that?"

"The dogs and Josef did the same," Henry said.

Ian turned to him. Blood ran down the corners of his mouth as he spit out the wood. He smiled, teeth bloody. "Old friend, I fear you catch me at a disadvantage."

"Father, what is wrong with Master Ian?" George shrank against the wall.

"Son, Ian is very ill. We must help him, you understand? It's like securing our horse during a thunderstorm, because he is afraid."

He nodded.

"It is just so with our friend, for he is ill and can't control himself just now."

"Ian," Maggie said. "We'll help you to bed."

"No, no. I can't lie still."

"You must, or you will hurt yourself."

"I don't care. Just let me die. I will anyway."

He struggled as George and Henry used all of their strength to tie him.

"Ian. Please, let them help you."

"How can they help me?" The muscle spasms contorted his face into a macabre grin.

"If you are tied, you will not hurt yourself."

"I am going to die," he said. "Go away from me, Maggie."

A convulsion tore through him, then stilled. "I am thirsty. So thirsty."

She held water to his mouth, but it brought the spasms on again, turning him into something unrecognizable.

She looked helplessly at Henry. "It's hydrophobia, like Josef. Perhaps there's a way to treat this. I must try to read the Galen book, somehow, but it is in Greek. Maybe there are pictures. But I need someone I trust to take my place here."

"George," Henry said. "Go to Mistress Sarah's house and bring Samuel. Say nothing to anyone you meet."

Samuel was the strongest person they knew and could likely control Ian if he tried to get out of his ropes.

Samuel arrived soon. His face was passive as he

looked at Ian, but she saw the muscles of his square jaw clench and tighten.

"What must I do?"

"Try to keep him quiet. Use force if you must." *I'm sorry, my love.*

Her heart raced as she went behind the counter. How long did Ian have before he was beyond help, and she would have to watch him die? No. She would not lose him.

Her hands shook as she opened the book. How did she think she could make sense of these foreign words? A guttural scream from upstairs filled the shoppe, the legs of the bed jolted against the floor. She could not hear what Samuel said, only his deep soothing voice in response to Ian's struggle.

Ian screamed again. "I have always wanted to kill you."

The sound of a hand smacking flesh, then silence.

"Samuel!"

"I'm sorry, Maggie. I had to."

She began to pray, to open herself up to the will of God. But what if His will was not hers? Ian could not die. She grasped the stone, rubbed its hard, smooth surface.

Please, Holy Sister. Help this man, this good man. For he sings to me, to my heart, my soul. He opens me up to the newness of life. I cannot lose him. Please, I will do anything to save him. Use me.

She gave herself up to the Holy Woman.

The stone warmed in her hand, and heat rushed up her arm, her limbs, her body, roaring with the power of the sea. It washed her soul away from her body, and a new soul with a voice like thunder echoed within her.

The new hands overtook hers, found the mortar and pestle. "For this malady there is no cure, but I will save him. For the love between you has a higher purpose, and the kind man's music gives life to the dead."

The Holy Sister searched the jars and drawers, mixed the herbs together, ground them to a fine powder. "We must put Kind Ian to sleep. He must sleep deeply, and we will trust his body to rest and heal itself. Listen midwife: we must bring him close to death to heal him. He must take all of this and keep it down, or it will not work. Then, he will sleep as if dead for days."

Before the spirit left, she laid her hands upon Maggie's head in blessing.

"All will be well. All shall be well. And all manner of things shall be well."

Maggie stirred the mixture into a small portion of ale, and climbed the stairs, limbs shaking.

Ian lay quietly, his eyes childlike. "Mother," he said in a voice not his own. "Why do I feel so poorly? May I have some pudding? For I cannot seem to count to ten, and I think pudding will help." He smiled winningly.

At first she was relieved, for it was so like him to say something stupid to make her laugh, but then his eyes rolled up into his head and he convulsed.

She told Samuel and Henry what they must do. They took positions on each side of the bed. When Ian's convulsions stopped, they sat him up. He was limp, but his eyes raced around.

"Ian. You must drink this."

He looked at her again, with limpid eyes and utter trust.

"Is it my pudding, Mother?"

"Yes. Here's your pudding, lovey."

"Oh good."

When he took the first swallow, he spit it out and grasped his throat. "No." He shook his head. "You lied. Not pudding."

"You must drink it, Ian. It will help you feel better."

"I will not," he roared, the childlike voice gone.

With a strength she did not know she had, she grabbed his jaw. With each mouthful, she held his mouth closed and tipped his head back. "Swallow it."

He gagged, and she held it closed, praying when he choked, until the last of the mixture was gone.

"What do we do?" Samuel asked.

She kissed Ian's damp forehead. "Now we wait."

She sat on the edge of the bed and watched him.

"I love you, Mother," he whispered.

"I am sorry." She held his hand and sat vigil.

Henry discussed the need for secrecy with Samuel. He would return later, after the rounds were finished. Samuel barred the door.

She knew when the medicine had taken effect, for Ian took a deep breath and slowly let it out. His breathing became so slow at times she thought he had stopped breathing. He was still as a corpse.

The night and then the day passed, as she sat vigil. His hands lay lifeless in hers, but she rubbed lotion on them, into the rough pads of his fingers, put ointment on his dry lips.

The second day passed. What if she had given him too much of the remedy? What if he never awakened, or it did not work when he did? No. She must trust in the Holy Sister's words.

She did the only thing she could: moistened his cracked lips with a wet cloth, kept him warm, gave him droplets of water and broth to strengthen him, and waited.

The sun made its way across the room again and again, and dusk settled on the third day. She must resign herself; she might never see his face alight with joy again.

"Maggie," Sarah said. "You must eat something." She handed her a bowl of soup.

"I cannot."

"You must keep your strength up. Do it for the babe. Ian could awaken any time."

"Yes."

"It will not do anyone good for you to become ill. He will need to be taken care of."

"What if he does not awaken, Sarah?"

"Eat. Do not think beyond this moment, and the bowl of soup in your hands."

"I was alone, and now he is my life."

"I know, sister."

They sat together and watched him. Sarah told her about Mrs. Stowe and her son Pete's arrest and their imprisonment. Pete had confessed to helping his mother move the body, distribute the pamphlets, and mutilate the dog. But it was cold comfort.

Days passed, and Ian lay, wasting away, but breathing, as she tried to sustain him with sheer will.

One morning, she had fallen asleep on the bed beside him. Something woke her up, the absence of his steady breathing, light and shallow. He had stopped breathing.

She kneeled on the bed, shaking him. "No, Ian. You cannot go." She beat her hands upon his chest. It cannot be true. When he didn't respond, she laid her head upon his still chest and gave herself up to her sorrow. Then suddenly:

"I find it hard to breathe when you are sitting on my chest. Do you mind?"

She jerked up. His eyes were open, clear, and alive. "Maggie."

She could not stop but cried in great gulps, held his face in her hands, until he cleared his throat.

"My face is quite wet, and I find I cannot move my hands to wipe your tears."

"You cannot move your arms?"

"No. Nor my feet, actually. Why can I not move?"

With a sinking heart, she told him the story of his confinement and treatment. "I did not know this would happen. I'm sorry."

"Maggie, do you mean the holy nun helped cure me of the disease?" His voice rasped from lack of use. "How extraordinary."

"Yes, and I think there is power in the stone I found in the cave." She smiled, but inside, her stomach seethed with worry. What if he never walked again?

No, she would not predict the future. He was alive, and it was enough for now.

Just then, Samuel let himself in.

"Samuel!" She yelled.

He ran up the stairs and relief flooded his face. "Ian, you are awake."

"I am awake, but it seems I cannot move."

"I will pull you up in bed. Mayhap you are just weak from lack of food."

But Maggie knew. "Ian, the dose I gave you was strong. It was your only chance to live. I'm sorry."

"No, I do not blame you, Maggie."

Samuel smiled. "So you think you will live a life of leisure here, with your wife feeding you every day?"

Ian smiled, then stopped short. "Maggie, how long have I been...insensible?"

"A week."

"But I am well, other than the moving thing. Thank you."

Before long, she was feeding him as often as he would allow. In a few days, he looked immensely better. His face had color in it, and he did not seem so weak. Every few hours, she would take his arm and stretch it, hold his elbow in one palm, take his hand, and extend his forearm, slowly.

"It's good," she said, "to remind your muscles they are supposed to move."

"My clever Maggie." He grinned. "But you are wearing yourself out on my behalf."

"No. I am happy to minister to you." She clasped his hands in hers. "Ian, you're alive, and not raving, or mad."

"Well, just a little mad." A shadow crossed his face. "What will happen when my affliction hits me, and I cannot move or play an instrument?"

"Mayhap your affliction is gone," she said, praying it was true.

"I like the way you think, Maggie. If only."

"Let's not think about it just yet. We must exercise your other hand." She started with his fingers, uncurling one at a time. When she stretched them all as one, she felt the pull of resistance as his muscles answered back.

"Ian."

"I meant to do that."

"Do it again." She held her hand in his. He squeezed it.

She embraced him. "My love, you are getting your strength back. You will recover."

"With the help of your healing hands. But Maggie, you saved my life, and if I never walk again, it is enough to be alive, to love you."

"But what if you never play your music again?"

"I will be happy as long as my voice can sing your song."

****

Indeed, it took two fortnights, but by then, Ian could sit in a chair by the bed for a while with Maggie's assistance, although he could not walk or bear weight. A week later, he could hold a mandolin in his arms.

Maggie sat beside him. "How are you?"

"Maggie, I need to go outside. I'm tired of this room."

"Would you settle for some good news?" Maggie grasped his hands. "I felt the babe quicken." She placed his hands upon her belly, held them there. "It feels like a fish flopping inside of me. Perhaps you can feel it."

He grew still, then smiled. For the rest of her life she would remember the joy upon his face. "Oh, Maggie."

"It's our child, Ian." The wonder of it!

"Pray God he is not like his father."

"Pray God *she* is."

She would celebrate a love that shone in spite of Ian's affliction, in spite of her imperfection. Her Ian brought light to the darkness, love to the lost. She would hold in her arms the child they'd created, and love them both with all the power she possessed.

Maggie laughed, joy unencumbered, next to her, and inside of her.

A word about the author...

Jennifer Taylor spent her childhood running wild on an Idaho mountainside. Although she's lived across the U.S., she's still an Idahoan at heart and a notorious potato pusher. She has a degree in Human Services and has been a roofer, a hoofer, a computer data entry operator, and a stay-at-home mom.

She's dreamt of writing historical romances since reading *Wuthering Heights* at the tender age of twelve, and is now living her dream of writing love stories set in eighteenth-century England. She feverishly lobbies for the return of breeches and would love to see her husband of thirty-four years in a pair.

Jennifer lives in rural Florida with her husband and enjoys the comings and goings of their three grown children and three grandchildren.

She is the author of *Mercy of the Moon*, Book One in the Rhythm of the Moon Series.

jenntaylor888@gmail.com
www.jennifertaylorwrites.com

www.ingramcontent.com/pod-product-compliance
Lightning Source LLC
Chambersburg PA
CBHW051517260626
47170CB00003B/666